THE CONNUBIAL CORPSE

A MALCOM WINTERS MYSTERY

Thorshammer Books
ISBN: 978-1-7358366-2-1
For ordering information,
visit: www.thorsonbooks.com

Designed by Stephanie Rocha
Image credits: istock.com, Upsplash.com, Vectoreezy.com

Printed in the United States of America.

THE CONNUBIAL CORPSE

A MALCOM WINTERS MYSTERY

THOMAS J. THORSON

Praise for
Heirs Apparent

"Thorson manages to deliver a story packed with mystery elements and secrets so deadly that no one is safe. *Heirs Apparent* is a thrilling ride into mystery, murder, lies, and greed..."—Anastasia Gkaitatzi with *City Book Review*

"One of the year's best thrillers"
—BestThrillers.com

"Thorson is as disciplined a storyteller as they come, revealing backstories and character insights in tiny, potent doses within a well-paced plot."
—BestThrillers.com

"Deviously delicious with relentless suspense"
—*The Prairies Book Review*

"a stylish novel...in the noir tradition of Raymond Chandler and Dashiell Hammett"
—*Mostly Mystery Reviews*

Acknowledgements

I write in a vacuum. Words don't start flowing until I'm totally secluded, away from all distractions, including friends, family, acquaintances, and strangers of all varieties. That being said, this book wouldn't have a chance of being released without the invaluable help of some of the very people I avoid. My daughters for their love and for pretending to care as I rant about word count or characters that insist on taking the novel in unexpected directions. My friends who tolerate interruptions to holiday dinners as I scramble to find paper and pen before a thought evaporates from memory. Steve Kirshenbaum of Looking Glass Books, the first to read and comment on my initial "final" draft. My patient editor Kristen Weber, who wishes I wrote cozy mysteries but who still finds ways to elevate my novel to a far better place. Stephanie Rocha, my supremely talented graphic designer, whose gift for producing incredible eye-catching cover art sadly overshadows all of the finer touches she adds to the book's inner realm. And finally to those strangers of all varieties, parts of whom inhabit and enliven the characters inside. I thank you all.

DEDICATION

Once again to my daughters Tierney, Lourdra, and Gilleece.
I write to make them proud.

ONE

My concentration level is acute and the tension palpable as my attention narrowly fixates on the task at hand. At this precise moment in time, the outside world doesn't exist. Every molecule of my being requires extraordinary focus on this most critical element of the unusual and difficult assignment I now regret undertaking. Despite my best efforts, a gray mist that portends peril begins to settle around me. I should have anticipated the odds of failure and turned down the job from the outset, but my client was persistent. It certainly didn't help that she approached me wearing that flowered dress that accentuates the curves of her calves. The scent of her perfume, an upper-range Chanel if I'm not mistaken, drifts in my direction along with the gaze of her expectant eyes. I'm at the breaking point, defeat is at the threshold. I need to do something, to say something, to salvage the situation and to avoid a crushing look of disappointment from the woman who swore that only I had the skill set to solve her problem.

"There should be four of them, but I only see three," I whine, breaking out of my noir daydream as I hold up a screw in Rebecca's general direction. "See…it's a #376 McPherson screw, which they stopped making seventy-five years ago, so it's irreplaceable. Two and a quarter inches long, sharp point, and a square head so that it will fit snugly into the square hole. One of four square holes, as a matter of fact, not three. Do you have any idea where it might be?" In truth, I have no idea if there's been anything called a McPherson screw in the history of mankind. I'm hoping to create the impression that I have enough of a familiarity with carpentry and degree of pride in my work that I require the use of genuine parts, which will then justify my storming out of the apartment in a rage over the missing screw. I've been at this for over two hours. For the last hour and forty-five minutes, I've been searching for an excuse to quit.

Considering all this effort and angst is for her benefit, Rebecca appears nonplussed as she peers at me over the immaculately manicured nail she's been examining for the past fifteen minutes. She stifles a yawn, manages to convey her apathy about anything screw-related without saying a word or uttering so much as a sigh, then returns to the study of her bright pink digits. Perhaps sensing my annoyance at her lack of involvement, she changes tactics and picks up a tattered copy of Vogue and disappears behind it, out of sight of the hired help.

Exasperated, I look for sympathy from Leo, my other tenant, whose creaky bones settled back in the only comfortable chair in Rebecca's apartment at the outset of my misadventure and who hasn't moved a muscle since. I would feel for a pulse, but my brilliant powers of observation have detected that the level of amber liquid in the glass nestled firmly in his gnarled left hand has gone down steadily. I'm not sure why he's here, unless I'm his entertainment for the day. It was, after all, at my doorstep Rebecca appeared late last night, breathlessly explaining that she was 'going to start a blog and had found the perfect antique rolltop desk at which to write it and I put a deposit on it but they'll only hold it until noon tomorrow and could you please help me get it back to my apartment that would be such a sweet thing to do thanks doll.'

She knew I would assent, just as she knew it wouldn't be due to her big doe eyes, or the earnestness of her plea for help, or the damsel in distress act, or even the fact that she pays her rent on time every month. Six months ago she saved my life from behind the business side of a sniper rifle, and while we have an unspoken understanding not to mention that disturbing episode again, she isn't above riding the undercurrent of that night to request favors that wouldn't otherwise be granted. There may be a statute of limitations on playing the 'you wouldn't be alive if it weren't for me' card, but damned if I know when that expiration date is and I'm not sure it's up to me to decide. From Rebecca's point of view, I suspect it ends at the exact same moment I draw my last breath.

All of which explains why I drove a rental truck to the South Loop at 6:30 this morning, bribing my brain to wake up with a thermos of steaming hot Assam black tea, whose hint of sweet honey tastes much better savored with a cheese bagel in the comfort of my kitchen, while Rebecca happily hummed a vaguely familiar show tune from the passenger seat. Had I known that the assistance she sought involved not simply throwing a piece of old furniture into the back of the truck, but also single-handedly disassembling a desk that had been put together over a century ago by someone who cared about his craft to the point that it was never meant to be taken apart, then carried down three flights of steep and narrow stairs, then back up another flight and a half, I might have simply killed myself to save her the trouble of doing it by giving me a heart attack. Rebecca's assistance consisted of telling me to be careful and not to scratch the wood. She made sure to point out that she would certainly have lent a hand, but she paid good money for that manicure and wasn't about to chip a nail; Denise the nail tech would just die. Besides, she was just a girl and would leave the heavy lifting to a big, strong—and might I add gullible—man.

Except she isn't, well, not entirely, which explains part of my irritation at being left to do the heavy lifting alone. Underneath the multiple layers of mascara and blush lies Ted, the tenant who signed a lease to rent this apartment from me. To put the most positive spin possible on him, Ted is a nasty, mean, selfish, greedy pile of masculinity who probably pulled wings off of flies and set ants on fire as a kid. From 8:30 to 5:00 Ted inflicts his toxic aggression on unfortunate souls working under him at some sort of corporate job down in the Loop. Once home, though, Ted sheds his pants for a dress and becomes Rebecca, a softer, kinder soul who isn't entirely unpleasant to be around. This transformation used to be occasional and furtive, only becoming an everyday thing when she discovered that Leo and I knew of her cross-dressing and didn't judge her—if anything we welcomed a respite from Ted—so now she leaves her male side at the door as soon as she returns from the office. She still doesn't have the role of erstwhile woman down pat, but she's getting there.

Maybe I'm not as accepting of her feminine persona as I think I am, though, because I would have been happy to put up with Ted and his sharp tongue for a couple of hours in exchange for borrowing his muscles while moving the world's heaviest piece of furniture. Once we got back to my three-flat in Ukrainian Village, Leo came out to assist, if you count warning me that I was too close to the bannister and offering several estimates of how heavy the damn thing is, each guess higher than the previous one. All of which was prelude to my present position on the floor of Rebecca's living room holding a screw and sitting in a pool of sweat. It's the second week of September but Mother Nature didn't get the memo that fall is here. Even Rebecca appears to be suffering from the effort of reading about the latest fashion trends, as tiny beads of sweat run down her forehead, taking her foundation with them. Leo, on the other hand, is wearing long sleeves and looks perfectly comfortable, as if this is nothing compared to the weather he grew up with in Cuba or the heat he's exposed to while working the fryer in his restaurant. Except I'm convinced he's never been to Cuba and nothing I've tasted indicates that he spends a whole lot of time cooking.

Leo responds to my griping by shrugging his shoulders slightly, digging into his left pants pocket and pulling out a screw that looks suspiciously like a match to the one I hold in my hand. "McPherson," he says softly, almost indecipherably behind his thick accent, a slight smirk working the corners of his mouth. I throw my best evil-eyed glare his way, which only seems to add to his veiled mirth. I suspect that watching as my misery builds is better than anything he watches on his ancient television, so he purloins a few essential parts of the desk to hand out at intervals timed to rescue me just as my frustration begins to peak. Not that he'll ever admit it. I learned long ago that Leo holds his secrets, and his liquor, well.

As time passes, the desk starts to take shape. Rebecca celebrates by enthusiastically offering neon-colored snacks she prepared herself, modeling them after something she had eaten in a restaurant with a chef that had actually been trained, but both Leo and politely decline. Been there.

Just as I test the rolltop and feel a long-overdue sense of satisfaction, my cell phone chimes. I smile when I see that the text is from Vinn, my teaching colleague, best friend, and sometimes partner in both bed and adventure. My cheer turns to puzzlement, however, once I read the message.

"7:00 a.m. in the café. Bring your picks."

TWO

The café that doubles as a meeting place before and between classes for Vinn and I is conveniently located on the first floor of the building housing my office on the campus of the University of Illinois at Chicago. Frequented mostly by students, it's not surprising that the tables are mostly deserted when I arrive at this ungodly time of morning, but the early hour isn't the only reason for the echoes of my footsteps. Now in my second year as a creative writing professor, a position I'm eminently unqualified for by anyone's definition despite the popularity of my classes, I've sampled virtually everything on the menu at one time or another and winnowed the "mostly palatable" choices down to, well, none of them. I don't glance over at the register as I pass by but can feel the glare of the owner burning into my back as he sees my steel mug of hot tea enter his domain. Sorry, Manuel, but the weak and flavorless swill generated by those tea bags you sell just doesn't cut it.

Despite my still-blurry vision, Vinn is easy to spot at her usual table over by the window. Even when the café is at its busiest and seats are scarce, she'll be found sitting alone with a buffer of seats in every direction. Men who know her, or anyone who chances to initiate a conversation, are intimidated by her off-the-charts intelligence, women by her ravishing beauty. Not that she cares, but Vinn doesn't help her cause due to her general lack of conventional social skills. Sit down to make small talk with her and before you know it the conversation morphs into the latest trends in gene sequencing or Nerd Monthly's article on monoclonal antibodies. Me, I'm intimidated by both her intelligence and her looks, and my eyes glaze over half the time we talk, but that hasn't stopped us from becoming close friends and sometimes more. Almost from the time we first met our relationship has been complicated and, to put the best face on it, fluid. One thing that hasn't wavered is the place we've made for each other in our lives, platonic or not, and the pleasure we each seem to take in starting out most workdays sitting across from each other in these very seats in this very café.

From the look on Vinn's face as I approach, on this day pleasure is the furthest thing from her brilliant mind. Worry lines stretch across her forehead and her normally placid expression has been replaced by an anxious compression of her lips, her eyes dark and tense. I approach with no small amount of trepidation, bite back my usual witty greeting, and sit down in silence.

"This is totally out of character for her, not like her at all," she begins before I can settle down in my chair. Vinn tends to get right to whatever's on her mind, which often means starting conversations in the middle of a thought and forgetting to provide the preliminaries such as essential facts. I take a quick gulp of my tea, a steaming Yerba mate, which by my standards is pedestrian fare and technically isn't even considered tea. Consuming it would normally qualify as blasphemy in my book, but given the haze I found myself in when the alarm went off this morning (which I'm sure had nothing to do with the celebratory sip or two of rum consumed with Leo after "we" finished reassembling the desk), I decided to trade in the subtle pleasure of a delicate Silver Needle white tea for the smack between the eyes provided by this bastardized hybrid. Its 85 milligrams of caffeine may have been a factor in my choice as well. In retrospect a good decision, as I send an urgent mental note to my brain to let the caffeine start working its magic asap. It's clear that there will once again be no prelude and I need to get my faculties working fast.

"She was always the first one to class, sat in the front, seemed to hang on every word, turned in her assignments early—they were impeccable—and asked intelligent questions. Other than that, quiet and intense. The kind of student we dream about, you know?"

Vinn looks at me for a reaction, so I nod and try not to appear wholly befuddled. Before I can actually formalize and verbalize a thought, she continues.

"So that's what makes it all the more disturbing, don't you agree? I mean, I know it hasn't even been an entire week, but that doesn't make me wrong, does it? I'm not overreacting, am I?"

Her expectant eyes meet mine, waiting for me to draw upon my vast warehouse of wisdom and say those words that will make everything better. Unfortunately, my mental fog is only now beginning to lift and I may have missed something as a result, but I have no idea what she's talking about. I have to find the exact right words that are both comforting and responsive.

"Vinn, I have no idea what you're talking about." Brilliant.

She looks at me in either wonderment at my ignorance or dismay at my idiocy before slumping back in her seat, running her hands through her hair. After a long few seconds she looks up and meets my concerned and, yes, befuddled gaze.

"I'm sorry, Mal. I ran this conversation with you through my mind so many times during the night that I mixed up my imaginary discussions with reality. That happens to me sometimes when I'm sleep deprived. Should I start over?"

I use my free hand to grasp one of hers and use my other to pour a large portion of my tea—sorry, my mega-caffeinated tea imposter—down my throat. I make a concerted effort to sound sympathetic instead of simply hung over. "I think that would be a good idea, Vinn. For starters, who are we discussing?"

Vinn takes a deep breath, gathers her thoughts, and begins to resemble the scientist I know and love. "Her name is Lily Cheng. She's here from China, not one of the big cities I don't think, maybe somewhere in the country. You're the linguist, you might figure it out from her accent. Anyway, this is her first year in the U.S. and first year in college, although she tested out of so many credits that she qualifies as a second-semester sophomore. She's in my mid-level organic chemistry class and might be overqualified for it. Very smart, very diligent. Did

I mention punctual? We sometimes exchange a few words before the other students get to class. Most of my kids dread this subject, but she seems genuinely enthusiastic. That's what worries me."

She pauses so long that I need to prod. "You're worried that she loves your class? Am I missing something here Vinn?"

"Sorry, my mind is drifting. She stopped coming to class. With some students that wouldn't raise a red flag, I would actually expect it, and every semester I have numerous kids drop out without telling me. But Lily isn't like that. We have class five times a week—an intensive course. Not including labs. She never missed a minute and was there Monday and Tuesday as usual last week. But not Wednesday or Thursday, or for two labs on those days. I was worried she was sick and might fall behind. I left messages on her phone and sent an email. No response. Checked with her other teachers, and she hasn't been to their classes either. They didn't seem worried so I tried to convince myself that I'm overreacting. When she didn't show up on Friday or respond to any of my messages I knew—I knew, Mal—that something was wrong. I need to know if she's okay. For that, I need your help. She needs your help."

I weigh my response carefully. It's only been half a year since Vinn joined me in tracking down the killer of my former girlfriend, and in the process we became reacquainted with the darker side of humanity and the dirtier parts of city life. It would be easy to discount her fears and write them off as an overreaction based on that experience alone, not to mention our past lives working in the shadows, Vinn with one clandestine and semi-legal government agency and I with another equally murky one. With anyone else, I'd reassure them that not going to class for three straight days is practically a requirement in the unwritten student handbook. In some revealing and painful conversations with Vinn, though, she's talked about the loneliness she felt growing up as a child too smart for the room and how the hurt from that experience has translated into an extreme empathy for anyone who appears isolated. Beyond that, I've learned to trust her instincts, and she's a friend in need. What should one friend be expected to do for another?

She tells me.

"I should have guessed when you asked me to bring my lock picks." We're standing outside of Lily Cheng's apartment door, each of us nervously glancing up and down the hallway to make sure we're not discovered. "But why do you need me for this? You've demonstrated more than once that you're better at breaking and entering than I am."

"I don't really need you. I need your tools." As she speaks, Vinn grabs the set of picks out of my hands, selects one, and in seconds has the door open. She meets my stare sheepishly. "Okay, maybe a second set of eyes can't hurt. And half of our dates seem to involve committing a felony."

She has a point, and with that we both slide into the apartment and gently push the door shut. I'm momentarily stunned by what greets me inside. Memories of my first dorm room, essentially a nondescript closet barely large enough to fit two beds and a shared desk, had me unprepared for both the size and comparative opulence of Lily's quarters. The short entryway containing a wide coat closet gives way to a large rectangular living area with floor-to-ceiling windows. The adjoining kitchen is small but still large enough to hold a full-sized refrigerator and stove and a breakfast bar. The bedroom is a more traditional box shape with the exception of a nook roomy enough to hold an L-shaped desk with track lighting above. Lily has started to add personal touches such as curtains and a poster or two. Not much yet, but enough to indicate a refined taste and, more to the point, an intent to settle in for a while.

Vinn apparently reads my thoughts and her voice breaks into my reverie. "Things have changed since you and I were in school. A majority of home-grown students rely on financial aid and grants just to afford the cost of attending and many colleges help out to the extent they can. Foreign students, though, are expected to pay full freight, so they're worth their weight in gold. Schools actively recruit kids from abroad, especially Middle Eastern students and Asians from affluent families. These same families don't consider traditional dorm rooms as suitable for their offspring, or don't want them to share a room, or are reluctant to throw a kid into a residence where not having a good grasp of English would add to an already-high stress level. Attitudes like this gave rise to university-approved private housing aimed at students from abroad. Most American kids can't afford a room in this place. I guarantee you almost all of the residents here are foreign.

"Now, if you're done gaping, can we get on with this?"

"Absolutely," I reply. "But what exactly is the 'this' we're getting on with?"

Vinn sinks onto a pristine flowered couch that appears to have had very few butts grace its cushions, cupping her chin in her hands. The weariness I spotted in the cafeteria is even more evident now. "I'm not sure," she says softly. "Anything that would indicate that she's okay, I guess. Receipts from local food places from the last day or two, recent notes from other classes. A printout of a plane ticket back home. Some sort of evidence that shows either that she's still alive and well in Chicago or that she gave up and went back to China."

From her tone it's clear that she expects our endeavor will turn up nothing, a view with which I happen to concur. Rather than state the obvious and add to her melancholy, I keep my mouth shut, move to the bedroom, and sit at Lily's desk.

The laptop sitting before me is the most obvious place to start, but I save it until after going through the drawers. It doesn't take long. A few pencils and pens, some Chinese currency, a pad of Post It Notes, and a box of paper clips are neatly organized in the top drawer. The bottom drawer contains several hanging files, each labeled with a class name and partially filled with spiral notebooks and some loose papers.

I open a blue notebook and page through Lily's neat scrawl in perfect English summarizing what I assume are either class notes from an advanced calculus class or the language of beings from another planet. Fortunately, I didn't need to understand what she wrote, I was only trolling for dates. No luck there, but I did notice that Lily seems to start each set of notes on a fresh page.

I take my phone out and pull up the school's registration portal to look up the math class. It meets three times per week. I go back to count the number of sets of notes in the blue notebook and divide by three. I repeat this task with each of the other four notebooks and consult the calendar on the wall above the desk. I'm not liking what I'm finding, but it's certainly not definitive.

One final folder is unlabeled but appears to contain assorted documents related to the program that brought Lily over to the U.S. A printout of plane reservations initially gives me a jolt of adrenaline, but a cursory examination shows it was the trip that brought her here from China. Stapled behind the flight itinerary is another printout, this time of the first leg of her journey, a train ticket from somewhere I've never heard of to Beijing. Another document stuck between her class schedule and tuition receipt falls to the floor. Her passport. I pick it up, flip through it, my heart dropping as I carefully place it back. The fact that it's here most likely eliminates the possibility that she returned to China, but I need to be sure.

Powering up the laptop, I pray that it's not password protected, but of course it is. It may not matter anyway, as the few words that appear on the screen are in Mandarin. I look down at the keyboard to confirm my suspicions. Sure enough. Each key contains an English letter but has up to three Chinese symbols crammed in as well. Even if I knew Lily, guessing at her password would be a chore. The fact that I've never spoken to her and that the password is probably in a foreign language makes the task impossible. And most likely fruitless even if I could get past the firewall. Any documents I would uncover would be in Mandarin as well.

Discouraged, I quickly go through the rest of the bedroom. Even a hasty search is time wasted. The only things of interest are how neatly her drawers are organized, with each garment folded like it was in a display. The hospital corners on her bed reinforce my growing impression of a meticulous young woman. Moving to the bathroom, the first thing I notice is the single toothbrush inside the medicine cabinet. A quick check of the bristles indicates it's dry. No medications to show when they were filled or if they were being taken. The towel hanging on the rack is notable only by the fact that its corners are precisely aligned. It too is dry. No moisture in the shower or tub. The wastebasket is empty and spotless.

I join Vinn in the kitchen where she has every drawer and cabinet door open to expose what lies within. Most are empty and un-used, the rest contain stacks of plates or pans and other essentials, the drinking glasses arranged in neat rows and columns like so many well-trained soldiers. The utensils sit precisely stacked in compartmental-ized containers. A kitchen towel hangs from the bar of the stove door. Like the bathroom towel, its corners are matched up exactly.

Out of habit I begin to tap the drawers for false bottoms and to look underneath for documents that might be taped there. "Mal, I don't think we need to do that. She's a student, not a spy," Vinn reminds me. She's right. Vinn sighs, a slight slouch in her shoulders, as she closes the drawers while I move around her to attend to the cabinet doors. Our eyes meet and she gives the slightest shake of her head, an unnecessary gesture, as her facial expression does nothing to hide her frustration. Together we move to the last untouched area, the fridge. Vinn pulls it open, our heads touching as we peer inside. Un-surprisingly for a student, it's mostly empty. Before closing the door, I pull out a quart container of milk. Half full, it expired three days ago. Unscrewing the lid, I position the opening beneath my nose and wince. Sour. Vinn pulls my hand over and repeats the smell test with the same result.

We move to the couch and sit among the patterned posies, turned slightly to face each other. We're barely settled before Vinn starts in.

"I gave the living room, kitchen, and hallway closet a fairly good going-over, including looking in the pockets of her jackets. I didn't really expect to find anything and I didn't. Students as bright as Lily, especially those who excel in the more esoteric areas of science, are as a rule organized, fastidious, maybe even a little obsessive compulsive. They also tend to be loners who spend a lot of time keeping everything important to them close by." Vinn's eyes take on a distant sadness and I know she's referring to more than just Lily. She quickly recovers and a slight upturn makes it to the corners of her mouth. "That's not that unusual for my students. It's part of what makes them good.

"But that's also what makes one item stand out. Did you notice—" Before she can go on, I hold up my hand to stop her.

"Before you say it, let me tell you what I found and then we'll determine if we're on the same page. I agree, she's galaxies beyond the normal neat freak." I tell her about the towels, folded clothing, and the bed. "It's also reflected in her classwork. She has a separate notebook for each class, each a different color, with handwritten notes that are so precise they look like they could have been typed. There are no dates, which seems a bit odd, but by counting the sections of notes for each class it's clear that she attended every one for the first four weeks. The number of sections of notes matches up with the number of classes for each subject. Until the middle of last week. Nothing. Either she stopped taking notes, which is unlikely, or she didn't attend any classes after Tuesday.

"Which brings us to what you noticed. The milk, right?" Vinn nods in response. "There is no way a woman who is this meticulous, this obsessively neat, should I say this anal, would have sour milk in her fridge. Clearly, Lily hasn't been in this apartment for almost a whole week."

Vinn looks deflated. "It doesn't make sense. Maybe she was overwhelmed. Strange country, difficult curriculum, no friends or family. All by herself. In a way I hope she just decided to go home. At least that way I know she's safe."

I cast my eyes downward before meeting Vinn's questioning gaze. I can't put off telling her any longer. "She didn't go home, Vinn. I found her passport in her desk. Wherever she is, it's not China."

THREE

"Vinn, just because she hasn't been in her apartment for a week doesn't mean she's been the victim of a crime. She could be touring the country, visiting a friend, or shacked up with a lover. Maybe even in the hospital with a bad case of the flu." All true, and along with a thousand other possible explanations more likely than something more sinister, but Vinn ignores me as she hastily mounts the few steps leading up to the entrance of an old brick building on Maxwell Street that houses the campus police department. She'd heard me out when I used the same arguments earlier and I'm sure had considered them herself, but she's one to follow her instincts and I can't say I blame her. There's probably a completely innocuous reason for Lily's dropping out of sight and the only mystery is which one, but it doesn't take much imagination to think of other, darker scenarios. If she's disappeared against her will, the passage of time isn't her friend. Vinn knows this as well.

My hesitation at taking the obvious precautionary step of consulting the authorities is more due to my past history with the men and women in blue than to doubts about the accuracy of Vinn's intuition. A career in the shadows chasing bad people doing bad things often brought me to the attention of law enforcement, never in a good way. The fact that I was prohibited from explaining my actions or for whom I was working only confirmed their assumption that I was culpable—they didn't always reveal of what crime—and for cops anxious to close a case a suspect arguing logic only increased their animosity and desire to pin something, anything, on me. More than once I was their unwilling guest until shady figures representing the good guys sprung me, usually to howling protests by my hosts. I've been beaten, spit upon, tortured, questioned for 48 hours straight, starved, and more that I've spent years trying to forget. Granted, they often had cause to do some of it, and I might have done the same in their place, but that doesn't mean I want to walk into a station full of cops if I have any choice.

Vinn hadn't shown much sympathy for that argument either, which she shouldn't have, but she may have chosen to go to UIC's police department instead of to the City of Chicago's finest in order to increase the odds that I'd accompany her. Campus cops are employees of the university, not the city, and as such whether fairly or not aren't always perceived as real officers of the law. But maybe they also aren't as jaded, or cynical, or busy, and will have the motivation and time to chase down a missing student despite the near certainty that they'll also assume Lily is spending a little mattress time with a campus hunk.

I've straggled behind a bit and Vinn is already addressing the desk sergeant when I catch up. Things don't seem to be going well.

"But I'm telling you something isn't right." Her voice is rising just short of shrill and her frustration is obvious. "I insist on filling out a missing person's report and it's imperative that someone starts investigating right away."

The woman behind the desk peers down at Vinn with tired, unsympathetic eyes. She has the look of someone who's put in too many years listening to people demand one action or another. I can see the words forming in her mouth that will politely but firmly tell Vinn to go to hell, but suddenly her visage changes as a better idea clearly intervenes.

"You know what, you should talk to Detective Jenkins. Let me see if he's available." A slight smirk plays around the corners of her mouth, which immediately puts my bullshit detector on high alert. I don't think Vinn notices. "Detective, there's a lady down here who needs to talk to you right away. It's important."

Savoring her moment of triumph, Vinn completely misses the condescending tone of the desk sergeant's conversation with the detective on the other end of the line. I wonder if we'll be escorted to an empty desk or outside a door that leads to a fire escape. At best we're pawns in workforce politics and are being used as a salvo against a detective in the doghouse. We're instructed to proceed up the stairs and then to turn left at the top and ask for Detective Jenkins. I hear the sergeant let out a large, satisfied sigh as we head toward the stairs.

The directions lead us to a room crammed with eight cluttered desks and an ancient whiteboard with the faded remnants of hundreds of case summaries staining its surface, a typical home base for detectives, real or not. It appears vacant. Vinn calls out a "hello" which echos off the filthy walls. At first there's no response, then I sense motion in the vicinity of a desk in the far corner of the room that I hadn't noticed when we entered. Unlike the others, it's clean and abnormally tidy. In fact, it appears almost completely unsullied by papers of any kind. Rising from behind it is a short, spindly African-American man nattily attired in a beige suit and striped tie. As we approach I see a badge identifying him as Jenkins. Detective Jenkins looks like he's about fifteen years old.

"Please, sit down. How may I assist you today?" His voice is incongruously deep and to his credit doesn't break as he talks, but Vinn seems immobilized as she stares disbelievingly at him, forcing me to adjust her chair so that she doesn't end up on the floor as she moves to sit. Since she appears temporarily paralyzed by Jenkins' appearance, I clear my throat.

"My name is Malcom Winters and this is, um, Professor Achison." It's always awkward introducing Vinn since despite our relationship as best friends and sometimes lovers, I don't know her real first name. I'm not sure anyone does other than Vinn herself. "Vinn" is the sound you get from saying the letters 'V' and 'N,' the initials of her first and middle names, quickly in sequence. She clearly embraces her privacy but just as obviously takes a perverse enjoyment from my discomfort. "We both teach here at UIC. We'd like to report a missing student."

Vinn's recovered her composure by now and takes over the narrative. "She's in one of my classes, here from China. She—" Vinn pauses, ponders an issue, then makes a decision mid-sentence. "I'm sorry, I don't mean to be rude, but how old are you?"

A momentary flash of irritation passes through Jenkins' eyes before he gets it under control. He's heard this before. "I'm twenty-three. I've been on the force here for four months, but don't let my youthful appearance deceive you. I'm perfectly capable of handling any matter you may have."

He comes off as defensive, a natural reaction, but in the few seconds it takes him to speak the situation becomes clear. He's the new guy on the force and has yet to earn anyone's respect. Maybe he got the job his fellow detectives wanted to go to someone else, a cousin of the desk sergeant perhaps. Maybe he said the wrong thing to the wrong guy and pissed everyone off. Maybe he's just an asshole. Whatever the case, since Day One he's been in the doghouse, and his baby face hasn't helped his cause. For now he's an outlier, and the smirk on the sergeant's face begins to make sense. Detective Jenkins just became her convenient outlet for getting rid of unwanted visitors.

"I didn't mean to suggest otherwise. I assume you get that a lot." That's Vinn trying to save face. She quickly moves on. "Anyway, her name is Lily Cheng. She's a first-year, really smart, very attentive. But she seems to have disappeared. She hasn't been in class—anyone's class—for a week now and I'm worried. Foreign students can be so vulnerable. She has no family here so I thought I should take action."

"I see." Jenkins can't hide his disappointment that this isn't the type of case that'll catapult him into acceptance from his fellow officers or even stardom. Like murder or a cheating scandal in the language department. I anticipate what's coming next but am still disappointed when it happens. "It's only been a week and we generally don't consider someone of her age missing at this point. She could be out of town touring the area, or visiting a relative, or maybe she's, well, hooked up with someone." Hearing my own words hang in the air, I look at the detective with a newfound respect. Vinn looks at both of us like we graduated from the same clown school. Jenkins ignores any slight Vinn's expression conveys and continues. "I can have you fill out a report, but I have to be honest that I'm not sure how many resources we can devote to looking for her at this point. Maybe if you want to follow up in a week?"

Fury erupts from Vinn's eyes before I see the realization hit that this is exactly the reaction she deep down expected. Arguing will get her nowhere and may even be counterproductive. She sighs, with great effort bites back the comment she yearns to make, then grabs the single page that Jenkins holds in her direction, borrowing my pen. It takes her all of about forty-five seconds to fill in the blanks. Standing, she thrusts the document across the desk and in one fluid motion turns to walk away. Jenkins looks a question in my direction. I simply shrug my shoulders, toss my card in his direction, and move to follow Vinn. I have no doubt that her pent-up wrath will find a convenient outlet in the form of a someone who looks exactly like me as soon as we get outside.

FOUR

My role as supportive friend obligates me to put forward a façade of optimism for Lily's safe return, which becomes more difficult with each passing day as my own doubts rise. Contrarian voices from deep within my brain loudly dispute every word of comfort I offer based on the knowledge that the odds of Lily's survival diminish with every sunset. I try my best to ignore them and instead focus on helping Vinn return to some sense of normalcy beyond the weekly routine of preparing for and teaching classes, enduring endless and unnecessary committee meetings, and navigating all of the trappings of academia, which explains why I drop by her place in Lincoln Park early on this Saturday to escort her to the Green City Market, one of our favorite warm-weather activities.

The sun is up but has little effect on the chill in the morning air as we head east toward the lakefront. Each of us wears a jacket that smells a bit musty from months of being buried in the back of a closet. I reach my hand out to her, which she instinctively takes as we wander past the converted three-flats and historic homes lining the streets. Any notion that the distraction of our outing has pushed thoughts of Lily to the background is quickly dispelled.

"It's just so difficult, you know?" Vinn says, breaking our silent reverie as we dodge cars crossing Clark Street. "I work hard to convince myself that it'll all work out, but each day when I'm forced to lecture over that damned empty seat in the first row, any bit of hope I've managed to build up just shatters. The worst thing is the sense of helplessness, that there's something that we should be doing. I know, I know…" she quickly cuts off the comment she sees forming as I open my mouth, "we talked about this. We've both been here before, where every lead in an investigation has been followed multiple times and, in your words, the well runs dry. Here we ran into a wall almost before we started, because we have nothing to give us a place to start. So instead we're forced to wait until either Lily returns or she sends word where she is. We may not have a choice, but I'm not happy about it. It's frustrating. Dammit, Mal, look at the two of us. If anyone can do something, it should be us."

There it is, the implication that we're better than this. And she's right. Each of us has a background and the types of resources that could be utilized to find an individual, even if they don't want to be found, but without any family or friends in this hemisphere that we know about, no idea as to her interests or habits, and with no car or credit cards to her name that could be traced, we don't have so much as a starting point. It doesn't help that as far as we can tell, Lily has absolutely no history in North America beyond the few weeks of classes she attended before disappearing. Her passport was issued four years ago and only shows the single, recent entry right before the start of classes.

"I feel the same way, Vinn. 'Frustrating' is exactly the right word, and I don't like being inactive any more than you do. In fact, I have a confession to make. To scratch the 'doing something is better than nothing' itch, I let myself into Lily's apartment one more time a couple of days ago without telling you. A quick walk around was enough to see that she hadn't returned since the last time we were there and I didn't find anything we didn't see the first time."

Vinn stops, presses my hand in appreciation, and pulls me into a hug. "As long as we're confessing to things we didn't tell each other, I should tell you that I called Detective Jenkins once just to check in. It wasn't a helpful conversation for either of us." I smile inwardly. I knew this, and also know she called him more than once because he reached out asking me to reign her in. Clearly he doesn't know the first thing about my fiery colleague. I'm not sure, but I think she also tried calling the Chicago cops. She and I discussed the possibility of approaching them despite my reservations, but she never mentioned that avenue again. I assume she tried by herself and got the royal brush-off, which would explain her foul mood on Thursday.

For a long moment, we hold onto the hug, to all appearances a happy couple enjoying the weekend. In truth our relationship is more complicated than that. When I first joined the faculty at UIC just over a year ago, parlaying a case of mistaken identity into a job I didn't qualify for—and still don't—I carefully avoided social attachments with the other teachers as a defense against exposing my fraud. Vinn, on the other hand, gladly embraced being shunned by her peers, if you can call anyone less brilliant than Albert Einstein as her peer, and fate's sense of humor being what it is, we two loners found each other. I was dating a woman at the time, so any romantic entanglement was off the table, or at least was supposed to be. As we were unwillingly drawn into an emotionally draining investigation, stressful situations that required support and long hours in each other's company tested our platonic status. We both felt the sexual tension but fought it and fooled ourselves into believing that we won the battle when we were unknowingly on our way to losing the war. A near-death experience and the emotions that spilled out as the investigation came to a violent, albeit successful, end led to a summer together in the middle of nowhere, where alternating soulful confessions and passion glued us together in an everlasting bond.

Now that we're back on campus and forced to once again face real life, our status as a couple so far has remained unwavering. How far we want to take it beyond an undying friendship and infinite respect for each other, with occasional submissions to lustful endeavors, though, is still being evaluated. Our summertime conversations were informative, surprising, and difficult, but failed to completely lay our souls out to bare, as we each held back certain aspects of our past out of fear of losing the love of the other. If we want to totally commit to a lifetime together, there can be no more secrets. I'm scared that revealing everything will frighten Vinn and push her away, and I'm sure she feels the same about candidly discussing her own history. For now, we bask in our friendship, take it beyond when we're both in the mood, and wait for one of us to force the issue. We've each dated others a few times, which has only resulted in amusing stories to share with each other the next day. As of now no worthy competition has appeared.

And so we arrive at the farmer's market hand-in-hand. At the dawn of this beautiful early fall day on the lakefront, it's almost easy to push all of our troubles to the periphery of our consciousness while we partake in one of the great pleasures the city has to offer. The Green City Market, a mecca for locals craving freshly picked organic produce, sustainably raised meats, and incredible people- and dog-watching, is situated adjacent to the Lincoln Park Zoo and within view of the Lake Michigan beaches. The smell of roasting cheese wafts in our direction as we approach, making it hard to focus on anything else.

I leave Vinn to peruse the apples and late-season blueberries to join the line for a raclette sandwich, a glutton's vision of melted cheese carved off a heated wheel onto a fresh baguette. When I return and offer half to Vinn, she almost smiles. Hot, dripping cheese will do that do a person. She pays for her apples and we silently munch on our treat as we stroll past the booths, each offering more temptations than we could possibly find the appetite—or cash—to indulge in.

When the schedule of cooking demonstrations at the market was first released, we each circled today's use of a grill to bake apple pies on our calendars. Given our moods it no longer holds the allure it once did, so we move on. Vinn pets every hound that comes within reach, I chat with a vendor of pickled products, and on occasion we actually stop to purchase jam or a vegetable or two. We've nearly completed the circle, stopping to consider if we want to tempt our waistlines with fresh peach pie, when a distant buzzing interrupts our reverie.

Vinn's the first to realize that it's her phone, buried some-where deep inside her purse. By the time she's pulled it out the call has gone to voice mail. We retrace our steps to an exit point and walk past a sea of yoga mats to find a quieter spot behind a small grove of trees. Vinn listens intently to the message, frowns, then listens again. Without clueing me in on its content, she jabs her finger impatiently to return the call.

"Hello, you just called me but I couldn't make sense of your message…. I'm sorry, who is this again? Oh, I apologize, but you're a bit difficult to hear." Vinn pushes her phone hard against her left ear and puts her finger in her right to block out the noise of the market. As I watch, her face slowly drains of all color and her mouth drops open slightly, a look of panic entering her eyes. She mutters a quiet "Thank you, I'll be right over" into the phone before disconnecting.

She remains silent for an interminable moment before looking in my direction. I don't need a degree in human behavior to tell that something's wrong.

"That was Detective Jenkins," she finally says, her voice breaking as she speaks. "They've found a dead person. A young Asian woman. He wants me to go to see if I can identify the body."

FIVE

After a seemingly interminable ride, our Uber pulls up in front of a drab, angular stone building conveniently situated among several medical centers about a mile west of the UIC campus. Despite its proximity to the university, I've never seen it before. I didn't even know where it was and fortunately up until this moment never had any reason to know. As we exit the ancient Ford Focus and the proximity of its aromatic driver, it occurs to me that I've never been inside any morgue with the exception of one time when I was mistakenly brought to one in Miami as the guest of honor. That memory does nothing to ease the discomfort I feel as we make our way to the entrance.

A high school freshman, who upon closer inspection reveals himself to be Detective Jenkins, is waiting just outside the front door, looking tense. He steps forward to intercept us before we can get inside.

"I appreciate your coming down. Just so you know, this matter isn't within my jurisdiction. What I mean is, it isn't my case. Ever since you left my office, though, I've been monitoring police bulletins for any mention of a body. Specifically, any reference to a deceased Asian female. That's how I found out about this Jane Doe."

"She hasn't been identified?" I ask.

"Not yet, but her age seems about right, that's why I called you. I also called—"

"Where did they find her? How did she die?" Vinn's lack of patience with the detective's self-appointed role as gatekeeper to the dead mirrors my own, although she probably also shares my reluctance to actually go inside to see the body. Jenkins hesitates before he replies.

"Um, I'd rather not go into any detail at this stage. Actually, the medical examiner requested that I not say anything at all for privacy reasons. You're not related to the victim, which means I'm already pushing limits by revealing her race. And they're not telling me much anyway. You understand, I'm sure. I called ahead and explained who you are and that you had filed a missing persons report, so they're expecting you. Us."

"Victim?" I mouth to Jenkins as Vinn strides purposefully away toward the door. He gasps quietly, bringing his hand to his head as he realizes he's once again given away more than he should have. He really is new to this, but I'm in no mood to care. I catch up to Vinn to offer moral support. I don't have a good feeling about what we're about to see.

Vinn takes the initiative and identifies herself and her purpose to the uniformed middle-aged woman at the reception desk, a virtual clone of the on-campus desk sergeant. She eyes us suspiciously, gives Jenkins a look like they've already done battle once, and finally picks up a phone and mutters indecipherably to an invisible soul on the other end. We stand impatiently for a few minutes before a young man in a soiled lab coat passes through a door and heads in our direction. His eyes reflect a weariness of someone who has gone through this process far too many times. I wonder how often he questions his career choice.

Introductions are brief and perfunctory. "If you would come this way, please. Officer, please wait outside."

Jenkins is perturbed, whether for not being invited, for being demoted in rank in the eyes of the examiner, or for having Vinn thrust a bag of apples, turnips, and jam into his hands, I couldn't tell. I wouldn't be surprised if he's never seen a dead body before and feels it's a necessary rite of passage in his profession.

Vinn and I follow the lab coat down a hallway, turn left, then walk a bit more before pausing outside a door labeled, appropriately enough, "Viewing Room." The antiseptic smell that was faint at first has grown stronger with each step, and it's now nauseatingly overwhelming. As the young lab tech reaches for the doorknob I panic slightly and intercept him.

"We don't need Vaseline or anything?" I half-plead. Vinn would never forgive me if I embarrass her by getting sick in front of the lab tech, although I'm sure she would also enjoy adding my failing to her arsenal of jibes to save for an appropriate occasion.

"What? I'm not sure—oh, I understand. No, well you see, I guess I should have explained. You won't be in the same room as the body—er, the young woman. It's done on closed circuit television."

Sure enough, we're escorted into a cozy room with one distinguishing feature—a large flat-screen television hung on the far wall. Other than that, the room is sparsely furnished beyond a few chairs and a side table. I take note of the oversized box of tissues on the table and an overflowing wastebasket below it. We're not the first visitors here today.

My daydream causes me to miss the beginning of an exchange between Vinn and the examiner. "Lily Cheng," Vinn is saying. "She's a student of mine. Asian, probably 18 or 19, average height, dark straight hair. No distinguishing features that I'm aware of."

The man nods. Vinn has just described every teenage woman in China, so he makes a tacit decision not to bother questioning her further and to proceed to the next step. I don't see a signal, but the television suddenly springs to life, the seal of the medical examiner's office filling the screen. Vinn acknowledges she's ready with a nervous nod. I reach for her hand, as much for my benefit as her own.

We've each seen our share of dead bodies but were still unprepared for the shock of the sudden appearance of a dead woman's face up close in high definition. I ponder if the old method of pulling back a sheet might have been better. The poor woman has bruising on her face, the discoloration marring what was as recently as yesterday a pretty visage. Marks around her neck suggesting strangulation are faint but obvious. A couple of cuts stretch across one cheek. Vinn looks away at first, then steadies herself and forces her head back in the direction of the television. She stares at it, tiny tears forming at the corners of her eyes, before steeling herself and bending her head to the side as if that will give her a better angle. The silence in the room grows eerie, but the young aide stands patiently, allowing Vinn to take her time. After several minutes she bobs her head slightly and as if by magic, the screen goes dark.

Vinn turns to the man, who waits expectantly. "I'm sorry," her voice waivers slightly. "But I had to be sure." He nods, encouraging her. "The answer is no. It's definitely not her."

A look of surprise or disappointment or a mixture of both flashes across the man's eyes before he regains his neutral demeanor. It's me that has my jaw dropped open, disbelief flooding my senses. I've been thinking ahead, mapping out the best way to comfort Vinn, struggling to find the right combination of words to convey both my support and sorrow. It never occurred to me that this would be a complete stranger.

"So what happens now?" Vinn asks.

The young man shrugs his shoulders. "If no one identifies her over the next day or two, we post her picture and details of her death on our website." Vinn and I both shudder and he takes notice. "I know, it seems gruesome, but we get a surprising number of bodies each year that no one claims. At any given time we have about sixty Jane and John Does on the site, stretching back for years." He sighs in resignation and a look of sadness descends over him. "Sometimes it works."

What do you say to that? He opens the door, allowing Vinn and I to precede him. On the walk back I don't even notice the odor, if it ever existed at all. My focus is solely on getting out of there. Jenkins is still in the lobby, staring out a window. He rushes over, passing by Vinn when she deliberately avoids making eye contact.

"It wasn't her," I tell him in response to his questioning look as I reach to retrieve our bag of produce. He doesn't do any better at covering his surprise than I did.

"Are you sure?" he begins before catching a glimpse of Vinn's expression out of the corner of his eye. She does not like to be doubted. Flustered, he decides to continue anyway. "Well that's good, right? I mean, we can still hope that she's alive then." He turns to face Vinn directly as he finishes, perhaps expecting a more positive reaction that he gets.

"Now can you tell us what happened to that poor girl?" she asks.

Jenkins glances in the direction of the woman behind the desk before whispering his reply. "Not here. Let's go somewhere where we can talk."

We follow him to his car.

Five minutes later we're parked near a fire hydrant in front of a small coffee shop on Taylor Street just off campus. From its window etchings to the prominent signage visible as we enter, it's hard to miss that this shop proudly proclaims its passion for java. Nearly hidden on the colorful chalkboard listing options from caramel macchiato to maple bacon latte is a single reference to a selection of tea. Over the past year I've visited every bakery and coffee shop within walking distance of campus and have yet to find one that has even a rudimentary grasp of how to properly brew tea. I pass on ordering and grab a table in the back corner while Jenkins gets coffee and Vinn visits the ladies' room. Jenkins joins me first.

"So what's with your friend? This isn't her girl, why does it matter to her what happened to her?" His eyes dart nervously toward the restroom door as he speaks. For the first time, I realize he's afraid of Vinn. Maybe he's smarter than he seems.

I could give a lengthy speech about Vinn's compassion, love of life, and the anger that arises from within whenever anyone is abused, as well as the occasional discreet actions she undertakes to set the universe right. Instead I simply reply, "She cares."

It seems to be enough. "Man, I know how she feels. Maybe I'll get jaded when I've been on the job for a while, but right now it just kind of gets to me, you know?" Jenkins balls his fist and lightly taps his heart. His eyes take on a distant stare and he involuntarily gulps. "That was my first body." I guess he got to see her after all.

Before I can respond to his confession, Vinn draws up a chair. I've been on the other side of the staredown she gives Jenkins as she sits and know that it can pierce your soul. Unable to endure her gaze, he looks down as if the tabletop has all of the answers before composing himself with a sip of coffee. He winces. Maybe the barista wasn't passionate enough today.

"Look, I don't know much. Chicago cops, the medical examiner, even paramedics, all of them, they don't respect us. Kiddie cops, they call us, like all we do is babysit a bunch of students and find their lost laptops or help them when they lock themselves out of the dorm. And it doesn't help that I'm new and I know I look young. Most of what I can tell you is what I overheard before you got there.

"They found her at O'Hare, in the cargo section. An airport cop got suspicious of a crate headed to China and opened it up. Probably lost his cookies. I don't care how long he's been on the force, if you open up a box thinking it's contraband jeans or Garrett's popcorn and see a dead woman, it's going to hit you. They said she was beat up pretty bad, she fought her attackers."

Jenkins pauses, taking a longer drink as he conjures up an image. No sour face this time. He takes his time before looking directly at us. "That's all I heard before they noticed me and moved away."

Vinn and I exchange glances. I know what she's thinking, and she knows I know. This attack may be related to Lily's disappearance, which means we need to look into it, or it's not, which means we look into it anyway because Vinn won't let anyone get away with doing what they did to that poor woman. Either way, I'm going along for the ride. No convincing or dragging me into it against my will is necessary, though. I saw the woman too.

Jenkins begins to rise. As he does, I stand and extend my hand out across the table toward him. "We appreciate it, thank you Detective. If you find out anything else, do you think you could let us know?"

His eyes narrow as he looks from me to Vinn and back again. Wheels spin in his brain and I know he's figured us out. This is the time for him to try to shut us down and make life difficult. Instead, he simply picks up his coffee and tips it in our direction.

"Will do. And you can call me London."

SIX

As motivated as Vinn is to blindly throw ourselves into an investigation of the death of a Jane Doe about whom we know nothing, she's also emotionally exhausted from the stress of the day's events and reluctantly admits that she needs some alone time. After having my ego assuaged that her decision has nothing to do with any lack of skill in the empathy department from yours truly, I just as reluctantly accede. We agree to reconvene at her condo for dinner tomorrow, which suits me fine. The break will give my brain time to begin working on finding a thread, any thread, to start unraveling so that I can at least offer a suggestion of some sort of a starting point to Vinn. Fully energized and ready to fulfill my duties as close friend and fellow sleuth, I fall asleep on the couch watching an old Ernst Lubitsch movie on Netflix.

Neither the movie nor a night of sound sleep get me any closer to square one. As I sit in my kitchen nursing a cup of a lesser Jasmine Pearls tea, I try to move past my pessimism and concentrate on breaking the roadblock thrown up by a complete lack of information about the woman in the morgue. Clearly, treating this as an isolated killing, even if true, will get us nowhere. Time to change my assumption that we're working in a vacuum and adopt a different approach. If I start with the assumption that Lily's disappearance and the murder of the other woman are connected—admittedly a huge leap—where does that get us? They're both about the same age, female, and of Asian descent or, at least in Lily's case, actually from China. Were they targeted because of their ethnicity? Could this be the work of some deranged white supremacist? Are we looking at cases of sexual assault, and if so, would that lead us to someone with a preference for Asian women?

I'm now confronted with the opposite problem, as simply assuming a link as a way of jump-starting my brain spins me off in far too many directions. Many of them are intriguing, but all of them are also far too speculative, with no supporting facts, and therefore not worth devoting much time. Or any time for that matter. Maybe brainstorming with Vinn will help us focus, but for now I have to admit to once again being stuck with no idea where to go from here. It's not a good feeling. As difficult as it is to do, I force myself to clear my mind of all things murder for now so that I have can start fresh tonight at dinner.

Dinner. I'm not sure, as the events of yesterday are a bit of a blur, but I may have promised Vinn that I would provide it. Not trusting my memory, I decide to play it safe just in case. Time's passing quickly and I need to get moving. I rummage through my fridge and freezer, then the makeshift hamper in one of the kitchen cabinets, and am pleased to find most of the ingredients for fish amok, a dish I learned to love during a stint in Cambodia. My version may not be quite authentic, but it's a treat nonetheless. We could use one.

I spend the next half hour calling around to a few local fish markets and Whole Foods until I find one with some fresh halibut, a suitable substitute for the Trei fish traditionally used in Asia. I throw some banana leaves into a cooler full of water to soften while I go out to gather the remaining ingredients. It takes me all afternoon to make the curry, but the smell of lemongrass and galangal tickles my appetite and indicates I must be doing something right. I just finish wrapping the fish mixture in the leaves and packing up the steamer when I see it's time to head off to Vinn's.

She answers the door in a sweatshirt adorned with a drawing of a gene sequence across the chest and a pair of comfortable-looking, tattered sweatpants, and immediately I sense that she's a bit more relaxed than she was yesterday. She looks genuinely pleased to see me but also throws a puzzled glance at the large green insulated cooler I have strewn over my right shoulder.

"What's that? You didn't bring food, did you? I thought I

told you that I was going to throw something together. It's my way of bribing you to get involved in this mess."

As I cross the threshold, I can smell cheese and lemon and notice pasta noodles sitting on the counter next to a tall stockpot full of water. A loaf of crispy bread is already on the table. My brain immediately sounds its internal warning bells and tells me that I need to make a choice. Do I blame my own defective memory, or should I redirect the cause of the miscommunication to Vinn's stress level of the day before? Ever the quick decision maker, I do neither.

Vinn watches as I ignore her questions and place my cooler on the island separating her kitchen from the living area. At that moment I realize she has her own doubts about who was supposed to provide dinner. After a moment of complete and awkward silence, we both break into spontaneous laughter.

"So what did you bring? I'm making lemon fettuccini with seasoned chicken."

"Um, fish amok. Unfortunately, I'm not sure if it'll keep for another day," I say guiltily.

"I'm too far along preparing mine as well. I guess we'll just have an international buffet tonight."

We smile, hug, and move to the kitchen where I set up the bamboo steamer over a large wok. Vinn starts the burner under the pot of water before grabbing a bottle of Beaujolais and two glasses and heading for the couch. We're each happy to avoid the subject of death and decay while the food is cooking and even manage to engage in some enjoyable small talk. Both the simple pasta dish and my more elaborate fish curry exceed anything we've eaten in a long time, but we're stymied as to what to do with the amount of leftover food. Vinn pulls a large plastic container out from beneath the sink, scrapes the pasta in, then pours the curry over the top. Using a couple of wooden spoons, she tosses the two dishes together, seals the container with a lid, and finds room on the bottom shelf of her refrigerator.

"Italian-Cambodian fusion," she says with a smirk. "The next big thing."

We both stand in the kitchen, stall by refilling our wine glasses, then move once more to the couch and face each other. After several moments, Vinn breaks the silence.

"I'm sorry if I've been a nuisance lately. I'm not sure why Lily's disappearance and then the murder of that poor girl have affected me to the extent they have. Maybe it's just that they seem so alone—Lily here by herself from halfway around the world and this other young woman who endured so much pain and then in death has to suffer the ignominy of lying there with no family or friends coming forth to claim her. They deserve someone to stand up for them, and if no one else will do it I will."

"No need to apologize. Your compassion is one of your more endearing traits. Besides, I'm right alongside you on this. Seeing that woman yesterday made me both sad and angry. With no one advocating for her, I don't know if we can trust the police to put much effort forward. Frankly, I'd rather find this person ourselves before they do anyway. My problem is that I've given it a lot of thought and I still don't know where to start." I choose not to share my strategy of searching for answers by falling asleep during an old movie.

Vinn sighs. "I know, me either. I'm sure you've considered that both women are Asian. Maybe there's some sort of connection there. You did more international work than I did. Do you have any connections from your former life that you could reach out to?"

The fact that she would ask this is a clear indication of how deeply affected Vinn is by the situations of the two women as well as how desperately she wants answers. We've had an understanding ever since our cautious confessionals during the summer, occasionally bent but never broken, to leave our pasts in the past. We're each afraid that revealing who we used to be will shatter our friendship in the present. Some things are better left unsaid and unshared.

Nevertheless, I nod in acknowledgement. "Maybe. I've been contemplating that route as well. But even if I make contact, what would I say? We have one missing woman about whom we know very little and one dead woman about whom we know nothing. Not exactly fertile ground even for a pro."

Her silence and melancholy fill the room until I feel that I have to offer her at least a little hope, despite my own similar outlook. "Let's do this. I'll follow up with Detective Jenkins tomorrow to see if he's got any update, then I'll poke around the Medical Examiner's office and find out which cops have been assigned to the case. Let's see if we can find something we don't already know."

Vinn says nothing but leans over to nestle her head on my shoulder. I wrap my arm around her and we sit still and close as the room grows dark. Eventually I sense a steady breathing as she falls into a deep sleep. Carefully I turn, move my arms beneath her, and carry her off to bed.

Not wanting to appear before my students in a rumpled shirt and pants that I clearly slept in, along with a few food stains I hadn't noticed the night before, I have to rush home to shower and change before heading off to my 9:00 class. The fates are with me as I catch the el as soon as I step onto the platform and it runs without delays, allowing me to walk into the classroom just in front of the last student to arrive. I throw my briefcase on top of my desk, gulp a healthy portion of strong tea, and face my young charges, all ready to begin. First, though, I have to remember which subject this is.

Just looking at the eager faces before me is enough to jog my memory. Almost entirely male, they could be clones of one another. Thick glasses, notebooks and pens at the ready, all a bit pasty as if they spend more time in front of a computer or television screen than in the great outdoors, each one looking like they just stepped out of the junior high rocket club, they're stereotypical geek. This is my "Fanta-

sy Fiction Writing 101" class. The first day of class, looking out over
the sea of faces for the first time, I thought someone was playing a
practical joke on me. A cohort in the English department eventually
clued me in. The prior professor who taught this class handpicked his
students and had a clear preference for a certain type until the administration caught on and took the class away from him. Too late, as its
reputation now scares away most women and anyone who doesn't want
to be perceived as a Dungeons and Dragons addict.

They're actually good kids and dedicated students, but they're
also terrible writers, at least so far, and have a difficult time delving into
their own imaginations instead of borrowing from Tolkien, Gaiman,
and Le Guin. I definitely have my work cut out for me. Today's assignment was to write a spellbinding opening paragraph without using
dragons, elves, magic, or time travel. It does not go well.

I have to pry myself away from a few hangers-on who want to
continue a debate that started in class about whether using a wizard
in the assignment was cheating because wizards are really overgrown
elves. I take the elevator up a few flights to take refuge in my office
for a few moments, but as the doors at my floor slide open they reveal
a delighted Stuart Vanguard, the head of the English Department as
well as my boss. Now I need refuge from my refuge.

"Ah, Mr. Winters, how fortuitous to run into you." Right.
Knowing Stuart, he's been camped out by the elevator since 7:00 this
morning waiting for my arrival so that he could arrange this coincidental meeting. While he's never said anything, I believe that Stuart
discovered late last school year that I wasn't the author he took me to
be and that I in fact have no credentials or experience that would support my teaching creative writing, or any other subject for that matter.
He's not about to report me, though, since he's the fool that hired
me, and it would reflect badly on him to have to reveal his error. He's
also probably worried that Vinn would beat him up, which frankly
is a legitimate concern. That hasn't stopped him from trying to find

or manufacture some other basis to let me go, but it will be an uphill battle. My classes are among the most popular on campus.

"I have to bring a small matter to your attention," he squeaks. Did I mention he squeaks when he talks? Or maybe it's more of a cross between a chirp and a warble. "You really do need to start locking your office door. Leaving it accessible to just anyone who happens to walk by, well, word will get out and before you know it the whole building will be swarming with ne'er-to-dos. Why, just this morning I had to chase off a young ruffian who I found coming out of your office. I could have been hurt. We just don't know if he might have had a switchblade or brass knuckles or something. You really must be more careful."

I stand corrected. It's definitely a whine. I stare at Stuart for a few minutes, add in a bit of a glare just to see how many beads of sweat I can induce, then smile and move on my way. I don't say a word, including the fact that I'm fastidious about locking my office door, a habit acquired over many years under different circumstances. I ignore Stuart's sputtering behind me and pick up my pace. I need to see what the "young ruffian" took from me.

Entering my office, also and more accurately referred to as my walk-in closet, my first pass-over doesn't reveal anything amiss. My files, the few that there are, haven't been touched, nor has the rock still graced with the DNA from the head of a fake Sherpa whose body may still be buried under thick layers of snow, that serves as my paperweight. Most importantly, my collection of teas that help me make it through a full day without also bashing Stuart in the head are untouched. Puzzled, I move around to the back of my desk and pull out my chair.

Sitting conspicuously in the middle of the seat is an unmarked manila envelope. Carefully holding it at arms' length as I open it, as if that will save me when it explodes, a thin file falls to the floor, scattering its contents. As I pick the papers up and tap them into a neat pile on my desk, the few random phrases that catch my eye are enough to reveal what the 'ruffian' left behind. In my hands is a copy of the Chicago police file on the woman Vinn and I saw in the morgue.

SEVEN

"Jenkins? You can't be serious." Vinn is sitting cross-legged on my living room floor, her back nestled up against the couch and the police file sitting on her lap. As tempted as I was to examine it in my office, Vinn deserves the first look, as long as I can be only a nano-second behind her. Our class schedules today conflicted too much to get together at work, so we came back to my place immediately after her last lecture of the day.

"Who else? I think he sees this case as his road to promotion, or at least some modicum of respect from his peers, or maybe a ticket onto the Chicago force, but without any standing in the investigation his hands are tied as to what he can do as a campus cop. He uses us as his proxies, lets us do all of the hard work, then steps in at the end and takes all of the credit. The success of his plan depends on our efforts, so he feeds us the report to get us started."

Vinn appears unconvinced, her unwillingness to give Jenkins credit for any positive intensions intact, but says no more. I slide down beside her and together we open the file. There isn't much there, which is understandable given that the body was only discovered two days ago and a Jane Doe doesn't merit priority handling. A case summary sits on top.

CASE FILE

File No: 20-479-OH

Victim's Name: Eileen Wong (ID'd by father)

Date of Birth: April 1998

Place of Birth: Shanxi Province, China

Race: Asian/Chinese

Date of Death: Unknown, range of 9/24–9/27/20

Next of Kin: Simon Wong, father Physicist, Argonne Labs
(contact found on cell phone)
1226 Apple Tree Lane, Batavia, IL. 630-555-9944
Mother lives in China, unable to contact

Residence: Chicago, father unable to give exact address.

Cause of Death: Asphyxiation (primary),
Strangulation (secondary)

Narrative: Body found in shipping crate in cargo section of
international terminal, O'Hare Airport. Crate targeted by security dog. On
site officer opened crate, body discovered under clothing labeled for export.
Specific destination written in Chinese, not translated, somewhere in China.
No return address. Local precinct notified, body transported to medical
examiner. Personal effects: diamond or faux gem ring (possibly engagement)
on left middle finger. Father says victim not engaged, not dating as far as he
knows. Six oranges, man's shirt
(folded, red and white), red silk slippers also in crate. Bagged.

When Vinn notices that I've finished reading—she's the faster reader—she turns the page. It's blank, eliciting a mild expletive from my foul-mouthed companion. Apparently that's as much detail as was written down initially. Handwritten notes indicate that the detectives working the case at that point were still unable to find her apartment and that her father didn't know where she worked or the names of her friends. The cops got the impression Eileen didn't share much with her dad.

The medical examiner's report is painfully detailed, but as far as I can tell does little to lead us in any useful direction. The official cause of death is listed as asphyxiation, although the examiner admits to some uncertainty as to the exact method that finished her off. He speculates that she was unconscious at the time and that the instrument used to strangle her was soft, like a scarf, not the more customary rope or human hands, but fibers in her lungs also suggest that when the scarf didn't do the trick she was suffocated with a pillow. I have to bite back a comment that this seems like overkill. Severe bruising to Eileen's arms and torso indicate that she tried to fight her attackers off but was overpowered; there's no explanation as to why she was unconscious at the time of death. No overt evidence of sexual assault but more tests were pending. There's no toxicology report.

We move on to the photographs, or more accurately out-of-focus photocopies of them, one or two to a page. There's a lot of them, as if whoever was behind the camera was trying to get every possible angle to chronicle something out of the ordinary. About halfway through viewing them, some quiet little voice from the deep recesses of my mind nags me, convinced that there's most definitely something discordant about this body. Without asking, Vinn gathers the pictures up and begins going through them a second time, more slowly than before. This time through I realize what seems odd. Based on the pauses Vinn takes with certain photos, I assume she sees it as well.

Once we've finished viewing the pictures, that's it. The investigation is in its early stages and the detectives don't seem to have devoted much time to the case yet, or perhaps the documentation we have isn't up to date, which would all explain the lack of any substantial detail. I believe there's something there, though, that gives us a starting point for at least some discussion. I wait before blurting out my thoughts. Vinn has a nose for this kind of thing and I want to hear from her first.

She's still holding on to the stack of paper with the photograph copies when she starts to speak. "There's a lot here that doesn't make sense. Did you notice?" She flips through the copies and sets several of them aside. Her selection confirms that we're both on the same wavelength. "For someone who was just killed, and who obviously fought back, her body is in remarkably clean shape. Not a hair out of place, as if it were brushed and then sprayed, but considering how violent the fight must have been based on the bruising, it's almost as if that was done after she was killed. She's wearing immaculate makeup, which the coroner must have removed before we viewed the body. She could have put it on herself before she went out, but then shouldn't it be smeared, at least a little bit? I haven't seen many pictures taken at crime scenes or in a morgue, but this strikes me as bizarre."

Relieved to hear her confirm my own thoughts, I'm more comfortable with my blurting. "I agree, but there's more. Let's take a step further back. We're in agreement that the bruising suggests a brutal confrontation where she resisted with all of her might, as if her attackers had difficulty subduing her. But then the actual killing was almost gentle. I'm speculating here, but in reading the examiner's conclusions, the killers may have rendered her unconscious before actually finishing her off, because they tried to strangle her with a scarf and when that didn't work, held a pillow over her face. It's almost as if they had affection for her."

"Or maybe they were afraid of making marks and sullying her body," Vinn adds, making a face. "That would be consistent with fixing her up, prettifying her, after she was dead. Why would anyone want to do that? And wait a minute…" Vinn shuffles papers to find a particular picture. "Here, look at this. This was taken at the airport before they moved the body and before the medical examiner stripped her to do the post mortem. The quality of these copies is terrible, but it seems like she's wearing some sort of fancy dress or gown that wasn't mentioned in the report. Could even be silk. We don't have a shot of the whole garment, but it looks almost ceremonial because of the embroidery, if that's what those blurry patterns are. And are those dragons? It's not listed in the inventory, but the pictures show what might be a veil or some sort of netting. Not something a young woman in this country would wear out on the town."

We both sit in silence for a few moments. Something occurs to me and this time I don't hesitate. "What did the summary say? Can we go back to that page? Weren't there also some silk slippers in the crate she was in? See, there. Along with some other items that don't make any sense, like the oranges. And wait, take a closer look at this photo. It's from when she was first discovered. Is that a pillow under her head?"

Vinn squints and turns the photo in multiple directions, as if that will help. "Maybe. Can't tell for sure. I assume your point is the same as mine, right? We may be way off base here, but she was killed with compassion, maybe by assailants without a lot of experience considering it took them several tries, then dressed up, hair brushed, makeup done, and placed comfortably, so to speak, when she was packed in a crate. What the hell?"

"Sounds crazy, I know. But you and I both came to the same conclusion, so maybe it's not so farfetched after all. We need to do one other thing. Hold on a minute." I walk to my desk, rummage through the drawers, and come back with a device about the size of a paperback. "It's old but the Mandarin language has been around for millennia and I don't think the it's changed all that much in the last twenty years. It's my government-issued translator. Do you have the picture of the shipping label that was on the crate handy?"

It takes Vinn a second to find it. I ask her to hold it still as I scan it into the machine. Now we wait. Even machines get slower with age, or maybe my patience gets thinner. "Here we go. I guess this is a name, or maybe just a drop point. But look at where the crate was headed. Didn't we see the name of that place somewhere else?"

Vinn grabs a paper. "Yes! Shanxi province. Eileen's mother lives there." She reads my face too well. "Wait, you don't think she's involved, do you?"

We look directly at one another but neither of us speaks. That's a good question.

EIGHT

It's been two days since Vinn and I conferred over the contents of the police file. Our initial euphoria at being gifted a starting point quickly faded when neither of us could come up with a single idea as to where to go from here. Vinn's frustrated, and more than a little angry, at her overwhelming feeling of helplessness. This is normally my cue to step in with a magical solution that opens up a door to move us forward. A nice concept, and it's never a bad thing to be a hero to the woman you love, but the sprites whose job it is to sprinkle me with the fairy dust that opens my eyes to a solution that's been in front of me the entire time can't seem to figure out the next step themselves. Either way, Vinn's frustration has become my own vexation, a state of mind so consuming that I can't sleep. Staring at the ceiling in the middle of the night doesn't seem to be accomplishing much, so I throw on some clothes, swallow my pride, and head down two flights.

Leo opens up the door before I have a chance to knock. I don't know how he does that and it's beyond disturbing when I think about it, but I'm in no mood to delve into the issue tonight. Wordlessly we move to our usual places across from each other at the kitchen table, Leo staring me down with a frown on his flushed face. I know him well enough not to go directly into the reason I'm there until he indicates he's ready, which usually means prior consumption of large amounts of alcohol. Tonight is no exception. We start in on a bottle of exquisite rum, then at some point move on to mezcal. Leo is very sly with the refills and I almost never notice him topping off my glass, so while I think I'm still working on my first or second drink it's entirely possible that I've consumed half a bottle or more of high octane booze. Leo is both perceptive and patient and the minutes tick by as we sit in silence for some time as we drink, make innocuous small talk, then drink some more. I'm not sure what time it is except that it's late, or maybe early morning. I glance at the clock on his wall but the numbers are all out of focus, there seem to be too many of them, and I can't find the hands at all.

Leo must sense that I've reached a state of inebriation where I'll feel comfortable freely bringing up the details of the reason I'm there, and that he's stoned enough to hear them. He nods, his signal to get down to business. It takes me a minute to sort out where to start, but once I get going the words spill out, slightly slurred but coherent enough to tell the story of the murdered woman. Leo sits silently and stoically as what I hope is reasoned conversation morphs into more of a drunken bitch session.

When I stop long enough that he can tell I'm not just catching my breath, he closes his eyes and sits eerily still. Time is a bit of a muddle, so it may have been only a few minutes, but I'm beginning to sober up and am just about ready to poke him to make sure he's still alive when he speaks.

"No. No mother would do that to her child. No." He seems angry that I would even suggest it.

"I agree, Leo, I'm sure she's not involved. But we can't ignore the fact that the body was destined for the same province in which she lives." I don't mention that I had done some research earlier that day. Shanxi province has over thirty-five million residents living in an area the size of Georgia. That leaves 34,999,999 people I've never heard of that could be the intended recipient. "I don't like coincidences so until we can eliminate her, we have to consider the mother's involvement a possibility." Leo's scowl suggests that he prefers his view of human nature to my own.

His eyes stay open but now take on a faraway look. I recognize this as a sign of deep thought on his part and know to stay quiet until he comes back to earth. Sometimes that can mean an hour or more. This time it's only a matter of seconds. I think.

"That girl. Not the dead one, the other one. The student. The missing one." I nod to show I know who he's referring to. In my impaired state, it's more an acknowledgement to my own brain that I'm following his train of thought. "Where's she from?"

I admit that my jaw may have just dropped open. Being drunk at this particular moment excuses my fuzzy thought process, but it never occurred to me to look into that when I was sober. Now that Leo has raised the question, I want an answer and don't want to wait for it. I grab my phone. Leo starts to say something and to move his hand forward, but I'm already furiously typing out a text. Sometimes words I use all the time look very peculiar through bloodshot eyes, so it takes me a while to compose something that makes sense. Even if I weren't an English professor, text-talk annoys me to a degree that I refuse to use any abbreviations or shorthand and my spelling has to be perfect. Time seems to stand still until I'm finally satisfied and press "send."

Leo shakes his head slightly with the corners of his mouth upturned as he reaches across to fill my glass. I'm about to take a swig of whatever we're drinking when my phone sounds with the funky sounds of Thomas Dolby's old classic "She Blinded Me with Science." Vinn returned my text. She's never told me what she thinks of my ringtone tribute although I'm sure she's honored. Well, maybe not all that sure.

I bring the phone about five inches from my face in order to read her message. "DO YOU KNOW WHAT TIME IT IS!!!???" Well, no I don't. I would if Leo's clock would stop moving all over that wall and if it had hands.

I'm disappointed that she doesn't actually answer Leo's question and instead drops into an awkward silence, punctuated only by Leo's quiet chuckling as he reads my expression. A few minutes later another text comes in.

"Damn you. I know where you're going with this, good question. Don't know the answer. I'll find out. Dammit, now I won't sleep until I know. I hope you don't either. Later." She loves me, I can tell.

Leo must be sympathetic, or maybe I just appear more pathetic than usual, as he rises and begins to heat water for tea. I keep a stash of my own teas in his apartment to avoid the crap he uses himself, and he's learned to brew a fairly decent cup. I can't stand to see anything go to waste, so I quickly swallow down the last bit of alcohol in my glass. Big mistake.

Fortunately, the tea begins to mellow me out and after a while my head starts to clear slightly. The homemade stew he also thinks to heat up and set before me is making me nauseous, but that's not the booze talking. His food has that effect on me even when I'm sober. I stir it around with a spoon and try to find a way to make it look like I've eaten some. The alternative of actually having to do so does more to bring me back to the land of the living than if I'd actually consumed it. Maybe Leo knew what he was doing after all.

"Leo, thanks for listening, and I appreciate the suggestion about Lily. It's distressing that this is eating Vinn up so hard and we can't seem to grasp onto even the most insignificant detail to guide us in the right direction. Or the wrong direction. Or any direction at all."

Leo looks concerned. He likes Vinn and I'm sure he doesn't relish the thought of her in distress. He reaches over and pats me on the back of the hand. "Leo knows. Tell you what. I know someone who knows Chinese people. I will have him ask. Maybe they know something. Maybe people talk."

I appreciate the sentiment and say so but can't imagine that whatever is happening here is the subject of general conversation in the local Asian community, or that Leo actually has the kind of connections that would have an ear to the ground on subjects such as this. It's true Leo has his secrets, and I've learned not to underestimate him, but I see what he's saying as his effort at encouragement rather than a true offer.

I don't remember rising from my chair, but I suddenly find myself exiting his door heading for the stairs bringing me up to my apartment with a leaky bag in my hand. Somehow Leo found time to pack up his stew before sending me on my way. Dammit. The misery of the hangover that awaits me in just a few hours will be nothing compared to discovering this meal in my refrigerator later in the day.

NINE

Vinn gained access to Lily's file from admissions, thankfully keeping me in the dark as to how she did so, and confirmed that she came from the same Chinese province as Eileen. Our initial euphoria at the connection quickly faded when we had to admit we had no idea what to do with that information, which we filed away in our memory banks in the hope of making a withdrawal later. The end of the work week has now arrived without a word from Leo or his source, if this person exists at all. I never mentioned Leo's offer to Vinn so as not to get her hopes up, which considering the lack of any outreach from an Asian stranger appears to have been a good decision. We've continued to meet in the café before classes to banter a few wild ideas back and forth, mainly to convince each other that we're actively moving forward with the investigation, but we aren't fooling ourselves. I can see the dark circles under Vinn's eyes and know that they're a reflection of my own.

Whether due to my tossing and turning for yet another night or simply characteristic laziness—I suspect the latter—it's now mid-morning on Saturday and I'm still not dressed for the day. I'm procrastinating at my breakfast bar with a steaming cup of Keemun black tea, a fairly pedestrian Chinese import that won't get my taste buds cheering for more. My selection of teas lately has been my own form of self-flagellation, penalizing myself for not being the investigative genius my background would suggest. There's nothing wrong with the level of caffeine in this swill, though, as the clouds begin to lift and my eyes start to focus for the first time since I slipped out of bed. I've been sitting here staring in the general direction of my front door for at least fifteen minutes before I notice an envelope sitting on the floor just inside of it. My first thought is that I need to check my seals, as it shouldn't be possible to get anything past my security measures, but that'll have to wait. I put my mug down, not unhappy to leave the remaining tea behind to cool until it's totally undrinkable and I can justify dumping it in the sink, and move to pick up the envelope. Not labeled, no indication of what may lie within, and best of all it doesn't explode when I jostle it. My first thought is that the Jehovah's Witnesses are getting sneakier.

I grab my letter opener, a long, thin blade responsible for the scar above my left ribcage and also the reason its former owner no longer has need of it, and slit the top. Inside is another envelope, a standard #10, which gets the same treatment from the opener. I pull out a small piece of notebook paper with a computer-generated printout in a jagged font taped to it:

"12:30 p.m. Chinatown. Where those who served are honored."

I'm intrigued, wary, and more than a little pissed off. What kind of game is this? If this is Leo's idea of a joke, I refuse to give him the satisfaction of confronting him with the note. On the other hand, if this is legitimate in an amateur sort of way and there's any possibility that showing up will lead to information about Eileen's death or Lily's disappearance, I might as well play along. It's not like I have any better ideas or plans for the day. I call my fellow investigator, dress, select which parts of my arsenal to take along, and head out the door, but not before pouring the remainder of the tea down the drain.

Vinn sits next to me in a half-empty el car on the Red Line heading south to the Cermak-Chinatown stop, enthusiastically punching buttons on her phone. She wears one out about every six months. Despite my sympathy for her keyboard, I'm fine with letting her do the research here. She's better at it than I am and could use the distraction of staying busy. While I wait, I occupy myself looking up general information about the neighborhood.

It doesn't take her long. "Pretty obvious, unless I'm missing something. There's the Chinese-American Veteran's Memorial on the corner of Cermak and Archer, a straight shot down from the station. If that's not it, I don't know what else the note could be referencing. I've only been to Chinatown a couple of times and the last time was at least two or three years ago. It's fairly compact, and other than a lot of restaurants and some gift shops aimed at tourists, there isn't much there. This has to be it. If not I can look some more, but let's at least start there."

Within minutes we're down the stairs and leaving the station heading west. Unlike Vinn, I've never been to Chicago's Chinatown, so all I know is what I just read on the train. It's larger than Vinn led me to believe, ranking in size and population only behind New York's and San Francisco's. Cermak Avenue appears to be the dividing line between the older section of the neighborhood to the south and a newer section on the north side. About half of the people we pass are Asians walking purposefully with a clear destination in mind. The other half are tourists wandering aimlessly, appearing lost. We pass several gift shops with the same smiling Buddahs and ornate cats with bobbing heads in the windows as well as several restaurants just starting to fill up with hungry diners. The scent of ginger and garlic fills my nose. I regret not snacking on the way.

"There—see?" Vinn points up ahead in the direction of something that no, I can't see. She picks up her pace and within a few steps I make out the outline of what appears to be a memorial of some sort. Only when we reach the street corner do I get a clear view. It's a simple but strong structure of dark marble, tall in the center before sloping down on each side. There's no doubt what it is, as large lettering identifies the structure as the "Chinese American Veteran's Memorial," with what I assume is the Mandarin translation below. For a brief moment the creative writing professor in me ponders which particular veteran it honors based on the location of the apostrophe but decide not to bring that thought up to Vinn. This isn't the time to play grammar cop. Besides, she's already three paces into the street and almost out of shouting distance before I move to catch up.

"Uh, Vinn, can you slow down? Can we take a few seconds to at least scope out the area before charging in?" I don't sense danger, but there's no point in being careless.

She glances back at me, annoyed, but does stop as soon as she reaches the far curb. Other than a few pedestrians hurrying by on the sidewalk, no one else is in view. Nevertheless, we're cautious when we move into the small plaza. Several moments pass.

"So now what?" Vinn asks as if she's reading my thoughts. "Does Boris Badenov come to meet us? Is someone perched behind a window somewhere watching us and laughing?"

Or aiming, I think, but I don't say it. "Well it doesn't do much good for us just to stand here. Let's at least explore the area."

Without a word, Vinn moves to the left and I move to the right, each of us quickly closing in on the memorial with each step. I walk to the far end to peek behind it and am just considering what to do about the tree that blocks my way to the rear when Vinn calls out from the other side.

"Mal, I could use your help." I do a slow jog to where she stands beneath one of a series of flag poles. I follow her gaze upward to a yellow Post It Note taped to the pole about two feet beyond her reach. Even with my additional height it's just past my fingertips. For the first time in ages I feel a surge of adrenaline. The note was clearly placed there intentionally by someone who didn't want a casual pass-erby to be able to reach it.

Vinn looks at me expectantly with her finger pointing down-ward. I raise an eyebrow in her direction, knowing the gesture annoys the hell out of her, but eventually accede to my new role as cherry pick-er. I squat down as Vinn first steps over my left shoulder then my right before grabbing hold of my hair. I rise slowly, resisting the urge to make beeping noises, gripping tightly onto her thighs. "Got it!" I hear, my signal to gently lower her back to the ground.

The note is folded in half and taped shut. Vinn carefully opens it with her fingernail so as not to tear whatever message may lie within. I'm not sure what we were hoping for, but another cryptic clue wasn't it. Vinn reads it out loud.

"Nine breathe fire for good fortune where a flower blooms." I don't think the expletive she mutters at the end is a part of the message. This time it's me who knows where we need to go and I don't need an assist from Google. We passed near a ceramic wall as we left the el station and even though it didn't merit more than a quick glance at the time, if the powers of observation I gained from years of training and experience aren't failing me, there's a long line of dragons on that wall. Enough that there could be nine. I pass my brilliant piece of detective work on to Vinn, who doesn't react as positively and with as much adoration as I had hoped.

"What is this, a scavenger hunt?" she hisses, once again using a very unladylike word in the middle of the question. The same thought is going through my mind, my brain also adding the same nasty word, but for the time being I'm willing to subject ourselves to this irritating form of manipulation for the sake of the missing and murdered women. My patience is running thin but unless another option magically appears I don't know what other choice we have. Going home empty-handed out of pique won't make everything better.

We retrace our steps and cross Cermak in order to reach an elaborate, pagoda-style tiled wall sitting behind protective fencing under the shadow of the expressway above. There are, in fact, nine large dragons on the panels, although if we count the smaller ones the total increases by several hundred. Contrary to the message on the note, nothing nearby is blooming, so we lean against the fence contemplating our next step. Just as we do, a young Chinese girl approaches with an armful of tissue-wrapped roses.

"Pretty flower for the pretty woman?" she asks me without

any trace of an accent. As I reach for a rose, she pulls it back. "Five dollars."

I scowl, bite back a comment about the value of a single wilt-ed stem and pay the young extortionist, who hurries away. Carefully avoiding the multitude of thorns, I peel away the tissue and a business card drops out. Vinn beats me picking it up and positions herself so that we can both read it at the same time.

No message on the front side, which advertises a local shop called Yin Wall City. On the back, in tiny lettering slightly smeared by unseen fingers, are the words "14 ounces ginseng." I watch as anger rises to color Vinn's cheeks, again reflecting my own mood. Silently she uses the GPS on her phone to find the shop, which turns out to be close by. Seething, neither one of us speaks as we head in its direction. Having fulfilled its function, I discard the rose on the way.

The entrance to Yin Wall City faces a grimy section of park-ing lot off of Cermak. As we enter, we're forced to navigate a long and narrow passage lined with dozens of barrels of bulk foods, with colorful bags populating shelves at face level on the walls. Hundreds more overflowing drums appear before us as we reach the main area of the shop. Each bin is labeled only in Mandarin, or maybe Cantonese. Vinn pulls a photo of ginseng up on her phone, which we match to the contents of one nearby bin. The shopkeeper hurries over as we reach for the nearby scoop, apparently worried that we'll abuse the goods. She motions to a scale with questioning eyes.

"Fourteen ounces, please." I say, masking my annoyance. It may be my imagination, but the woman's countenance seems to light up after I speak. She hurries away and returns with a paper bag identi-cal to those that sit directly next to the bin of ginseng. Without both-ering to use the scale, she scoops a healthy amount into the bag and quickly scurries to the cash register where she rings up my unwanted purchase.

"$118.00? Are you serious?" I nearly scream. The woman is

nonplussed and silent, probably used to hearing this from tourists on a regular basis. Whomever is behind this better hope that we never meet. Vinn places her hand on my arm to calm me before quietly retreating a few steps, leaving it clear who will be paying for this. Ginseng may have health benefits, but at this particular moment all it's doing is raising my blood pressure.

We leave the shop through a front door that exits onto a modern, cramped outdoor mall. Retreating to the doorway of a vacant storefront, it doesn't take us long to find the next message written in a tiny, neat scrawl on the bottom of the bag: "Go 4 Food. Order Fusion Chili Crab and Ma Po Tofu with shredded pork, nothing else. Have a nice lunch."

This latest message, rather than inspiring us to go on, has the opposite effect. We both deflate like old balloons. Vinn sinks to the ground but quickly stands back up when she realizes how dirty it is. Time to be the voice of optimism, if not reason.

"Might as well. I confess I am a bit hungry. But that's it. No more games. After lunch, we go home." She nods, pulls out her phone to find where we're going, and we start walking. It's only then I realize she slipped the bag of ginseng into her purse. Maybe not the best time to ask her for $118.00.

The restaurant is back on the other side of Cermak, just past the more touristy shops on 23rd street, off the main drag of Wentworth Avenue. I'm surprised to see a Michelin star on the window. At this point it's well past lunchtime, but the place is busy. The dining room is small but we manage to secure a table near the back. It's as if it were saved just for us.

The menu is typical in that it has way too many items from which to choose but our selection has been preordained. Keeping to the plan, we stick with water and order nothing other than the two dishes. Neither of us is in the mood to speak. My stomach lets out an involuntary growl.

The food arrives after about fifteen otherwise-quiet minutes. I spoon some of each out for Vinn, then fill my own plate. Vinn's eyebrows rise as she uses her chopsticks to sample the crab. I try the pork. Soon we're both hungrily clearing our plates. We don't utter a word until after the second helping. Vinn sums up what we're both feeling.

"Wow."

I nod my agreement. We may have wasted a good part of a Saturday for some unknown person's amusement, but at least we have a new favorite restaurant to add to our list. Eating has also improved our moods substantially. I ask for the check.

Vinn excuses herself to use the ladies' room just before the bill arrives, which after the ginseng incident is more than a little suspicious. I pull out my wallet but put it back again after reading the check. When Vinn returns I hold it up for her viewing.

"My treat," it reads in the now-familiar handwriting. "Meet me at the Chicago Chinese Table Tennis Club." Listed below is an address that's practically right across the street. Despite our vow not to pursue any more of these leads, we both agree that we might as well try one more since it's so close and our host went to the effort of paying for our lunch.

Not that it's easy to find. The address on the check leads us to a boarded-up shop that has the appearance of having last been open during the Nixon administration. After a few minutes of contemplation, we slowly move down a narrow passageway to the left of the building, only wide enough to go one after the other. We pass by a few closed doors beneath red awnings and are about to turn around when Vinn whispers "Listen."

It takes a moment, but I hear the faint and familiar sound of a ping-pong ball as it hits both table and paddle. We follow our ears to the rear of the building, where a door is slightly ajar. I feel for my weaponry before pushing it open. We both slide slowly into the room, all of our senses on high alert.

At first all that's visible are a few tables set up in a room painted green with Chinese language characters on the walls. Two elderly Chinese men furiously send a ball back and forth across a net. Motion to our left has us turn, hopefully to face the sadistic individual who's had us traversing the neighborhood all morning. He or she had better have something good to share.

Our clue-writing nemesis is indeed there, grinning. I freeze, jaw to the ground. Vinn does the same. For a moment neither of us speaks. Finally, I'm able to recover enough to squeak one, single word.

"You!"

TEN

Rebecca stands before us, a vision in flared high-waisted taupe pants leading up to an oversized blouse of some undetermined color, perhaps in the orange family, with a silkish scarf adorned with what appear to be tennis balls wrapped loosely around her neck. My immediate thought is that I'd like to get my hands wrapped around that neck, and my squeeze would be anything but loose. She's beaming, almost giddy, clearly amused at our shock.

It takes me a moment to find my voice again. "Rebecca, what in the hell are you doing here?"

My tone may be a bit aggressive, as the corners of her mouth turn down into the makings of a frown, but she recovers quickly and brings back the smile.

"Leo said you needed help. Did you enjoy your little adventure?" The joy in her voice seems genuine. "Wasn't it just the best time you've ever had?"

Vinn jumps in ahead of me. "That was you? You're responsible for sending us all over Chinatown on that dog and pony show? Couldn't you have just told us to meet you here?"

Rebecca looks hurt, unable to grasp why we're upset. "What would be the fun in that? I thought I would add the Rebecca touch to this cloak-and-dagger exercise. Tell you where to meet? How drab. How predictable." To emphasize how much we've damaged her feelings, she tosses her head back in the air and heads off past the players to the far table, hips swaying exaggeratedly, where she picks up a paddle and ball and pretends to be interested in sharpening her game. She's fooling no one. No one plays ping pong in three-inch heels.

In all of the commotion, I hadn't noticed the small Asian man who's now standing in the space Rebecca just vacated. His head moves back and forth between the colorful diva at the far end of the room and ourselves, perhaps not comprehending the exchange that just occurred. He notices himself wringing his hands and stops, then unconsciously begins again. His left foot taps the floor repeatedly. He's not just nervous, he's scared. Is he the reason we're here? One way to find out.

I move slowly forward, hand extended. "I'm sorry you had to see that. We've just spent the last few hours following a twisted trail, unnecessarily it seems, and our nerves are on edge. Rebecca was the last person we expected to find at the end of the line. My name is Malcom. Mal. This is my friend Vinn."

He bows slightly, pauses as if making a decision, then nods to himself and bows again. I withdraw my hand. "I am called Li Wei," he says in a heavy accent so quietly that I lean forward to hear. His voice waivers and his eyes continue to dart. Part of me wonders what his real name is. "Please. Come sit."

He leads us to a corner where three chairs have been arranged and waits for us to sit before he joins us. A wobbly table holds an ancient, purple clay teapot adorned with a wrap-around dragon and four mismatched cups. Without asking, he begins the traditional Chinese tea service, pouring tea into the cups to warm them before dumping them out and refilling. We take the proffered drink without comment. I glance at Vinn, wary of whether she'll insult our host by declining. I'm sure she would rather have Starbucks. I sip, find myself surprised, then sip again. "Exquisite," I say. I mean it.

This seems to please our host and he relaxes ever so slightly, looking over in the direction of Rebecca, who continues to pretend that we don't exist. "I am sorry. I do not know what games she play with you to get you here. I do not always understand her." He looks at us for our reaction and the corners of his mouth upturn slightly at our grinning faces. "She is also man, do you know? Many months ago went on date with my niece who came in to say hello. He asked to join club, I think to impress her. Man not so nice, I not allow to join. She is…" he stops, trying to find the right words, "not as bad. Bad player, but not bad person. No longer sees niece but keeps coming anyway. Members here only judged on skill with paddle."

I'm smiling widely now and Vinn snorts to hold back a laugh. Rebecca either doesn't want to be left out of the fun or thinks we're talking about her, which we are, and starts to casually slide along the wall in our direction. Alarmed, Li falls silent. I need to get him talking.

"I don't know what Rebecca has told you, but we're both teachers. Professors here in the city. One of Vinn's Chinese students has disappeared and we're looking for her. For too long now, and we're concerned. During our search we found out about Eileen Wong, so now we want to know what happened to her too, and to see if it will help us find Lily." I don't go into detail. I don't know how much Mr. Wei knows or wants to know.

Vinn decides to add a woman's perspective. "I like Lily very much. She's a good student and a nice person. I worry. I know her mother must be worried even more. I'll do everything and anything to find her." I glance over. The mother is a nice touch.

The old man's eyes are downcast and sad. "I did not know either of them. But I tell her," he nods in the general direction of Rebecca, who's been creeping slowly closer and is now nearly part of the circle, "that I will listen. See what I can hear.

"I do not like what I hear." His hands are clearly trembling as his grip on the teacup tightens. "Whispers. Rumors. No one wants to talk. Too dangerous. Tongs."

We wait as several minutes pass. The conversation appears to be over, but we haven't learned anything. I need to encourage him to continue. Easy enough to do, as the last word he said is one that I'm not familiar with. "Tongs?" I ask.

"Tongs are Chinese gangs." It's Rebecca who chimes in from behind me, using the opportunity to join our trio. There are no more chairs, so she leans against the wall, casting annoyed glances at me and my perch. I'm guessing the protocol is that I should offer her a seat when she's dressed this way, but I need to be on Mr. Wei's level if I'm to hear what he has to say. I'm also holding a grudge for our earlier game of hide and seek. I stay seated but look up at Rebecca as she speaks.

"Chinese gangs have mostly stayed under the radar, but that doesn't mean they don't exist," she explains, evidently having consulted Wikipedia. "They grew out of the old Triad system in China, highly structured. They have their hands in activities similar to gangs of other nationalities—drugs, prostitution, extortion, etc. They can be very violent. They've worked their way into the social and political structures of the neighborhood here, so they know everything that happens." She glances over at our host, who's turned pale and now seems petrified. "Mr. Wei may know more than what he's saying, but probably not. As soon as the specter of local gangs was raised, I'm sure his ears and eyes shut down for his own safety. His mouth would do so as well. Just telling you that tongs are somehow involved could get him in trouble. The two of you will have to take it from here."

Rebecca's earlier joviality has by now completely disappeared, and Mr. Wei's hospitality is wavering. I look at Vinn and read in her eyes that she's thinking the same thing that I am. We didn't get much, but it's all we're going to get, at least for now. If what Rebecca says is true, the last thing we want to do is drag anyone else into the danger zone. We rise, and I place our cups on the table.

"Mr. Wei, thank you so much for your hospitality. The tea is some of the best I have ever had." I bow in his direction. He acknowledges me with a nod but says nothing.

I turn to face Rebecca as we walk toward the door. "Thank you for the introduction and the meal." Might as well try to make amends. I have to live right above her, after all. "Do you really play ping pong?"

She looks affronted. "Ping pong? Ping Pong? You really are an idiot, Malcom. I play table tennis." She shuts the door in our faces.

ELEVEN

"Now what?" We're back in Vinn's condo, once again sprawled on the floor with our backs against her couch. I can't remember the last time I actually sat on the damn thing. We haven't said much since leaving Chinatown, probably because neither of us has an answer to the question on both of our minds, which is exactly what Vinn just expressed. Now what?

I decide to dispense with any optimistic happy talk. "I honestly don't know, Vinn. This investigation, if we can call it that, has brought nothing but frustration since we started. We run into a wall with no idea how to get over it, finally catch a break through no effort of our own, but are still stymied. Then just when things seem totally bleak, we're unexpectedly handed some additional information that probably means something, but also have no clue what to do with it. For all of our running around today, all we discovered is that there may be a link between Eileen's death, Lily's disappearance, and a Chinese gang—excuse me, tong—but where does that get us?"

"My thoughts exactly." She shifts to lean in closer to me. "Did you observe how terrified Mr. Lei was even to mention the connection? My guess is that the residents down there won't be talking about this to anyone that they don't know well, much less to strangers like you and me, and even then only in whispers. With our pale faces and lack of ability to converse in any of China's 297 languages, we'd be instantly shut off and maybe just draw unwanted attention."

I know Vinn wasn't looking for brownie points for being one of three people in the world who know how many languages are spoken in China. She clearly has been spending a lot of time on the internet randomly browsing for any information that might break our stalemate, and once a fact enters her brain it never leaves again. Nestled comfortably inside that brilliant mind of hers in the guise of general knowledge are a million and one obscure bits of information that she assumes everyone knows, like the color of the sky. I just let it lie. I also choose not to take the bait on her reference to the last time we exposed ourselves for the sake of bringing justice to a killer. Nothing good will come of revisiting that horrid incident.

We sit in silence, content to simply hold each other while watching shadows begin to intrude through her windows as the sun dips below the rooftops of the building next door. My body may be still but my mind is restless. Surely there has to be something I can say to provide at least a modicum of assurance that everything will work out despite my own opinion that it's hopeless. Right on cue, the flash of an idea tickles the periphery of my conscious thoughts. I close my eyes, slow my breathing to lull myself into a state of half sleep, and concentrate on bringing it back. Ten frustrating minutes pass before I'm able to successfully wrangle the elusive thought, but I'm more than a little disappointed to discover that all of that effort resulted in something less of a revelation and more of a desperate suggestion.

"Vinn, you asked me a while ago if I know someone who might be able to assist us. It just occurred to me that I may actually have a useful connection. Or had. Someone from my former life, one of the few from that time that I respected. Also one of the few who tolerated me or saw me as more than an instrument to use without concern for my well-being. Our paths only crossed a few times, but each time was in Asia where they were based. Should I reach out?"

Vinn doesn't jump up and down in excitement. We've already established that she's not dumb, and she obviously knows this isn't a clear path to solving our issues, but that it's better than nothing. Of course she assents.

Now the question is, how do I find someone who doesn't want to be found?

No one could credibly dispute the fact that keeping in touch has never been easier than it is in society today. Instant communication around the world is made possible through the miracles of email and telephones. Cell phones have the dubious distinction of making it nearly impossible to be out of reach of a call from your boss or jealous boyfriend. In the case of certain governmental agencies, spy satellites, drones, invisible tracking devices, and the like provide the technology to follow an individual from the dry cleaner to the sushi restaurant to the bathroom and beyond. Unless you're willing to settle in the middle of nowhere in a cave without a single electronic device and to live off the land, chances are you can be located whether you want to be or not.

All of which makes it doubly frustrating for someone like myself, who at one time had access to all of the latest technology and who was tied into a network where if I wanted or needed to drop a note to any of my coworkers, in a matter of a nanosecond my words would find their way to the second row, third prayer rug from the left in a mosque in Tabriz. Not that the hired help always used the customary channels. There were times where we didn't trust official communication methods, or didn't want certain higher authority ears to listen in, or were simply out of touch, and for those situations super spies used the fastest, most sophisticated method of spreading the word that the world has ever known.

Twitter. Yep, despite the impression they work so hard to convey, intelligence agencies are incapable of scanning even a fraction of all of the tweets and twerps in social media, making it the perfect medium to place an innocuous posting about kittens or food that the recipient will read in a totally different way. It takes me most of an evening of constant meditation to remember the handle of who I want to contact and almost another hour, this time aided by the consumption of a bit of liquid encouragement, to remember my own Twitter name and password that I used for such desperate times.

I can't risk committing them to paper—ironically that's against all sorts of unwritten rules—so I quickly pull out my laptop and get online before I forget. My account is thankfully still active, although the few followers I once had deserted me long ago, which is surprising in a way since most of them were fake. I compose a post about making waffles, and in the few letters that I'm allowed include a reference to traveling (I want to meet), egg rolls (hopefully a transparent indication that the subject involves China), and a picture of kitchen tongs, a reference which may be obscure but at least could be linked to waffles in a way that would make sense in a twisted way to most Twitter aficionados. I tag my individual, hoping they're still active and check Twitter periodically, and click the post button. Nothing else I can do now but wait. And hope. And maybe drink just a little bit more.

By Friday night I'd stopped checking Twitter every twenty minutes, and the small amount of optimism I may have felt when I sent the post out into space dwindled to almost nothing. With Saturday morning dawning dry but overcast, the gloom mirroring my mood, I prepare to meet up with Vinn. Today, in yet another effort to take our minds off of our lack of progress, we're heading down to Pilsen, a Hispanic and artsy area not that far from the UIC campus. Kind of like Wicker Park before gentrification and high rents drove out most of the very shops and restaurants that made it a desirable place to live in the first place. There's a neighborhood festival going on today where we can poke around some of the vendors' tents looking for Mexican clothing or goods without "Made in China" tags, munch on a birria taco with tortillas made on the spot, and listen to some music. Afterward we'll wander over to 18th Street to browse the vintage shops, an activity that usually raises Vinn's spirits. Nothing says happiness more than discovering a 1950s flocked tea dress in your size. Or so I've been told.

Public transportation won't bring us close enough to enjoy the additional lengthy walk in this weather, so I hail an Uber. Vinn is subdued as we travel south in a five-year-old Mitsubishi Mirage, whether due to the impasse on our investigation or terror that we won't make it to our destination in one piece, I can't tell. At least she knows not to ask whether I've heard anything since last night. For now, we'll try to get away from our troubles for at least a couple of hours.

We enter the street fair, paying the $10.00 "voluntary" donation that seems endemic to all outdoor events in this city, and our spirits are immediately raised as the aromas of cheese, beef, goat, and cumin fill our noses. Vinn even manages a small satisfied smile. We wander past one of the small stages, the tiny crowd of unenthusiastic listeners apparently sharing my own opinion as to the questionable skills of the accordion player, stop to look at some turquoise earrings, then join the queue outside a food truck for the tacos we've been smelling since we arrived.

As we stand in line, stomachs growling, I find myself glancing around, edgy for no apparent reason. Vinn notices.

"Are you okay? Is something wrong?" We shuffle forward a few more inches toward culinary heaven.

"Nah, it's probably nothing," I tell her. She looks at me like she's waiting for my nose to grow. "Okay, for the last few minutes it feels like we're being watched. I'm sure it's paranoia. Occupational hazard. Former occupation, that is."

"If it makes you feel any better, I've felt it too. From almost the time we walked in. I thought it was me, but now I'm not so sure. I can't imagine why we'd be of interest to anyone, though. Stay observant, but let's not let our imaginations spoil lunch."

Agreed. In the ten minutes it takes us to make it to the counter to order, two things happen. One, the feeling of being watched doesn't go away. Second, my appetite increases twofold and I'm not going to let anything prevent me from enjoying this taco.

Tables are in short supply but we find an open spot to sit on the curb and dive in. The taco is superb. The birria is seasoned perfectly and falls apart as I eat it, just the right amount of spice hits the roof of my mouth, and juices run down my fingers on their way to the street. Vinn has her eyes closed as she eats, reveling in a sort of gastro-nomical bliss. Alas, all good things must end, and eventually we rise, throw our wrappers in the trash, and attempt to clean off our hands with the cheapest napkins available on the planet. It's taking a lot of napkins.

I sense rather than see a presence behind me, and Vinn's wide eyes tell me my instincts aren't wrong. Turning slowly, moving be-side Vinn as I back away, I can now see what, or in this case who, I felt. Standing uncomfortably close before us is a tall, painfully thin, pale-complexioned woman with tangled red hair poking out from un-der a broad-rimmed straw hat that she may have purchased here. She's dressed casually, just another visitor to the festival.

When she speaks, her eyes, partially hidden behind a pair of sunglasses, appear to dart around as if looking for someone. Her tone is firm but soft, careful not to carry beyond our ears. "If you're done eating, I suggest you follow me."

Vinn speaks first, equally soft but clearly defiant. "And why should we do that?"

"Because the friends I brought with me will insist." She nods off to her right, where two very large, muscular men dressed mostly in black stand awkwardly, trying unsuccessfully to blend in. Despite the press of the throngs filling the aisle between the vendor tents, the flow of visitors gives them a wide berth. As if prompted, one of the men slowly moves his hand up to his vest pocket and pats it briefly, signal-ing a weapon. With biceps like he has, I don't think that was necessary.

Vinn and I turn our attention to each other, trying to speak telepathically. Maybe it works, or maybe I'm projecting, because what I'm hearing from her is what I'm also thinking. We could create a scene, making it uncomfortable enough that our new acquaintances would be forced to slip away, but they might also push back, not an option we want to encourage with so many innocent bystanders around. Add to that the fact that Vinn's earlier statement that there's no reason for anyone to be looking for us isn't quite accurate, at least in my case. There are plenty of people out there somewhere who would be happy to see me dead. I'm just not convinced these are them. Another factor has me leaning toward compliance, although I confess there's no logic behind it. My former girlfriend, "former" because she was murdered, had red hair. I'm a sucker for it.

Vinn nods almost imperceptibly. I give up on the napkins and finish wiping the oil coating my hands onto my jeans. Without a word, the red-haired woman turns and we follow. We no longer have to imagine that someone is watching us from behind. We know they're there.

TWELVE

It takes a tense fifteen minutes to move through the crowds, exit the fair, and walk several blocks to a black Suburban with heavily tinted windows. Apparently even thugs have trouble finding parking spots for special events. An instinct for survival has me eyeing escape routes along the way but it's overruled by curiosity as to what we've gotten ourselves into. Better to find out now than to be paranoid and looking over my shoulder until the next abduction. Once at the car, our young kidnapper places herself behind the wheel, leaving her two massive and silent bodyguards to wave us into the back. One of them climbs in behind us while the other moves around to the other side of the car and also gets in the back, squeezing Vinn and I virtually on top of one another. I guess asking for seat belts is out of the question.

Vinn is pushed into a position where she's mostly facing the back window, but I have clear eye contact with the driver, who appears to have a slight smirk on her face as she looks at us through the rearview mirror. "Don't worry," she tells us lightly, "we're not going far. But I'm afraid we still need to take precautions."

No sooner does she finish speaking than a blindfold descends over the top of my head, then is stretched tight and tied from behind. Based on Vinn's muffled and profane protestations, I have to assume that she's suffering the same fate.

The car pulls away slowly. My training automatically kicks in as I try to get my internal clock to time our journey while simultaneously memorizing the number and interval of the turns. I haven't been in this exact position often and the few times I've tried to recreate a route have been total failures, ending up in empty fields or mall parking lots. Any kidnapper worth their salt will take a circuitous route impossible to follow from a mental map later, but the red-haired vixen driving us hasn't given me the impression of being a seasoned professional. It's worth a try.

If the adding machine and stopwatch in my brain is any indication, we've traveled a minimum of sixteen and maximum of ninety-three blocks over somewhere between twenty minutes and three days by the time we come to a stop and move backward and to our right, apparently parallel parking. The engine stops without any adjustments. Either the spot was large or our host aced driver's ed.

Doors open and the passenger side of the SUV seems to rise about six inches. One of the giants has clearly left the vehicle, while the other gives me a nudge which I assume is an indication to move out toward the door. I slide over without brushing Vinn, which means she must already be outside. A voice from behind me that I recognize as the red-haired woman barks instructions.

"My friends will be leading you to our destination, and I'll be following behind you. It's in your best interests just to go along and play nice. If you do, you'll be on your way back to your tacos in no time."

We move only a few feet before my feet stumble over a step, my shoulder hits a door frame, and I'm pushed forward as a disembodied female voice tells us that there are sixteen steps to climb. I reach out blindly with both hands and find a rail on my left, which I grab hold of. Climbing stairs blindfolded is harder than it looks.

We reach a landing, I hear keys, then we're led through a door and into who knows what sort of a scenario. Lights are dim. Nothing happens for about a minute before my blindfold is removed. Vinn and I are standing together side-by-side, a spotlight in the ceiling casting light straight down, blinding us to any objects or villains lurking in the darkness beyond the few feet from where we stand. I hear movement but can't see any of the three people who brought us here.

The silence is broken by the shuffling of feet. Seconds later a woman emerges from the darkness in front of us. She's about fifty, white but maybe with some Hispanic in her genes, hair cropped short.

Despite her age she appears extremely fit, even muscular, although it's hard to tell under her starched pale blouse and dark blue business suit, which fits her like a glove. Tailored.

"You didn't have to dress up just for us." I read somewhere once that taking the initiative when in a position of weakness helps balance the power dynamic. It's never worked before and it doesn't appear to be any help today either. The woman scowls as she approaches, doing a good job of looking intimidating, then circles us as she gives us the once over with dark, piercing eyes. I return the favor, taking the opportunity to get a better look at our adversary. Judging her, sizing her up. There's something familiar here. Déjà vu big time.

"Did I ask your opinion?" she spits. "You're not in much of a position to say anything, chump. You can't have any idea what or who is watching from the darkness. If I were you, I'd stay very quiet."

"You're not me, bitch." I retort, trying to sound confident as she finishes pacing around us and faces me directly once more. "You need to tell us why we're here and what you want. Now."

Vinn turns toward me, nervous, uncertain. "Mal..." she whispers.

"Listen to your girlfriend, moron." The woman invades my personal space, moving chest to chest, then leans in within inches of my face, spittle at the corners of her mouth. "You're either brave or stupid, but either way you'll end up the same if you don't cooperate here. And you'll take your pretty little dollface down with you. Now shut the hell up."

"Do you think I'm scared of you?" Vinn pokes me in the ribs as I speak but I ignore her. "I'm not afraid. I've seen worse than you. Now tell us what you want or we're out of here."

Fury erupts in her eyes and her face turns a deep crimson. "You don't call the shots here, cowboy. In fact, I've had enough of you. What would you say if I tell you I'm going to take off your fingers one by one while the little lady watches, and then move south to the only part of your body she probably cares about? Would you like that, 'bitch?'" As she speaks she grabs my crotch and gives it a squeeze. Pain shoots through my entire body but I can't back down now. There's too much at stake.

"Listen, lady." I take hold of the lapels of her suit, eliciting a gasp from Vinn. "I'll tell you what I'm going to do. I'll…I'll…" Words fail me as I try to think of just what I will do. Another squeeze down below makes it impossible to concentrate. "I'll…" I freeze, at a total loss for words. Damn it.

My victorious adversary lets go of my privates, steps back, and breaks into a wide grin. "That was pathetic, Griff. Gone a little soft since you retired?"

I return her smile. "I've never been in your league when it comes to the tough guy act, Car. Grabbing the balls was a nice touch." We move forward for a firm handshake and move tentatively toward a hug before what little professionalism we have leads us to back off. Only then do I remember that we have an audience.

Something tells me that the look of astonishment on Vinn's face isn't something I'll want to remind her of later. There's an edge to her voice as she speaks. "Can someone tell me what the hell is going on here? And who is Griff?"

"I'm sorry, I need to introduce you. Vinn, this is…" I look to my right. "It is still Carlotta, isn't it?" I get a nod. "Carlotta. Car, this is my friend and sometimes co-troublemaker, Vinn."

Carlotta extends her hand in Vinn's direction, clasping Vinn's warmly. "Nice to meet you. Sorry, I guess he goes by Malcom now. I knew him as Griffin, although whether that was a first or last name I never did ask. We occasionally worked together in a past life. Past for him, anyway. Some of us will never get out."

By this time the lights have been raised, and I can't help but gawk at our surroundings. We're in a dungeon. Not the old, disgusting, Medieval kind, but a clean, modern BDSM playroom. A cage sits against the wall to one side, a large wooden cross with arm restraints on the other, and scattered around the room are a medical table, bondage bed, spanking bench, and equipment that I can't comprehend as to their purpose. A colorful array of whips, paddles, and ropes hang from every wall. As my eyes take a tour of the room, I notice that the red-haired woman has vanished, but the two giants remain. They appear uncomfortable in our surroundings as they shift from one foot to the other and try to avoid eye contact with pretty much everything.

Car sees the questions in my eyes. "She's my niece. Goes by the name Mistress Mayhem. Makes a very nice living catering to the kinkier side of men. Women too, I understand." Car's eyes shift into a more serious look and her tone loses any hint of nostalgia. "Griff, I got your message. You have to understand that after leaving the service the way you did, you're not exactly a favorite among certain people who are in a position to make my life miserable. I had to find a location that's off the grid and then get you here in a way that made sure our meeting isn't open to public view. Sorry about the blindfolds and the G-man charade. I didn't know she was going to do that. I guess she just wanted to have a little fun." What is it with people and their covert fantasies? First Rebecca, now this.

"No hard feelings. I appreciate your tracking me down." As I speak, three chairs appear at the hands of one of the apes from the car. A silent signal from Carlotta and they immediately step outside the door, closing it behind them. We sit, although Vinn continues to study the room, her jaw dropping periodically. I guess it's up to me to get started while she's distracted.

I fill Car in on Lily, Eileen, and what we were told by Mr. Lei. She listens intently, never once interrupting, although at least one time she raises an eyebrow in Vinn's direction when I reference our past investigative history. "I know you have expertise in the gang area and that you spent at least some time in either Cambodia or China," I tell her. "I don't know what you did or do for the company precisely, but I'm hoping that your time in Asia and your time studying gangs overlapped, so that you can give us some information about tongs, especially here in Chicago, and where we need to go from here. We could use a push in the right direction. In any direction."

As I speak, Vinn's focus returns and we both lean forward in our chairs, as if getting closer to Car will help elicit the assistance that we need. Car responds by sitting back, closing her eyes as she considers how to respond.

"Let me start by saying that this is all off the record. You haven't seen me since the old days and we never had this conversation." She pauses until we both nod our assent. "And I'm not sure I can help you a great deal except to provide some general background. Chinese triads, the umbrella criminal organizations based in China, have been around a long time, but not a lot of attention has been focused on them on this side of the ocean.

"They're not that much different from any other gang or organized crime unit except they're not as tightly controlled. Think of a cross between a highly structured and disciplined Mafia-style organization and a street gang where rules aren't always enforced, if they have rules at all. At the top of a tong is the "Dragon Leader," followed by an officer in charge of operations, an officer in charge of ceremony, and a deputy who oversees the next lower level, consisting of an administrator, a liaison officer, and an enforcer. That's where the structure pretty much ends. Beyond that it's just a mass of members and hangers on. The enforcer has some degree of control over the members, but once you get past the upper echelon of a triad, the lower-level members have leeway in conducting their own criminal activity as long as it doesn't interfere with that of the triad itself. In that way it's very different from non-Asian gangs."

The silence in the room is complete, broken only by the occasional squeaking of Carlotta's chair as she shifts to make sure has our attention. She does.

"There isn't a clear distinction in nomenclature, but a tong in my world is a kind of sub-gang made up of a loose affiliation of street level triad members, often with members of competing triads working together. Triads are into most of the usual vices—drugs, prostitution, extortion. Smuggling people into the U.S. from China is big, our estimates are in excess of 100,000 per year, and anyone who they bring over has to work off the cost of getting here. As you might imagine, that cost is high and the smuglees end up being virtual slaves for years if not forever.

"There are four main triads, mostly based in Hong Kong, but they've spread out all over the world. The main one in Chicago is the 14K Triad, also known as Sep Sie Kie. Much like the Italians from early last century, it gained power in part due to the oppression of Asian people, so its members and its influence are intermingled with legitimate Chinese social organizations. As you might expect, locally it's based in Chinatown. We think the main activities are run out of the Chicago Chinese Cultural and Benevolent Association, which has offices above a hot pot restaurant on Wentworth Avenue. Sources tell us that the leader in the city is a man by the name of Hop Leung, but that's a guess. His name is in the papers for raising money for parks, organizing festivals, assisting newly arrived immigrants, and so on, but no one we know has ever actually seen him. So of course, no pictures.

"I'm digressing. As far as your two women, if anyone knows what happened to them, or if the one is still alive and where she might be, it would be the officers of Sep Sie Kie. But it's also possible that they ordered the women killed so it's not like you can go up to them and ask politely. You do not want to be on the radar of these people, although frankly it might already be too late for that."

Car stops, looking contemplative, as if she's making a decision. She nods to herself, reestablishes eye contact with us, and continues. "There's another possibility. There are a lot of Asian students attending American colleges. Not all of them are here to study, if you get my drift." I don't, which must be clear to Carlotta as her tone changes to that of a frustrated teacher. I know because I use that same tone with my own students. "Spies, Griff, spies. China especially uses young people to come over here as students but their real function is espionage. Large cities are favorite targets. It's a long shot, but it's possible that your two women were sent here by Chinese intelligence. You of all people know that if our own agency discovered them, their disappearance may be home bred. Whether it's China or the U.S. involved here, government or gangs, tread very, very carefully, both of you. I know you, Griff, so I know I'm wasting my breath here, but stay away. Little good can come of you looking into this, but plenty of bad can."

With these last pieces of advice, Car looks directly at Vinn. She then turns her gaze back to me. "That's all I can tell you. But there is one more thing." She rises slowly and moves to the door, calling in the two agents waiting in the hallway. After a short consultation, they all walk quickly toward where Vinn and I sit. In a flash, before I can move, the men pin me to my chair. Car disappears behind me and I feel my arms being tied securely to the chair with rope, followed by my legs.

"Car, what the hell?" My voice rises, my yelling gets more profane, but it only serves to bring a frown to Carlotta's face. She scans the room, exits my line of sight, and returns to stand behind me.

"This should help." As I begin to scream in protest, I feel a ball gag being forced into my open mouth and secured behind my head. It not only prevents me from talking, it's uncomfortable as hell.

"Sorry, Griff." Car turns toward a wide-eyed Vinn and softens her tone. "Vinn, I don't know you, but I do know him." She points a thumb in my direction. "I just want to make sure that you know what you're doing. On the one hand, he's got one of the biggest hearts I've ever known and is far more intelligent than he looks. His reputation in the sack was stellar, or so I hear. Without more, he'd be a great catch, but it's the "more" part I want you to be aware of. From what I gather you have some awareness of what he used to do."

Car pauses, a faraway look in her eyes. "It was a rough business and the only way to survive was to be tougher and more brutal than your adversary. Griff was more than up to the task. He was one of the best before he burned out. I won't go into details, and most of what I think I know is rumor anyway, but the only reason he's alive today is because he did some things which no one should have to do, and which I'm not going to describe. He has a demon inside of him that came out when he needed it. If he's able to control it, there's no better person to be with. If not, I fear for you." She stops again, opens her mouth as if to say more, then decides against it. She avoids making eye contact with me, perhaps afraid of what she'd see, but she didn't need to worry. Nothing she said was untrue. It's something Vinn needed to know, if not from me, from someone.

Carlotta begins walking away before turning back and approaching Vinn.

"I just wanted you to know, woman to woman," she says softly. "And by the way, my niece said to take as long here as you need to. Just make sure the door locks behind you when you leave." Car walks to the door without looking back, the two giant agents trailing behind.

I begin to plead to Vinn around the gag, gesturing toward my binds with my head, which to any reasonable person is a clear instruction to release me. Instead, she pulls her chair around to face me, not saying a word, her eyes wandering to examine the implements on the walls, a broad smile spreading across her face.

ℑHIRTEEN

A week and a half have passed since our bizarre and oddly erotic rendezvous with Carlotta and her dominatrix niece. The information she provided spurned Vinn and I into nonstop action, newly energized to delve deeper into the death of Eileen and the disappearance of Lily. We've researched Chinese triads, Chinese espionage, Chinese businessmen and women in Chicago, and Chinese egg rolls, the latter of which required a field trip or two. We've filled pages of a notebook with notes about crime syndicates and tongs, possible links between Chinatown businesses and organized crime, trafficking arrests involving Asians in the Midwest, and much, much more, and about the only salient fact we've uncovered is that egg rolls as we know them were most likely invented in New York City. The sad reality is that nothing we've found for all of the time spent has gotten us any closer to solving the issue with the two women than has the discovery of the origin of egg rolls.

Vinn's frustration level has increased exponentially with every day that Lily hasn't returned to class. I try to remain positive to her face, but know from experience that with any inquiry sometimes, many times, you reach a point where you've exhausted every lead and nothing else can be done. You just have to wait for new information to spontaneously appear, which it almost never does. The fact that it already did once in this matter lengthens the odds even more. I know that Vinn understands this, but this cold reality remains unspoken.

My empathy for Vinn, along with a substantial amount of resentment at the unknown forces that have put us in this position, have me sitting in bed after midnight on a school night with my laptop sitting, naturally, on the top of my lap, just randomly inserting phrases into search engines in the hope that something in the results will activate a synapse in my brain and trigger a revelation that solves everything. Unfortunately, all it has done so far is numb my legs and make me sleepy and even more embittered. The cup of Gyokuro meant to keep me alert went cold on my nightstand long ago and I don't have the energy to go to the kitchen to reheat it.

The gradual awareness of a pounding inside of my head puzzles me until I realize that I fell asleep sitting up in bed with my laptop frozen on a map of central China, and that the pounding is coming from my front door. I stumble out of bed, grab my bathrobe from a hook on the back of my bedroom door, and stagger in the direction of the persistent banging. If I'm about to be asked if I've found Jesus, someone is going to take a tumble down my stairs.

Checking my security feed to make sure it's safe to open my door, I'm startled to see that the source of this middle-of-the-night intrusion is Rebecca, impatiently throwing her fist against my door. One glance is enough to tell me that she dressed hurriedly, as she would never match her black jeans with a brown sweater, her wig is askew, and she didn't take the time to apply makeup. She knows I abhor Ted, so I'm appreciative that she sacrificed her customary fashion fastidiousness to appear at my door in feminine mode, even as I'm baffled as to what would lead her to be there in the first place.

I throw open the door. "Reb—"

"Malcom, get dressed. You need to come with me, pronto. No phone calls, no questions, just come. Now."

I know better than to argue. Within thirty seconds I've thrown on whatever pair of pants and shirt were within reach inside my bedroom door, which probably also don't match, and emerge at a trot. My hurried selection apparently doesn't meet Rebecca's approval, as she raises an eyebrow after giving me a quick once over. This is apparently not the time to remind her of her own faux pas, so I ignore her as I pull a jacket out of a closet and step outside.

We're about halfway down the stairs when headlights flash on from a dark Civic double-parked outside the front gate. Rebecca pauses to give me a chance to open the front passenger door for her before I jump into the back. Following the instructions she whispered to me as we made the descent from my apartment, I remain mute, but do grant myself the opportunity to study our driver. Asian, mid- to late-thirties, thick glasses, with a cap pulled low on his head. He makes no move to greet me or otherwise say so much as a word.

We travel west on Division Street, which is for the most part free of traffic. I pull out my phone to check the time. 2:16 a.m. That explains the lack of cars on the street, as even most bars are closed at this time on a weeknight. We slow at stop signs and lights just long enough for the driver to glance around nervously before blowing through them. It doesn't take us long to get to the Kennedy Expressway, where we head south. Well before we exit at 18th Street, I correctly conclude that our destination is in or near Chinatown.

Driving more cautiously now, we turn down 28th Street before pulling into the shadows of an alley to park. To say my nerves are on edge would be a massive understatement, and I'm on high alert as we prepare to exit the car. If Rebecca had wanted to knock off her landlord, though, all she had to do was force feed me some of the experimental meals she prepares from time to time. Her presence assures me that we're not in imminent danger, but the question remains why we're here at all.

Rebecca leans over from the front seat, her finger over her lips. "We have to walk a little way. We thought it best not to park the car near where we're going, just in case," she whispers.

Duly informed, kind of, all three of us exit the car, the silent driver in the lead. Moving west, then north, we walk past a sign signaling the entrance to the Palmisano Nature Area. My extensive and up until now useless research into everything and anything near Chinatown finally comes into play. I know that this park used to be a limestone quarry, and after it closed became a landfill for construction debris. The Chicago Park District eventually used that to its advantage and transformed the dumping ground into its current use as a public refuge from the hustle and congestion of the city.

The skies are cloudy and moonless, so the park is one over-sized shadow, barely revealing its features even a few feet off the path we're traversing. We begin by walking straight but a sudden noise, probably a bird, spooks our guide and we backtrack, transferring to a different path. Moving faster now, we pass over a stream and through wetlands. I make a mental note to come back here in the daylight sometime with Vinn, but now's not the time to sightsee. Soon we're back on the path we originally set off on, but not for long. For the first time I notice from my position to her rear that Rebecca's feet are jammed into impossibly high heels. Despite her questionable choice of footwear for a hike, I have to admit I'm impressed that she's keeping up.

We veer off onto another narrow path which begins to descend slightly as concrete walls rise to our left. The path splits, the section on the right becoming a raised platform with rails, but we ignore it and continue straight. I can now see the outline of a pond appearing ahead of us, stone steps leading down to its edge. Towering limestone walls line the far sides. The raised path has circled around to meet us but we again hustle past it, hurrying down the stairs and staying to the right. The uneven steps eventually force us to slow our pace, but within seconds we join a small group of Asian men gathered closely together in the shadows.

"Wait here," Rebecca says softly as she goes to talk to one of the men, who I recognize now as Mr. Wei. The conversation isn't long but appears to be emotional. Rebecca returns, looking stricken. "Come with me."

We walk up to the group, which parts to allow us through. Immediately after bypassing them, I stop short and emit an involuntary gasp. Whatever my sleepy brain expected, this wasn't it. On the ground just in front of me, lying in the darkness of the path overhead, is the body of a young woman. I turn to Rebecca, who's turned pale and twists to face away from the scene. She continues to talk in hushed tones, barely loud enough for me to hear, whether out of respect for the deceased or fear of being overheard, I don't know.

"A couple of teenagers discovered her. Mr. Wei said that their parents don't approve of their relationship—she's been promised to an older man—so they sometimes sneak off when everyone's asleep and come down here where they can, well, you know. You can see they'd have plenty of privacy."

She falls silent and volunteers nothing more, which I take as my cue to view the body. I stoop down on my haunches and take hold of her arm. It's still pliable and slightly warm despite the chill in the air. I'm startled. She hasn't been dead long. Her neck is twisted and looks all too reminiscent of Eileen. She's about the same age and is clearly Chinese. Instantly, a feeling of dread spreads through my body. Be careful what you wish for I tell myself, realizing that my unspoken prayer asking for something to occur that would help Vinn and I in our investigation of Lily's disappearance may have just been granted. The odds of this being someone else are miniscule. I pull my phone out and take a couple of pictures from different angles.

The group of men has grown increasingly agitated in the few minutes since I arrived. Rebecca has returned to join them. As I approach her she again anticipates my question before I can ask it. "The police have not been called. The local Asian community have some trust issues with them, with good reason. You know Mr. Wei; these are a few of his friends. They want you to look into this. Mr. Wei says that they will talk to you, but not here and not now. We need to go."

No argument here. I signal my agreement by pointing in the general direction past the gathering, and immediately we all hasten away from the scene, splitting into smaller, less conspicuous groups as we walk. When we reach a fork, the rest of the men continue on a straight path but our driver leads us back to the left. We stop suddenly as Mr. Wei returns to whisper something into Rebecca's ear before hurrying away and disappearing into the darkness.

Rebecca is dumbfounded and seems uncharacteristically at a loss for words. I look a question in her direction, forcing her to compose herself. "Mr. Wei said that there's one more thing you need to know. When the couple discovered the body, that wasn't all they found. There was someone else there attempting to move the dead woman before they interrupted him. He fled as they approached, but not before the young woman saw his face. She thinks she knows who it was."

FOURTEEN

My alarm won't go off for another ninety minutes, but there's no sense trying to go back to sleep. I sit at the island in my kitchen the rest of the night, drinking cup after cup of tea, eventually rummaging through my supply to find my least favorites since I wasn't tasting it anyway. Despite my zombie-like state, I attempt to make a mental checklist of the pros and cons of this latest development. The only pro I can come up with is that the mystery of Lily's disappearance, if that's who I saw in the quarry, is now solved. Of course that comes with a very large con on the other side of the coin, which is that the worst case scenario came true.

A million questions race through my mind, flitting in and out of my consciousness and bumping into each other as they bounce off the walls of my brain, forcing me to use all the focus I can muster to wrangle a few of the more pertinent ones. Lily's been missing for around a month, yet her body was freshly killed. Where was she during all that time? Why couldn't we find her? And are we partly responsible for her death because of our inability to locate her? I try to push the last thought away for now. There'll be plenty of time—a lifetime, in fact--to second guess and judge ourselves and to evaluate where we went wrong if it turns out there's something obvious that we neglected to do. My energy for the moment needs to be applied elsewhere.

My biggest immediate concern is breaking the news to Vinn. I decided even before getting back to my apartment during the night not to text or call her. This is something that demands a personal touch, although I'm the first to admit that my skills in this area are limited. It's also best done in private, which rules out the school café. I need to get to her before she leaves her home this morning.

I depart in the gloom before the sun has even thought to peek above the horizon so that I have time to walk to her place and hopefully use that time to clear my head. If the body I saw was in fact Lily, I can predict Vinn's reaction down to the last sob. Shock initially, denial accompanied by a surge of hope that the body wasn't Lily, dismay, overwhelming sadness and tears, anger (at ourselves as well as the unknown killer), and finally a fierce determination to move past all that and to shift our focus from finding Lily to finding her murderer. Following up on that last resolution, at least, is more in line with my skill set, although she and I will have to have an open and difficult talk about whether to trust law enforcement to mete out justice. It's a discussion we've had before.

I luck out and arrive outside of her condo building just as a clean-cut young man in a $2,000.00 suit leaves, and I hurry to catch the outside door. As I climb the stairs to her floor my legs feel like they're carrying two-ton weights. I take a deep breath, stand motionless outside her door for not more than six or seven minutes, then finally screw up the courage to knock. Footsteps approach, I feel myself being scrutinized through the peephole, and the door finally opens.

Her face is already flush with tension before I even cross the threshold. I nod in response to her unspoken question as we move into the living room. For once we actually sit on her couch instead of the floor. Despite all the time I've had to prepare for this moment, when it actually arrives I'm at a loss for words how to begin. She prompts me.

"It's Lily, isn't it." It wasn't a question. "Dammit all, Mal. Talk to me."

I briefly recap the night's events up to my being led to the body, then pull out my phone. "It isn't pretty, Vinn. Let me know when you're ready."

She takes in a deep breath, closes her eyes briefly, then bobs her head. I hand her my phone with the best image of the woman's face already loaded. She stares at it for so long I begin to worry that she's in shock, but then without asking she begins scrolling through the other pictures. There aren't many, as the desire to get away before the cops came calling overrode any desire for a thorough documentation of the scene.

Eventually Vinn holds my phone out for me to take, a small nod and tears acknowledging her identification. She then proceeds to run through the gamut of emotions in exactly the order I expected, except the speed with which she does so is astonishing. Within a matter of ninety seconds, she faces me with the unmistakable visage of someone who has made a life-altering decision. I'm sure that it's the scientist in her that's responsible for how fast she arrives at the inevitable conclusion—review the facts, then determine what the next step will be without forming a committee.

"Mal, we need to find who did this. I won't rest until we do."

It doesn't escape my notice that she didn't say "find out" who did this, merely "find" this individual. That may not have been intentional, but my guess is that it accurately reflects her wish to mete out her own form of retribution in a way that doesn't align with police-approved protocol.

I fill her in on the rest of what happened last night while she finishes getting ready for work. She stops dead still for a brief moment when I mention the possibility that the killer could be identified but says nothing. In fact we don't say another word until we're squeezed together on a red line train heading toward the Loop.

Vinn looks around at the rest of the passengers, evaluating, before speaking to me in a low voice. "You said that Mr. Wei agreed to meet with us. When?"

"We didn't have a chance to talk about it. The priority last night was to get the hell out of Dodge." I find myself whispering as well. "I don't have his direct contact information. I'll check with Rebecca later today."

My focus isn't on creative writing today, and even the geeks in my science fiction class don't hold any amusement. Vinn's concentration level is apparently even worse. At lunch she admitted to missing the cosign on a formula she wrote on the board and a freshman called her out on it. Knowing Vinn, that has never happened before and will haunt her the rest of her life.

I'm just finishing office hours near the end of the day when Vinn appears at my door just as a fairly well-endowed blonde coed is exiting. Not that I noticed. Much. Vinn's subtle look of amusement and raised eyebrow are a clear indication that she's getting back to her normal self, in a vigilante sort of way.

I sigh. "She's a student, Vinn. Had a question about an assignment."

"Uh huh. Anyway, Officer Jenkins just called. You can probably guess what he wants."

Without another word I grab my jacket, lock up my office, and we head to the morgue.

Once again, Jenkins is waiting for us outside the entrance to the building. If anything, he looks even more anxious than the first time. And maybe about five years older. A second body will do that to you.

"Thank you for coming. This time the medical examiner reached out to me to ask if I could arrange to have you come by. As I mentioned on the phone, the victim is another young Asian woman, no ID, and they remembered you from last time. I don't know much and the ME's still reluctant to share details. She was found in a park on the South Side by a jogger early this morning. Her injuries are similar to the other one. Time of death is sometime between 9:00 last night and 4:00 this morning." Jenkins stops, waiting for a reaction that doesn't come. He casts an odd look our way and starts to say something before changing his mind. After a moment he simply says, "Okay, you know the routine."

We push through the now familiar doors, are met by the same

assistant as the first time, and follow him down the same hallways to stand outside the same door. This time, though, he skips the speech. I guess that makes us veterans in the body-identification world.

The television powers on as we enter the room. Vinn nods and a gruesome image, looking far worse than the body in my photos, fills the screen. Vinn studies it for only a few seconds before turning away.

"Yes, that's her," she tells the attendant, her voice steady. "Lily Cheng. She's—she was—a student of mine."

The young man eyes Vinn suspiciously. "Are you sure? You didn't look at her for very long, I know it's difficult, but maybe study her face just to be positive?"

"I said that's her!" Vinn snaps. The TV screen goes blank and the assistant tries to recover his composure. It's probably a bit unusual to deal with someone appearing as calm and in control as Vinn was when she saw the image of the body, but he should have known better than to question her identification. I choose not to tell him that she already had her moment of trauma when she saw the pictures I took of this woman roughly twelve hours ago. Some things are better left unsaid.

This time, we're escorted to another room containing a desk and a couple of chairs, much more spartan than the identification room we just left. The requisite box of tissues has a prominent place on the desk. Vinn is asked about a hundred questions about Lily, most of which she isn't able to answer. Finally her patience wears thin, she tells the poor guy that she'll send over Lily's UIC file, including next of kin information, and she stands up to leave. I throw a sympathetic shrug at the attendant and hurry to catch up.

Jenkins strides quickly toward us when we reach the lobby. Vinn apparently feels no obligation to talk to him and rushes by without saying a word. As she nears the door I turn to him to fill him in. "Yes, it's her. I apologize for Vinn, she's a bit upset. I'll call you later. And if another file happens to fall in your lap, we'd love to see it."

"File? I don't know what you're talking about." Jenkins tries to keep a poker face, but a slight upturn at the corner of his mouth gives him away. I wink then hurry to catch up to Vinn.

FIFTEEN

I haven't bothered to call Rebecca during working hours because only Ted shows up for his daytime job and I'd rather not deal with him. I'm not sure exactly what he does, and the job description on his application to rent the second-floor unit was vague, but from what little I do know about it from overhearing his cacophonous and prophane telephone conversations when he takes calls at home, it feeds into the more unpleasant characteristics of his personality. Limiting my interactions with him makes my life just a little bit more tolerable and besides, interrupting him at work to ask for a favor wouldn't get us any closer to setting up a meeting with Mr. Wei. As I debate whether to ask the student taking up two seats on the el with her backpack to make room, I try to recall the approximate time Ted usually gets back at night and estimate how long it takes him to transition to her. Not being a Friday, Rebecca usually doesn't go out at night or I would have to add an extra hour or two. Becoming beautiful takes time.

Arriving back home, I immediately see that all of my angst about when and how to approach her was unnecessary. Taped to my door, written in a purple Sharpie, is a note that simply says "Yummy Yummy on Broadway, 9:30 p.m. tomorrow." When she converses face to face it's usually difficult to get a word in edgewise, but apparently Rebecca is less verbose with the pen. I exchange my briefcase for my laptop and carry it over to the couch, pulling up Yelp as I walk. Yummy Yummy Asian Cuisine isn't far from Wrigley Field on the North Side, easily a half-hour drive from Chinatown, and I'm tempted to walk downstairs and threaten Rebecca if it's the first stop in another long line of destinations. After taking a deep breath and calming myself, I think better of it. I text the information to Vinn along with a note that tells her I'll drop by so that we can go together, then close my eyes.

As I let my mind wander it dawns on me that I've been up since the middle of the night before, and the emotions of the day's events have been slowly draining what little energy I began with in the morning so many, many hours ago. The couch is feeling more and more comfortable, my motivation to leave it to start dinner is rapidly growing weaker, and soon I'm enjoying that marvelous dreamland halfway between wake and sleep. Visions of sunsets and piles of puppies soon give way to fried wontons and sharpened chopsticks, though, and any calm I was beginning to achieve floats away. The sound of an alarm clock brings me out of my trance. It takes a moment to remember that it's nighttime, not morning, and that my alarm isn't telling me to get out of bed and ready for work. Another few seconds pass before I realize the intrusive noise isn't an alarm at all, but my phone's ringtone. Still a bid befuddled, I manage to answer it before it goes to voice mail.

"Malcom, is that you?" The voice sounds vaguely familiar, but I can't place it. The number on the screen is equally unfamiliar. "Hello, are you there?"

"Sorry, yes, I'm here. Who is this?" No sense trying to bluff my way through in my current mental state.

"This is London Jenkins. I thought I should tell you that there won't be any more files in your future. The locals have wrapped this one up tight. You can understand why—two young women, the chance of it being racially motivated, pressures from the Asian community. I can't get within two city blocks of that paperwork."

I don't hide the disappointment in my voice but I know it's not his fault. "Don't worry about it. I'm not sure that we're likely to get anywhere with this anyway, with or without your assistance. I'll let Vinn know. Thanks for trying."

"Don't hang up. I didn't say I pulled a complete blank. Would I have called you otherwise? I did hear something on the police radio band before they went quiet. They found a sandal at tucked into the crate with the first victim. We have a link."

Chicago is a city of neighborhoods, but exactly how many depends on who you talk to. According to official city records, there are 178 of them, and maybe there are in some bureaucrat's warped view of the city, when in reality they tend to overlap and blend and most residents adopt whatever nearby neighborhood name makes them feel better about where they live. Borders are fluid, it seems, especially when realtors get involved. Broadway a block north of Diversey Avenue, where Yummy Yummy serves its fare, is probably Lakeview or maybe Lakeview East, but look for a home around here and your realtor will try to sell it as part of the tonier Lincoln Park, half a mile or so just to the south.

It's also skirts the border of Boystown just a few blocks to the north. On this Friday night, Vinn and I encounter several all-male couples heading to their favorite restaurant or bar as we stroll the street for fifteen minutes killing time so as not to arrive at the meeting location too early. Just as the alarm on her phone notifies us that it's 9:30, we arrive under the faded green canopy of the restaurant. It's dark inside and its neon "Open" side is likewise off even though the hours stenciled on the door show it's not due to close for another hour. Just as I reach out my hand to pull the handle, the door opens and an arm extends out to grab the front of my jacket and pull me inside. Vinn follows dutifully and the door quickly closes and locks behind her.

I immediately recognize Rebecca as the owner of that powerful arm, but it takes a few moments for my eyes to adjust to the dimness of the room. The interior is narrow with room for only about six two-person tables, the furnishings cheap and well-worn. Two of the tables have been pulled together in the back, where Mr. Wei sits impatiently drumming his fingers on the table. He's either perpetually nervous or this situation makes him so. He's not the only one.

We follow Rebecca to the back, which only takes about three

short strides. Rebecca claims the spot next to Mr. Wei and we slide into chairs across the table facing them. No sooner do we settle into our seats than an Asian man old enough to have dined on chicken feet with Chairman Mao silently brings steaming dishes of food to the table before departing. Rebecca and Mr. Wei transfer dumplings and rice to their plates; Vinn and I both pass for now, although the food smells better than the ambiance would suggest. I do accept Mr. Wei's pantomimed offer of tea.

We're guests at this party, so protocol requires that we wait for someone else to speak first, but for what seems like an eternity our hosts keep themselves busy attending to their food. I observe with some level of amusement that Rebecca is struggling with her chopsticks and that there are no forks in sight. Finally, what little patience I have runs out and I clear my throat. Mr. Wei takes the signal and taps his lips with a paper napkin before refilling hot tea into our customary small cups.

"My apologies," he begins in his heavily accented voice. "But I have been unable to take meals lately. Please, eat if you wish. My nephew owns this restaurant, but the cooking is done by his grandfather, who you just saw. I did not want to be seen meeting with you, and few people from my neighborhood travel this far up here to dine. It's too bad, as his food is good. But for us tonight it's better not to be in Chinatown, where everywhere there are eyes and ears.

"It would raise suspicions if the young woman I told you about accompanied me tonight. It was already difficult to arrange to speak with her. Same with the young man. They are both very frightened and do not wish to expose themselves. If the wrong people knew that she could identify the man they saw that night, they would be in serious danger. So it's best that you do not increase their risk. I will pass on to you what she told me."

Mr. Wei pauses long enough that I wonder if he's having second thoughts about the wisdom of giving out information to us.

It takes self-control I normally don't possess not to interject words of encouragement to him, which could just as easily have the opposite effect. A quick sideways glance at Vinn reveals her biting back a comment as well. I distract myself by putting a spoonful of food on our plates. Neither of us touches it, but the movement seems to have brought Mr. Wei out of his trance and he continues, speaking softer than before.

"If she is correct, his name is Delun Shen. His is a well-known face in the neighborhood so it's not likely she is wrong. He is a punk, always causing much trouble, but he is also under the protection of the triad. I don't know where he lives or what he does for money. Drugs I think. That is always a good guess. He and other boys like him sometimes meet to smoke dope in an empty store on the second floor of a mall on Wentworth. Here is the address." Mr. Wei slides a scrap of paper across the table, which I pocket without reading.

"I cannot take the chance of taking a picture of him, but you will know him when you see him. He is tall, muscular, and wears a ponytail. His hair is dark like most Chinese, but he has a spot of white above his left eye, and two ugly scars across his neck. But the easiest way to spot him are his tattoos, one on each bicep. On the right one, a green dragon with a yellow belly. On the other, a red one with a white belly."

Mr. Wei seems to be tiring, staring down at his plate as if mystified how it became empty, but makes no move to rise. He pushes the plate away and reestablishes eye contact. "One more thing. Delun is seldom alone when he is out making trouble. He likes to have someone with him to spread tales of his exploits. That person is usually Ji Jiang, who is also easy to spot because he is very fat for an Asian. Together they are unmistakable. You will see.

"Most people in Chinatown are very good people, Mr. Winters. They want justice done for those two girls, but do not trust the police and are too scared to act against the tong. They will not assist you, but they will secretly wish you good fortune. Do what you need to do to. But be aware that every action has consequences."

He seems to have said what he came to say, but I need more information from him before he departs. "Mr. Wei, I appreciate your help, and I will do what I can. But before you leave, can I ask you a few questions? The first woman, the one from the airport, was found with some odd items. Six oranges, a man's shirt, and red silk slippers. A similar silk slipper was also found by the body in the quarry. Does that mean anything to you?" I take out my phone. "Here's a picture of the slippers from Eileen's case. Sorry about the quality, it's a picture of a picture."

As he looks at the photo, a glimmer of a thought lights Mr. Wei's eyes before instantly disappearing again. He stares at it for at least thirty seconds then lowers it to the table, his hand still clasping it tight. "What else was she wearing? The first woman?" We tell him, bringing up one additional picture which he also stares at before nodding as if we just confirmed his suspicions. His eyes take on a sad, distant look. He turns slightly in his seat and calls out softly in Mandarin to the rear of the restaurant.

The old man who served the food returns to stand next to the table. Mr. Wei talks to him for a long minute, gets a response twice as long and much more animated, then takes another turn, his voice rising. He picks up my phone and holds it up to the older man's eyes. The man gasps softly then excitedly but firmly speaks at an accelerated pace. We sit still, fascinated as if watching a play unfold. The two men appear to be having a debate, talking over one another, their voices getting louder, then eventually calmer as if they've come to a consensus. The old man looks over and stares directly at Vinn and I before shaking his head and hurrying back to the safety of the kitchen. He returns shortly with a pot of tea and fresh cups, pulling up a chair to join us.

Mr. Wei pours tea and pushes the cups in front of each of us.

"Drink. This is Mr. Zhang, who is older and knows more about what I am about to tell you than I do, so he is here in case I need him. He also speaks better English and will interrupt when I have trouble. I have a story to tell you which I believe has some relevance, but that will be for you to determine."

SIXTEEN

"To understand what I am about to say, you must understand that China is a country of contradictions, with its front foot striding confidently toward the twenty-second century while its trailing foot is still dragging in a time period a thousand years ago." Mr. Wei closes his eyes as he speaks, seemingly reciting from memory words he picked up long ago for some unknown purpose, perhaps giving tours for Westerners. It's an awkward transition from his usual speech patterns, but only lasts for the one sentence. He opens his eyes and his voice returns to normal as he continues. "Traditions die slowly and the old ways linger, especially in the rural areas. Superstitions have been passed through so many generations that they are ingrained in our culture as fact. Customs are critically important and often mingled with the need to avoid shame.

"One such custom that survives very strongly is that a child must marry to bring honor to his family. Or her family. If a woman dies single, she disgraces herself and is often not allowed to be buried with her ancestors. For a man, the shame is even greater. It has been this way for thousands of years. For just as long, the Chinese people have sought solutions when a loved one dies young. That is how ghost marriages came about."

Vinn and I exchange glances, intrigued but puzzled. Simultaneously, we take a sip of our tea. Smooth, soothing, and extraordinary, this clearly isn't the tea served to regular customers. I sigh with pleasure, earning a 'hmrmph' from the coffee drinker at my side. Mr. Wei looks upon us with strained patience before continuing. "I know, the term sounds strange. The truth, I'm afraid, is even stranger. The concept is as simple as it is bizarre. If someone does not marry in life, their family arranges for them to marry after death. Often it is to avoid dishonor, but there are other reasons as well, as when the deceased has younger siblings. Tradition demands that marriages take place in the order of seniority, so that a younger man or woman cannot wed until their older brother or sister does. In some families, the death of the elder child does not alter that rule, so in order for younger siblings to marry, an older one must do so first, even if they're no longer alive. There is a significant barrier when the prospective groom is male. For so long by law in China women could only have one child, and sons were more highly prized than daughters, so after generations of this rule, there are far more men of marrying age than women. It is hard enough for a living man to find a bride. What woman would want to marry a corpse?

"In those rare instances in which a living woman marries a man who died, immediately after the nuptials she's declared a widow. She will then be welcomed into the man's family, and his next younger brother can now marry the woman he's been engaged to for years. Other times a marriage is arranged where both bride and groom are already dead, so both sides of the family are released from the shame of an unmarried child. These ghoulish weddings still take place today. Usually paper cutouts symbolizing the deceased bride and groom are used. But not always."

I suddenly have no taste for my tea, fine as it is. I don't like where this is going. Mr. Wei looks hesitant to continue, has a brief muttered conversation with Mr. Zhang, then begins again. "The large discrepancy in the numbers of men and women also means many living men will not marry. Women in China are so outnumbered by men that they have their pick of husbands, leaving millions of men unmarried and in disgrace. So both living men and dead men need to find a way to marry. Women have no reason to agree to marry a dead man, except maybe money. Families get desperate. If there are no living women to wed to their dead son, or if their living son cannot find a live woman to take as his bride due to the competition, well then..." Mr Wei didn't finish the thought. He didn't have to.

"There are stories coming out of central China, which I always hoped were exaggerated, of a black market in corpses, especially women, for use in such marriages. Years ago a man in the Hongtong area supposedly was arrested for killing a woman to be used as a ghost bride for a man—I don't remember if he was alive or dead himself— for which he received a large fee from the groom's family. When you mentioned the sandals, and showed me how she was dressed, the red silk dress with dragons, that is what made me think of this. Mr. Zhang agrees. Those are traditional forms of dress for a wedding. There is no other reason to wear them. Oranges are a traditional gift for a bride. A fine shirt serves the same purpose for a Chinese groom. It is possible that with not enough women the right age in China, families are looking for Asian women living in other countries, willing or not.

"One more thing for you to think about is the time of year this is happening. Each year, the seventh lunar month of the calendar is the time for Yu Lan. Another name for it is the Hungry Ghost Festival. During this time, which lasts four weeks, the gates to the spirit world are said to open and the dead are free to walk the earth searching for their relatives, from whom they are seeking food. But they are also looking to have their families resolve any of their open issues. People believe that misfortune will fall upon those who do not help. One of the biggest causes of unhappiness among the deceased is dying before they can marry. Their families will try to remedy this and avoid the wrath of the dead by arranging to marry them even after death. If no living woman will marry their deceased son, they will often look for a bride among the dead, who have no say in the matter.

"This year the festival ran through most of August. The women's bodies were found shortly after that. It may be coincidence, but that is for you to determine." Mr. Wei looks around the table. "That is all I have to say. May it guide you to bring a resolution to this problem and peace to the families of those two women."

He stands and bows slightly, as does Mr. Zhang. I have a million questions but the interview is clearly over. We watch, stunned into silence, as the two men depart through the kitchen.

Rebecca recovers first, picking up a menu and hustling to call after the owner. "Wait a minute! Can I order a milk tea to go? Red bean and coconut please. And don't forget the tapioca pearls!"

This morning finds me once again sitting and yawning in my kitchen in the pre-dawn darkness. I'm sipping a steaming cup of gotu kola tea I obtained many years ago in a remote village of southwestern China. It's a huge step down from the ambrosia Mr. Zhang served last night. My supply has lasted for an especially long time because I'm not overly fond of the bitter, astringent taste, but the herb from which it's made supposedly promotes mental clarity and focus, and at this moment I need all the help I can get. It was late when I got home last night and I postponed looking further into the whole concept of ghost weddings in favor of trying to get some much-needed slumber. Before hitting my pillow, however, the idea of murders to fulfill requests for mail-order brides and raging guilt that I wasn't doing enough led me to send another underground message to Carlotta asking what she knows about this phenomenon and also requesting—okay, begging—her to use her resources to check into Delun Shen and Ji Jiang. I have no idea if she has any motivation to assist me, and given the circumstances of our last meeting, I have mixed feelings about if I even want to get together again, but at least I can tell Vinn I've done something.

For the second morning this week, I'm suddenly pulled out of my reverie by the ringing of my cell phone. I have very few friends or important people in my life, meaning the number of phone numbers I store is so small that I've assigned a distinct ring tone to each of them and can tell instantly who's calling. This isn't one of them. Normally I wouldn't even bother to look at my screen, but curiosity about who would be dialing me before 6:00 a.m. leads me to take a peek. At first the number doesn't look familiar, but then a memory pulled from somewhere deep inside my brain clicks. Maybe the tea works after all. I punch a button.

"Good morning, Car. What in the hell are you doing up at this time?"

"I'm impressed, Griff. Wasn't sure you'd remember your old number. Sorry, did I interrupt your beauty sleep? Or did I interrupt you and that hot little professor in the middle of something?"

I muzzle my irritation while at the same time wondering what strings she had to pull to sniff out my former phone number. "What can I do for you, Carlotta?"

"You reached out to me, remember? Look, I may have some information for you. How does 11:00 sound? Do you know some public place we can meet where there won't be many people around? Preferably out of the cold."

"Eleven is fine." I pause, trying to think of a safe spot where we can be confident there won't be a crowd. Inspiration hits; it has to be the tea. "I know exactly where to go." I give her the address.

Vinn has never been to the Kuban Kabana, Leo's tiny restaurant on the near South Side of Chicago within hailing distance of the UIC campus. It's become something of a running joke between the two of us after my vivid description of the first and only time I ate there shortly after I moved to the city, when Leo decided to go all out to impress his new landlord. The culinary disasters that he proudly served that day have reached legendary status and still rank among the worst food that has ever passed through my digestive system, including the time I spent in a Tibetan prison. I've long held the belief that Leo, like each of us, has a hidden past. He himself claims that he's been set up as a Cuban cook as part of some sort of witness protection program. That would not only explain the quality of his food, or more accurately the lack thereof, but also the facts that he never seems to actually be at the restaurant and his multiple five-star social media reviews, which have to be manufactured. He may have done something to deserve government protection, but who's going to protect unsuspecting diners from his culinary crimes?

Despite my reservations and the loud anticipatory objections from my stomach, I chose it as our meeting place because it's located on a side street in a sparsely-travelled area of the city, and as far as I know I've been his only customer in the last eighteen months, so privacy won't be an issue. Vinn lets out an involuntary giggle as we approach from across the street and she sees a dilapidated shack held together by a blue and white striped paint job apparently referencing the Cuban flag. She tenses suddenly though, as do I, before we enter.

"Did you notice?" she whispers. "I saw two."

"Three," I reply. "There's an old guy in the Amazon van up the block. And for every one we see there's at least one more we don't." I wonder why Carlotta has felt the need to bring in the troops. Throwing caution to the wind, I hold the door open for Vinn and we walk in together. The smell of grease immediately assaults our senses.

The apparent reason for the presence of the detail outside is sitting next to Carlotta in a booth near the back of the narrow dining area, past the window. He takes up most of the seat, his broad shoulders supported by an impossibly wide girth which forces Car to hang precariously off the edge of the vinyl seat. His most prominent feature, though, is the rubber Vladimir Putin mask covering his face. Whether that's his—or her—idea of irony or humor I don't know.

As expected, the restaurant is empty other than the two of them. We slide into the booth. Car immediately takes charge.

"Griff, Vinn, I won't introduce this gentleman by name. Suffice it to say that he's my best source for any and all information on China. If he doesn't know it, you don't need to know it either. What you wanted to know isn't exactly top secret, but since he was in the area anyway I figured you could hear it straight from the Russian President's mouth." Car smiles slightly. Vladimir remains passive.

Without preface, Vlad starts right in. His accent is more New Jersey than Moscow. "First, the two names you gave us. They're not in the system. Be aware, though, that any activity in Chinatown would draw the attention of the local triad, the 14K. If the assholes who murdered those women weren't shut down after the first one and then killed again, chances are they either acted at the instruction of the triad or are a part of an affiliated tong and have free reign. Either way, going after them is dangerous. From what I've learned about you, I understand that these punks may not see another New Year. If you want to see one yourself, no one can know you're behind whatever happens to them."

I glare at Car, who simply shrugs. Before Vlad can continue, Leo emerges out of nowhere with heaping platters of unidentifiable food. The smell of black beans and cumin fills the air, but other less pleasant aromas cancel out any pleasure of the more familiar scents. To avoid hurting Leo's feelings, Vinn and I each dish out a little bit of everything on our plates before Leo disappears again. I use a fork to spread it around and make little piles to make it look like I ate something; Vinn takes the hint and does the same. Carlotta actually samples one of the dishes that may or may not have had plantains in it before making a face and discretely spitting it back into her napkin. Vlad's mask prevents him from partaking, which has the advantage of keeping him alive long enough to finish his talk.

"Ghost weddings originated as a means of casting aside shame from desperate families with unmarried children and have been around for 3,000 years. They were outlawed in 1949, and as larger cities moved more into the modern age many younger people abandoned the older superstitions, but residents of remote villages have been slow to change. Grave robbing on behalf of families looking for a bride for their son or brother, living or dead, is enough of a threat that the parents of young women who died have been known to sleep on their daughter's grave for weeks or even months. In the Hongdong district of the Shanxi province—"Vinn and I exchange glances at the familiar name— "over a recent four-year period twenty-seven female bodies were reported stolen. The actual number would be much higher. Shame prevents bringing attention to most of them. And that's only one sample area.

"Intelligence tells us that eleven men were arrested in another province in 2014 for raiding graves and selling the corpses. Understand that this is a lucrative business. Families are willing to pay a premium to find a bride for their son, preferably alive but dead will do in a pinch. Prices as high as 200,000 yuan, that's around $25,000.00, aren't unheard of for a female body. The cost depends on factors such as freshness and the beauty and socio-economic status of the dead girl." He notices the look of distaste on our faces. "My point is that the motivation is high. That's a lot of money for a peasant in China.

"And that leads us to how this anecdotal information may relate to your women. In 2016 a man in the Shaanxi province was convicted of murder when he killed a woman to provide a body for a ghost wedding. There are a couple of other examples that we know about as well, so it's still going on to a limited extent over there. But a government crackdown on stealing corpses has led some Asians to look elsewhere for their victims. Note also that there are thirty-three million more males than females in China, so the supply of Chinese women is limited. As a result, a criminal element has moved outside of China to find brides for deceased Chinese men. In some ways it's less risky to kill a woman here in the U.S. than to dig up a grave. Besides, as I mentioned, freshness counts, and the bounty will be higher if proof of beauty can be provided.

"Your first victim was bound for Shanxi and dressed for a wedding. The man's shirt was for the groom and the oranges were also a gift for the hungry male corpse waiting in China. A ceremonial slipper was found near your second victim. In my opinion you're on the right track. They're linked by the ghost wedding. You're dealing with dangerous men who are probably desperate as well. They've failed twice. Odds are they'll try again. Whatever you have planned, it may be a bit quixotic, but it's also necessary to protect the city's young Asian women."

The entire time he'd been speaking, Vlad's eyes periodically left us to scan the bounty of food on the table. A distinct rumbling of his stomach echoed in the room. His professional discipline eventually won out and he once again met our eyes, albeit through the holes of the mask.

"But be forewarned. Chinatown in Chicago is a close-knit and relatively small community. You've probably already been observed. Your chances of finding these two guys without drawing attention to yourselves is small, maybe not possible at all. If they disappear or end up dead and the trail leads to either one of you, the consequences will not be long in coming."

Carlotta reaches across the table and grabs my arm. She has a strong grip. "Griff, Vinn, be careful. This will be our last meeting. Don't communicate any more. I don't need the exposure, especially if you end up dead. Besides, in a couple of hours I'll be leaving the country. I couldn't help you if I wanted to. Now vamoose. And good luck."

Vinn and I rise and walk slowly to the door. As we leave, I overhear Vladimir talking to Car. "Are you going to want any more of this? Do you mind if I pack it up to go?" He doesn't know it, but he just made Leo's day.

Seventeen

"Which brings us full circle all the way back to the question of 'now what?'" Vinn and I are wandering the Maxwell Street Market, an occasional Sunday morning favorite of ours. The first time we were here, like the knowledgeable native that she is, she filled me in on its history. A precursor of the modern flea market, it started as a produce market loosely operated by Jewish immigrants in the late nineteenth century. Over time it expanded to a mile-long cacophony of carts and stalls selling everything from fresh fish and vegetables to toys, tires, kitchen goods, electronics, and more. If you needed it and didn't mind rubbing elbows with the tens of thousands of shoppers looking for a bargain and shouting at their kids in a dozen different languages, or the possibly questionable provenance of the goods, you could find it there. While you were browsing you could grab a red hot or a blintz while listening to a soulful jazz saxophone trying to be heard over the nearby blaring of a boom box. For nearly a century this rag tag collection of vendors survived in the shadow of the Loop.

Eventually its location led to its doom as businesses looked to expand away from the main business section of the downtown area and gentrification began. Its fate was sealed when The University of Illinois at Chicago, the very same institution that signs the paychecks for Vinn and myself, expanded its campus and evicted the merchants. The city responded to the resultant uproar by relocating the market further west, in the process attempting to sanitize it. You can still find an occasional bargain among the junk, but what apparently once was is no more. Still, if you want to sample some of the best Mexican street food north of the border while watching an ancient Hispanic woman make fresh tortillas, it can't be beat.

"I wish I knew," I respond honestly as I take a big bite of my taco pastor, pico de gallo dripping down my chin. "We have more than enough reliable information, a lead on the possible killer, motive, and absolutely no way to get close to him. You know why."

Vinn nods. She hasn't touched her tamale with red mole. "We're too pink. Even if we could get the locals in Chinatown to open up to us, which they won't to anyone at all regardless of race because of the risk, much less to an outsider, he'd know we're looking for him before you could say 'chopsticks.' And because we can't blend in, he or his minions would see us coming from a mile away. Not to mention that if he doesn't kill us, the tong or triad or whatever it's called here would be more than happy to do the job. I want justice for these women, Mal, but not at the cost of our lives."

"Agreed." Vinn's summary of our situation mirrors my thoughts exactly, but it's still depressing to hear it out loud. "What we need is someone on the inside, specifically a Chinese resident of Chinatown who can keep an ear to the ground without raising suspicions and who can tip us off at the appropriate time. I think we can agree that Mr. Wei doesn't fit the bill. We need someone younger, less conspicuous, who may even occasionally run in the same circles as this Shen character, or be Facebook friends or something."

Vinn looks at me with a sarcastic smile. "Facebook? Get with the times, old man. No one under thirty uses that anymore. But identifying this mythical accessory isn't our only problem. He or she would probably be too petrified to help. With good reason. And you're still ignoring the 'at the cost of our lives' aspect."

We both fall silent, giving us the opportunity to finish our lunch, this time with no intrusion by a crimson-haired dominatrix. Thankfully even the seemingly unsolvable quandary we're facing doesn't dampen my taste buds. Delicious.

"Okay," I finally say through sauce-covered lips. "Until we find a solution to the issue of tracking down and isolating this asshole and his pal, I'll focus on thinking of a way to take them out of commission without drawing attention to ourselves and giving us convincing deniability. Not only to keep us off the radar of the triad, but that of Jenkins and his cop pals too. The goal is to be prepared so that when the chance does come up, we already have a plan in place. That's assuming that we've verified that Shen and Jiang are culpable, and I guess we have to figure out how to do that as well."

"Fine," Vinn replies as she takes a wet wipe from her purse in lieu of the apparently universal useless paper napkins supplied by our vendor. That's why she's the genius, although apparently even geniuses don't always share and I'm left with sticky fingers. "And while you do all that, let me work on finding a volunteer to help us out down there. I may have an idea."

She chooses not to share her idea, just as she chose not to share her wipes. We depart the tent and head toward the exit, the dulcet sounds of an out-of-tune guitar accompanying our departure.

"I'm working on it," I assert defensively in response to Vinn's questions as we sit in our usual spots in the school café waiting for our first classes. Vinn munches on a blueberry bagel while she makes faces at the muddy river water that passes for coffee here. I sip my own weird but surprisingly wonderful mix of British breakfast tea and a Japanese sencha that I brought from home as I push the sweet roll I didn't want around on a napkin in the hope it will disappear without my having to eat it. I hate to waste food, but I dislike even more the threats by café employees to kick me out if I don't purchase something now and then. I grin to myself as I ponder whether Stuart has figured out that it's me periodically leaving pastries on his desk tagged with a Post It Note adorned with tiny hand-drawn hearts.

In my defense to Vinn's unspoken accusations, I have put together a tentative plan for dealing with the killers of the two women. My initial and admittedly strongest temptation is to use certain aspects of my past training to make sure that they'll never be a threat again by employing the "eye for an eye" approach, but that would violate an oath I took to myself when I abandoned my former life to leave the less savory parts of it behind for good. My internal debates over the past few days and nights were strong and passionate and ended with a compromise: I'll try other methods first, but if it comes to the point where my principles run up against a situation where these hoods won't pay for what they've done, that oath I took won't mean a thing.

I've also had to consider our overriding concern that Vinn and I don't put our lives at stake. This applies not only to our face-to-face confrontation with the two men, however that plays out, but also requires setting up a scenario which can't be traced back to either one of us. As things stand now, if word got out that something happened to Shen or Jiang, or even more conspicuously, both of them, all eyes of the Chinese community and the local tong will fall upon us even if we aren't involved. By default, we'll be viewed as the culpable parties, and in this life actions frequently get initiated before the facts are known. To offset this, we have to be insulated by a buffer in the form of a clear and obvious fall guy who won't be subject to the wrath of the triad and who'll take the heat off of a couple of clearly innocent college professors.

And I think I've got a strategy that will do just that. The downside is that it involves committing a felony, requires information I don't have and don't yet know how to get, and may get me arrested or killed before I'm able to put it into action. Other than that it's perfect. The illegality and personal danger are the main reasons I don't want to draw Vinn into my plan of action, but another is the fact that to a discerning ear it sounds like there are so many holes in it that it doesn't constitute an actual plan at all. Vinn is no idiot. For the time being, then, deflection is in order.

"Any luck on finding a volunteer?" I pride myself on how clever I am to throw the onus of plans back into her lap. Naturally, her response is a mirror image of my own. Two expert vacillators at work.

"Maybe," she begins. "But I haven't decided if I should approach this person or not. There're some moral issues here considering the risk involved. For now I want to give myself a few more days to see if I need to continue wrestling with this quandary or just leave it be. And just so you know, my inclination is to not to get them involved even if it's just to provide a pipeline to someone else."

Vinn's careful avoidance of using any pronoun to reveal the gender of whomever she has in mind, even with me, reveals how seriously she considers the dangers here. Just as I'm trying to protect her by not discussing what I have in mind, she's doing the same on behalf of her own potential co-conspirator. Our reticence to draw anyone into this mess and our overriding wariness of risk are prudent precautions but may also act as effective roadblocks which prevent us from getting anywhere near a path to the justice we so desperately seek.

"Okay," I say as I rise, carefully wrapping my roll up in the pink tissue paper I bought on my way into work. "Good talk." Vinn grimaces as she also gets up. She knows as well as I do that as long as we walk on eggshells, progress will be slow. Together we head for the door.

The distance between Stuart's now pastry-enriched office and my own is one short stretch of hallway, but with each step my intuition that something is off grows stronger. I don't always know what my subconscious registers that sets off warning bells, but I've learned not to ignore them. It could be the subtle scent of perfume or a cigarette or the vision of a smudge on my door handle that wasn't there before, but as I approach there's no doubt in my mind that someone is or recently has been in my office.

I cautiously push open my door with two fingers as I stand slightly to the side so as not to provide a target for whoever is inside. Glancing around the door jam, I quickly process that the dark figure perusing my books is familiar and non-threatening. It takes me about two nanoseconds more for my brain to recognize the face and assign a name to it.

"Jenkins? What are you doing here? Are you waiting for me?" Brilliant deduction, Winters. As if he thought Scarlett Johannsen would be wandering into my office.

"Funny thing." His voice doesn't seem to be carrying any overtones of humor. "About an hour ago I received a text."

"Wow. That is odd. A text, you say? Very unusual." If he's going to play games, I'm more than willing to meet him in that happy place.

"The sender asked me if I knew who the biggest drug dealer on campus is. And what kind of drugs he sells. And where to find him."

"Incredible. Weird and stupid that a student would have the guts to ask that of the local constabulary. Although smart in a different way, since if anyone would know the answers it would be you. But what does this have to do with me?"

"The text came from your phone."

"Ah, did it now? And you came here personally to deliver the information. I must say I'm quite impressed with the personal service of the campus police force." As I speak, I step around Jenkins, no easy task in the tiny and cluttered space, and move to my chair. As I lower myself into a sitting position, Jenkins does the same on the other side of my desk. Without the uniform, he could easily pass for one of my students or even a high school senior on a college visit. He glares at me.

"Malcom, I know you're not a moron. At least I thought I did. So cut to the chase. What gives?" Jenkins' interrogation technique could use a little work. At least bring along a hot spotlight or threaten me with unjustified parking tickets. Nevertheless, under the circumstances I decide a little candor might be appropriate.

"I don't suppose you would believe that it's for a research paper for one of my classes?" He glowers at me, which I take as a no. I lean back and sigh. "You know that Vinn and I have been looking into the deaths of those two women?" Jenkins nods but his eyes narrow. "I'm just considering options in the event the legal system moves too slowly or ultimately fails us. Believe me, Jenkins, at this stage it's all theoretical. Just one of a myriad number of possible schemes we throw out to each other to help us feel like we're doing something. There's nothing imminent if there's anything at all." I don't mention that I'm relying on my assumption that Jenkins' ambitions for advancement and respect within the department will encourage him to play along in order to take credit for bringing down a gangbanger.

I'm not sure he believes me that this is all simple brainstorming, but my explanation allows Jenkins to relax enough to settle back into the student chair, which almost swallows him up. The scowl remains.

"I take back my earlier statement. Maybe you're a moron after all. I see where you're going with this, and I can picture exactly the result that you'd hope for. Yes, it would be satisfying. But I can't help you. First, whatever made you think that I would give you information with the foreknowledge that you would use it to commit a crime? Not only is it against my oath of office, I'd be considered an accessory. Secondly, and thirdly and fourthly and so on, there are so many things that could go wrong every step of the way that you'd end up under arrest, in the hospital, or dead. I'm sorry, Winters, but you're not going to get that name from me."

I nod sympathetically. "Yeah, that's pretty much what I thought you'd say but I wasn't sure where else to turn. Although, I'll bet I could pick a student at random from any one of my classes and ask if they knew where I could score. Once I explained that it wasn't for me but for the greater good in helping bring justice to two women who were brutally beaten and who had their young lives cut short for no good reason, they would probably give me a name or two without worrying about being arrested as an accessory. Oh, don't do that. My mom always said that my face would freeze that way if I did that."

What's the next stage beyond scowl? Grimace? Whatever it is, that's what's staring at me from Jenkins' face right now. Not a pretty sight.

"You're nothing but a piece of trouble waiting to happen, you know that Winters? Like I said, I can't help you. What I mean is that I won't help you. Besides, as far as I know Reid Baxter is probably behind bars right now. It's common knowledge that he hangs out in that green space across from the library most weekend nights after dark, so the Chicago cops would have definitely been on to him by now. Most likely, he was arrested weeks ago."

Jenkins leaves his chair and turns before he even finishes talking and bustles out my door. I grab a piece of scrap paper, which turns out to be a student essay waiting to be graded, and scrawl down the information. Hopefully I'll remember to erase the addition of drug dealer contact information before returning it to my student. I swivel to my laptop and begin researching prison sentences for the possession of various drugs. I make a list of the top five. I assume Baxter either has or has access to at least one of them.

EIGHTEEN

"No. Absolutely not. Never. It's out of the question. A non-starter." I realize I'm babbling but it's better than using the language that first crossed my mind, and internally I'm fuming at Vinn. She must sense this as she fidgets uncomfortably in the same student chair Jenkins recently occupied on the other side of my desk. The color in her cheeks is rising with each word I utter but I can't help myself. "How could you possibly consider such a thing? Vinn, you're not stupid. You're by far the smartest person I know, or maybe ever have known. Following through with even a part of what you're suggesting is just insane. You must know that."

More shifting, a couple of false starts as her mouth opens and shuts, then when she finally does begin speaking her eyes avoid looking into mine. "I do know how it sounds, Mal. First of all, let me be clear. I didn't approach her. I thought about getting one of my Asian students to help out in some way, even if it was just to keep ears to the ground—with a different student actually—but after a lot of soul searching decided against it. It would be morally wrong to bring someone else into our private quest here. Not only wrong, but risky. Dangerous. And unfair to even ask. So yes, I do agree that it's insane, to use your description.

"But I didn't search her out; she came to me. And after she did, I reevaluated and came to understand that this really isn't our own 'private quest.' There are bad people out there that are targeting women, Asian women, and that community is involved whether they want to be or not. It's not a choice they have the luxury of making. You saw that with Mr. Wei. He made it clear without actually saying it that most of Chinatown wants these men stopped. They're petrified and they feel helpless. That's why he came to us. And it's why Maggie approached me. Well, not only that in her case. I made a call to her journalism advisor and Maggie is ambitious, to put it mildly, and intent on making her mark in the field as soon as she can in any way possible. He called her 'an unstoppable force.' She's going to involve herself with or without us. And face it, Mal, we're not getting anywhere and could use some help. This could be the break that we've been looking for. A way in. A spy, if you will. Someone who would blend in and be given access to information that we could never get on our own. Yes, it's crazy. In a smart kind of way."

As she finishes Vinn raises her head to stare directly into my eyes. I see the passion but also the nagging doubts, which have to be the same ones that are bouncing around inside my own brain. I sigh, press my lips together to avoid the temptation to speak before I think, then lower my head into my hands as I mull what she's saying. A dull throbbing headache distracts me and makes it hard to push away the discomforting idea that what she's proposing actually does make some sense, but only if you're willing to downplay the danger. I make a conscious effort to soften my tone.

"On the one hand, I agree with everything that you're saying. It's a logical way to overcome the obstacle that the color of our skin presents and could build the bridge we need to find these bastards and to bring an end to the terror that they've imposed upon the Asian community. Maybe even prevent further killings. But there's one factor that I just can't get past, and that's knowingly putting another young woman in harm's way. I just can't do it."

"I know," Vinn replies gently, sympathetically. "That's where I keep getting stuck as well. But there's something else that you need to know and to factor into the equation. Something that maybe I should have told you as soon as I sat down."

Vinn pauses, hesitant, forcing me to wait as the seconds tick by. She's having a hard time getting her mouth to work, or perhaps she's worried at how I'll react to whatever she's about to say. A reasonable precaution. We won't know for sure, though, until I hear it. My patience gives in quicker than her resolve pushes her to talk.

"Well?"

"This young woman I started to tell you about. The student. The one that's at the center of our discussion." Vinn licks her lips before sitting up straight and blurting it out. "She's been standing right outside the door this whole time."

The student may have been in the hallway when Vinn began that sentence, but by the time she finished the young woman was a blur in motion, covering the few feet into my office quicker than I could say "You've got to be kidding me." Standing at the edge of my desk, hands tightly wound into fists as she leans forward, she's a study in fury. She's also quite short, stick thin, and looks to be about twelve years old. More to the point, I assume, she's Asian.

"Mr. Winters, I mean Professor, I heard everything you just said and I just want you to know that it's complete and utter bullshit! Let me tell you—"

Before she can go on, Vinn stands, puts her hand firmly over the young woman's mouth, and guides her to the front of the chair, pushing firmly on her shoulder until she was planted exactly where Vinn had been a moment before.

"Maggie, before you go on, take—uh, no, quiet for a minute— take a deep breath and let me make a proper introduction." The bluster of this Asian volcano and Vinn's exasperation is in some perverse way amusing to me, maybe because it takes so much to make Vinn lose control in any situation, and I can't help but stifle a grin. Part of it must have been visible anyway because as Vinn looks in my direction she visibly relaxes slightly and the hint of a smile turns one corner of her mouth skyward.

"Maggie, this is Professor Winters." She stresses the "Professor" part, Vinn's proffer of an olive branch to me and also a less than subtle message to the poor girl as to the hierarchy at work here. "Mal, this is Maggie Wong. She's a student here, a journalism major, or so she tells me. She's not a student of mine but sat through a lecture in advanced structure and mechanisms just so she could capture my attention after class. She would like to—very calmly and professionally—present a proposal for your consideration." Vinn keeps a hand on the young woman's shoulder the whole time, squeezing it when she got to the 'calmly and professionally' part. The student winces but seems to take the hint.

"Professor Winters," she begins, speaking fast but at least without profanity, "I'm not from Chicago so I live near campus, but I spend time down in Chinatown. The food reminds me of home and my mother's cooking. San Diego, not Beijing." She smiles, a bit whimsically, before getting back on point. Or at least hopefully on her way to the point. "Anyway, I've heard the rumors. About the two young women. So I started investigating, you know, like all good journalists do? I'm a journalism maj—oh, wait, you know that already. I didn't get very far down there, Chinatown I mean, not San Diego, before I must have caught the attention of an elderly gentleman whose name I keep forgetting. I have it written in my notepad—did you know I keep a notepad? All good journalists do, you know, so that you don't forget something important. Mine's red, so that I can always find it quickly in my purse when I need it. Anyway, his name's in there if you need it."

I'm fascinated and more than a little entertained watching her struggle but decide to save her from herself. "Might it be Mr. Wei?"

She perks up immediately. "Yes, that's it exactly! Mr. Wei. Anyway, he found me in Qing Xiang Yuan Dumpling House, you know the one on Wentworth? They have a delicious sea cucumber dumpling but it's kind of expensive and I'm only a student so I usually get the one with leeks and shrimp which is pretty good too. I think that's what I was eating when Mr. Wei found me. Is that important?" She didn't wait for an answer, so maybe the question was rhetorical. "He seemed kind of nervous and I was too because I didn't know who this old man was that sat down at my table. You know? Women have to be careful, but maybe you don't know that because you're a man. Anyway, I'm careful. But he didn't seem threatening but you never know. He said that word had got around that I was asking about the women who were killed and that it wasn't a good idea to draw attention to myself. He wouldn't say why, but I'm not dumb, you know?

"But maybe he thought I wasn't smart because he said that there were some bad people who might wonder why I'm asking questions and he didn't want anything to happen to me. No, wait. It wasn't the leeks and shrimp. I think it was the tomato and egg. I like that sometimes too. So after he said that I looked him right in the eye and said 'I'm not scared' and then he said maybe I should be and I said 'I'm going to keep investigating no matter what you say' and he said just keep quiet and eat your dumpling and listen to me. That's when he gave me your name and Ms., I mean Professor Achison, her name too and I thought it would be better to go to her because you know she's a woman and sometimes women relate to each other better, but no you wouldn't know that because you're a man." I swear she said that entire speech in one breath. It's exhausting listening to her but she's apparently not done yet. "He said that I need to talk to you because you two are looking into this stuff and maybe you would talk some sense into me but that's not why I went to the class, which I really didn't understand but then science isn't my thing, it's because I want to help and you can't stop me anyway. So it's not really a proposal it's kind of a demand. Either we work together or I do it on my own. If you're worried about my safety wouldn't it be better to know what I'm doing and to work together than to know I'm investigating on my own and you'll never know where I'll be or what I'll be doing?"

She has me there. I look up at Vinn, who shrugs her shoulders with an 'I told you so' expression on her face. I utter my own profanity, hopefully too low for our new assistant to hear, then look back at the diminutive Maggie Wong. Strands of hair fall haphazardly across her face and not a single muscle of her body seems to be sitting still as she fidgets in the chair, her eyes shining intensely as she focuses on some unknown point behind me. Before I can even open my mouth to respond to her question she's off again. I guess she didn't expect an answer.

"I've thought it all out. I can be researching a paper. I'm a student, right? Did I tell you that? Oh, right, I did. So I'll have a reason to be asking questions. It doesn't have to be on the two murders themselves, that would be kind of obvious, don't you think? Right, too obvious. I agree. It could be something like violence against Asians in general or how immigrants blend into a community or something like that. Or maybe how the school deals with the death of a student because they've been pretty quiet about it and I could expose that. I have a notepad, that will make it look real. See? I've thought of everything."

Not nearly everything, I think to myself, not even close. I feel trapped and don't want the blood of this well-meaning and totally exasperating young woman on my hands. I learned long ago that when it's impossible to prevent a catastrophe, the next best thing is to try to control it. I put on my best authoritative, professorial voice, or at least what I think one should sound like.

"Maggie, what you say makes a lot of sense. I'm pretty sure we can find a way to use your journalistic skills." I swear she did a little clap with her hands. Vinn is rolling her eyes, whether at me or Maggie is unclear. "But we have to make it as realistic as possible. That means that I'll pose as your supervisor on this fictional research paper. You don't do a single thing without my approval, or that of Professor Achison, is that clear? And every time, and I mean EVERY TIME, you venture into Chinatown for any reason other than chowing down on dumplings, you will be followed by a team of expert surveillance personnel who will be monitoring your every move and if it appears you are in the slightest bit of danger, they'll swoop in and carry you away and that will end your participation, is that clear? This is non-negotiable and I need to hear that you understand and agree."

At least one sixty-fourth of a second passes before Maggie squeals, bounces in her seat, and says something with so much enthusiasm that I can't make out the wording, but her expression gives her away.

"Fine. Great. Welcome to the team. We're having a strategy meeting later in the week and I'll expect you to be there. Write down your phone and email and I'll send you the details." The infamous red notepad comes out along with a purple-inked pen and soon I have the contact information for our newest investigative team member, who literally skips out the door.

Vinn and I both stare at the door as if we wish we could start the last twenty minutes over. She finally turns back to me and breaks the silence.

"Surveillance team? Strategy meeting?"

I respond in the only way I know how, which is to bury my head in my arms and wait for my desk to swallow me up. I hear Vinn move beside me, open the bottom drawer, and pull out a bottle. She knows where I keep the good stuff and that I save it only for moments of celebration or as an aid in dealing with despair. This seems to be one of those occasions.

ℕINETEEN

ℳy late-night sessions at Leo's kitchen table have become a
frequent occurrence but fluctuate wildly in nature. The norm
is topical conversation fueled by the consumption of an inordinate
amount of strong liquor, the type of which has also varied depending
on Leo's mood and what he has on hand in quantity. Typically it's
the standards: rum, tequila, mescal, or a powerful, unlabeled brand
of whiskey that I've never had the nerve to ask where it comes from.
Other times he digs into his treasure trove of bootleg spirits, including
Brazilian catuba or pox from some remote village in Mexico. The traits
they all share is that they're always potent, always overwhelmingly in-
toxicating, range from mildly to severely addictive, and without fail are
the reason behind my throbbing headache the next day. Some nights
Leo is sullen or I'm contemplative and we drink in silence. Occasionally he hands out unsolicited advice on what's going on in my life—but
never the other way around—and once he sewed up a bullet wound
in my arm. There's no regular schedule. When the mood strikes me I
head downstairs, where Leo always appears to be expecting me with
two shot glasses at the ready on the table.

The one constant in all of these boozy confabs has been the
unstated entry fee of testosterone. It's a manly journey into the dark
haze of alcoholic masculinity full of sweat and bluster and uncensored
drunken behavior. Since proving her mettle through her skills with
firearms, Rebecca has been allowed to join us now and again while
Ted remains forever banned, but even in a padded bra and mascara
she's more manly than most men. Leo and I also believe that she still
has certain genitalia that most of society continues to use to define the
male sex, although we've both been either too polite, or too embar-
rassed, to verify that assumption. If this were a club the bylaws might
require a doctor's note or visual proof, so it's a good thing that we have

no rules that I know of and tend to be flexible in defining gender.

All of which is a way of setting the stage for the highly unusual and unprecedented scene that lies before my eyes in the wee hours of this particular evening. Leo and I are settled into our accustomed spots, but tonight we're joined by both Rebecca and Vinn. Rebecca is resplendent in a dark blue, plunging evening dress with a gemstone necklace and matching earrings, although her red high heels seem a bit too garish for the occasion. Vinn, being Vinn, can't help but exude a high level of femininity despite having dressed down in tattered jeans and an oversized University of Wisconsin sweatshirt. Leo knows and likes Vinn but still appeared uncomfortable at first, as if his lair had been invaded, but the fact that Vinn is keeping up with him shot for shot seems to have gained her a modicum of acceptance from the big man.

We've been drinking and making small talk mixed in with a little background on the subject of our journalism student for over an hour, but Leo's room is beginning to move as its features blur, so I feel it's time to either get down to business or pass out.

"Anyway, that's where we stand. She's stubborn to a fault and is going to do what she wants to do with or without our consent, so the only way to reign her in was to agree to accept her assistance but with conditions. At the time it made a lot of sense to insist that she notify us of when she's venturing into Chinatown on her fact-finding mission so that we can have a team surreptitiously follow and observe her, and then to move in if things go badly. A lot of sense, that is, until as Vinn points out," Vinn is also fuzzy but not so much that her smug grin goes unnoticed, "we don't have a team.

"I know you've helped us with surveillance once before, Rebecca, and your assistance was invaluable." I choose not to detail the time that Leo had her follow Vinn and I without our knowledge, a decision that saved our lives. Rebecca doesn't need to be reminded and I'd rather not have to haul and assemble the twin to her rolltop desk. "But that was trailing one man who had no reason to suspect that he had a shadow, and frankly if anyone attacked him the last thing we wanted was to intervene." I turn my attention to Leo. "Here we're dealing with a young, inexperienced woman who might find it fun to try to give the slip to her followers, or who won't see the hazards of certain behavior, and there may be dangerous people not only tracking her but following instructions to look for anyone else who may be watching. The point is, we need help from more than the people here in this kitchen. We need a team, and as it stands we don't even have enough for a pickup game of hoops."

Leo peers off into a space somewhere in the middle of the room, his eyes bloodshot but alert and thoughtful. Vinn bores her gaze directly at him as if the intensity of her stare will magically draw out a solution. We both jump a little in our chairs when it's Rebecca who speaks up.

"Darlings, don't be such Debbie Downers." Her tone brings up visions of a clueless cheerleader rooting on a team that's behind by sixty points late in the game. "Leave it up to Rebecca, I can arrange everything. How many people do you need, Malcom? Five? Ten? Fifty? I do have connections that can be useful, you know. You just need to trust me."

It's a good thing that Rebecca's faced in my direction and doesn't see the look of open-mouthed incredulity on Vinn's face. Leo's expression remains frustratingly impassive, either implying that he knows something that I don't about Rebecca or that he long ago passed the point where his brain has been processing cogent thoughts. That leaves only one other person in the room with the responsibility of responding.

"Um, that's great Rebecca. Where are you going to find these people?"

"Oh, Malcom, details, details. Have I ever let you down before? Now let's see…" Rebecca draws her focus away from me as she loses herself in thought, silently counting on the fingers of her left hand with the brightly polished index finger of her right. Mauve is definitely not her color. We're all mesmerized as we wait for her to finish. "Okay, people, I can get at least seven, no eight, together by the end of the week. Malcom, be a doll and set up a meet with your little student and let me know tomorrow when and where. Right now, I need my beauty sleep. Vinn, it's always a pleasure. Ciao."

We all stare as Rebecca rises in one fluid motion and flounces...yes, flounces...toward the door. No one so much as exhales until the sound of Rebecca's footsteps above us breaks the spell. Leo rises without a word, puts his hand on my shoulder and shakes his head as he passes, then leaves the room.

Vinn and I silently bring the drink glasses to the sink, rinsing them out, then put Leo's bottles back in place. As we exit the apartment and head upstairs, Vinn quietly speaks for the first time in thirty minutes.

"Mal, I don't know what she has in mind, but I have two things to say. One, what do we have to lose? We haven't come up with any ideas of our own and if we don't like what we see, we put the kibosh on it. Two, I have to confess that I'm morbidly curious about what kind of group Rebecca is going to put together. It kind of makes me feel like I have tickets to the circus."

My thoughts exactly.

"Thank you all for coming. I think it's important that you familiarize yourselves with the faces of everyone you'll be working with as well as to meet Maggie herself, and also to go over procedure to make sure we're all working off the same page." I glance uneasily around my apartment at one of the oddest assortments of individuals ever gathered under one roof. I'm sitting on one of the barstools I've moved around to the living room side of the kitchen island with Maggie perched on another stool to my left and Vinn to my right.

Scattered around my living room on every available seat and spilling onto the floor are what Rebecca assured me are the absolute best local "gumshoes"—her word, not mine—who each have extensive experience in the art of surveillance with a special knack for not being seen.

At first sight, it's much easier to believe that rather than blend into their surroundings, each person here would draw special attention from every passerby for blocks around. At least two of the guests wearing dresses have five-o-clock shadows, and one in a particularly revealing green skater dress sports a full beard. Two women, if that's how they choose to identify, could be high-priced models due to their stunning beauty. If I can't take my eyes off of them, and I can't, it's a fair question how they'll fade into the background anywhere. The more customarily-attired gentleman leaning against the door is over six and a half feet tall and 300 pounds with a gleaming bald head. Not so the average-sized black man sitting at his feet, who would win the award for most conventional appearance were it not for his hair, which is braided into cornrows of every conceivable color. A twig of a woman in the corner has every inch of her exposed skin tattooed with mythical beasts. I've detected accents from at least five different regions of the world from the general muttering before I called this meeting to order. It's the Baker Street Irregulars flying under a rainbow version of the United Nations flag.

Rebecca said she could produce a crew, and she was true to her word. She brushes off my attempt to ask how she knows such an unusually diverse segment of the city's citizenry and to vet them with a simple "trust me" and a glare. A few times when she's joined Leo and myself in late-night drinking sessions she's made vague references to various offbeat clubs and organizations she's joined in her effort to gain acceptance. I assume that's where she met at least some of the individuals gathered before me. Like it or not, I backed myself into this corner and have no option other than to trust Rebecca. I just hope I don't come to regret it. Time to begin.

"Before we go any further, I want you to meet Maggie, our intrepid journalist who it will be your job to shadow and to protect if necessary. She's—"

"Ooohh, this is so exciting!" Maggie's voice as she talks is at least an octave higher than it was in my office. Rather than reign her in, I decide to let her get whatever she needs to say out of her system. "I feel so much better knowing you'll be watching me. And—oh, my, where did you get that skirt? Such an unusual color. I love it. Is that Escada?"

She's looking directly at Rebecca, who beams in response to being called out. "No, dearie, it's just a knock off I got from Poshmark. But you really can't tell, can you? And you know, I just happened to find these shoes on eBay that match so perfectly, don't you think? Or would basic black have been better?"

"No, they're simply wonderful. Don't you just love Poshmark? I'll have to try eBay too. Maybe you can give me some tips on what search words you use. It seems so overwhelming."

So much for not reigning her in. "Ahem." I clear my throat, drawing a hurt look from Rebecca. "As I was saying, Maggie will be doing a little investigative work for Vinn and myself. You don't need to know the details. While on the job she'll be spending most of her time in Chinatown, which is where you'll be every time that she is. Rebecca will be in charge of assigning teams and arranging the logistics of each surveillance. Maggie here will notify Rebecca every time she plans to venture out on our behalf and Rebecca will then contact you." I turn to look at Maggie, who nods.

"Your job is to keep your distance but to never lose sight of Maggie. It's critical that no one knows you're there, or it will draw unwanted attention to her. Unobtrusiveness is the key word here." I look directly at the bearded woman, although in all honesty my focus could have been on anyone in the room. "That being said, you have to be close enough so that at the first sign that Maggie's in trouble you're in a position that allows you to extract her safely.

"That's your primary objective. Keep your eyes open, though, for anyone who might take an unusual interest in Maggie. If you notice someone following her, or see the same face in her vicinity more than once, take pictures. In fact, take pictures whenever there are people nearby her and get them to Rebecca and myself at the end of each shift. Anyone suspicious, follow them and find out where they go, even if it means that one of you needs to abandon Maggie for a while. With luck, either the information Maggie gathers or the photos you take will save a life, and also provide the basis for finding justice for lives already lost."

"Will we be a part of that? The imposing justice part, I mean?" It was the bodybuilder, who appeared eager at this possible opportunity.

"Um, no, sorry. That will be left to Vinn and myself. Your jobs are limited to protection and fact-finding." His face fell with disappointment. "Of course, if Maggie can only escape possible injury or worse, do what you need to do." His eyes, and those of everyone in the room, seem to shine brighter as I speak those words, which I immediately regret.

"If there are no questions, then, why don't you mingle around to meet the others you'll be working with, as well as Maggie. And again, thank you for coming."

Most of the team comes up to say hello to Maggie, and to memorize her features, which doesn't seem to bother her in the least. Rebecca starts to follow up on her conversation about fashion until a look from me cuts her short. Mingling with each other doesn't seem to be a priority for our guests, however, which makes sense if the members of the group truly do earn a living doing work where it helps not to be noticed. Within ten minutes, the crew starts to filter out, Rebecca dutifully stationed by the door taking contact information, before Rebecca and Maggie exit together, chatting excitedly. One of the men trailing behind hesitates at the door before cautiously edging back to my side and holding out his hand.

"I'm Chuck and I'm mostly responsible for getting this group together. I used to specialize in this kind of thing and met Ted in that capacity, earning a pretty good fee for very little work at the time. So when he—uh, she—asked for my help I was more than willing to donate my services. I admit the people here are amateurs, especially those Ted—Rebecca—brought in, and they may not look all that professional, but I've used all but a couple of them in the past and there's none better." He looked at me with a sly grin, sensing my doubts. "I guess you've just got to trust my word on that."

As Chuck closed the door behind me, I realize that the future of our investigation relies an awful lot on believing people when they ask me to trust them. With that grim thought in mind, I flop on the couch beside Vinn, both of us letting out deep-throated groans that sum up our feelings and the chances of our prospects exactly.

"Is this the best you've got?" comes a loud, gruff voice from the kitchen, startling both of us. Leo stands with a bottle of cognac in one hand, one of gin in the other, and an angry grimace on his face. I didn't even know he was here.

Vinn and I sit back on our stools and release simultaneous sighs. "Welcome to the circus" she says with a soft smile.

ᵀWENTY

S tuart's under the radar crusade to find cause to get me fired or to make life so uncomfortable for me that I quit, and thus save him the embarrassment of anyone discovering that he hired a fraud, includes periodic threats to sit in on my classes, but until today he never followed through. Perhaps he's been worried that I would encourage him to join in on a discussion of something about which he's not familiar. It was an unwelcome jolt, then, when I walked into my 1:00 "Mystery and Thriller Composition" class to see him sitting tall in the front row of desks. My shock must have been evident and pleased him, as he used the opportunity to pounce.

"Well hello, Malcom. You look surprised. Did I forget to notify you that I'll be joining you today? I'm so sorry. I thought it was time to see my star hire perform in person. I'm not taking anyone's seat here, am I?" he sneered. He was clearly enjoying this.

"Actually, yes. Jamaal Forrest—you know him, he's a defensive tackle on the football team—usually takes that spot because he's so large that he needs the room up front to extend his legs. He got a little surly when a sophomore tried to cop it a couple of weeks ago, but we diffused the situation before the carnage got out of hand, and according to her friends the other student is recovering well. I'm sure he won't mind."

Stuart had to know I was fibbing. He should have at least known that UIC doesn't field a football team. Nevertheless, he glanced around nervously, a little tic twitching by one eye, and eventually slid down one seat closer to the door. He needn't have worried. Even my more interactive students don't like the front row. Either it gives them comfort to have a buffer between themselves and me or they don't want to get a reputation as gunners. Stuart will have the whole row to himself, which come to think of it might fuel his paranoia about not being respected. I smile inwardly.

He actually chose the perfect class to attend, at least from the perspective of saving my job. Composed entirely of juniors and seniors, the students enrolled in this class because they genuinely wanted it and have a strong interest in the genre. I never read many thrillers or mysteries prior to being assigned to this topic, but I did lead the life for many years, so I'm able give a prompt or two and then stand back and let the class do most of my work for me, discussing and debating with an unusual passion. I'm mostly an observer but they try their best to draw me in in order to get brownie points. After all, I issue the grades.

The class fills up a minute or two early, so to score points of my own I decide not to wait for the bell before starting. If Stuart is impressed, he doesn't show it.

"All right class, your assignment was to write a single sentence that starts your very own mystery novel. The goal, as we discussed last time, is for it to be of such interest that with just those very few words the reader is hooked and wants to read more. Who wants to go first?"

Virtually every hand in the class rockets skyward, although I know the real reason is that no one wants to look shy, while deep down all but a handful are praying not to be called on to be the initial reader. I came into class already knowing who I would choose, as her contributions usually provoke a lot of controversy and discussion.

"Sarah, how about you read what you've got."

Supremely intelligent and just as shy about revealing her talents, Sarah blushes a deep scarlet before standing, moving down to the front of the class, and clearing her throat. She gives Stuart a withering glance before beginning. She doesn't know it, but she just got extra credit.

"As she trudged slowly across the desert sands, Angie knew that it was impossible for anyone to follow her without being seen, but she also knew that she was being watched, that the watcher was nearby, and that she wouldn't make it until sunset alive."

Not entirely terrible and something about it causes a vague feeling of unease to rise within me which I can't immediately identify. For the rest of the class, it has the desired effect of setting off a wildfire of opinions. None are overly critical, as every other student knows that they still have to present their own work to the highly judgmental group, which is another reason why I chose my student most sensitive to criticism to read first. Others that follow are mostly good efforts but flawed enough to keep the discussion lively. A few try to sneak Faulkner-style eternal sentences without punctuation in and that leads to cries of fowl from the other students. Overall an entertaining and instructive class, with enough energy carrying past the bell that several students hang around my desk afterward to ask questions. Out of the corner of my eye I notice Stuart slink away, eyes focused on the floorboards. Safe for another day.

Once alone, I think back to Sarah's sentence that led off the class, which has continued to gnaw at my subconscious for the past fifty minutes and I finally realize why. I take out my cell phone and send a text off to Rebecca, who at this time of day will still be masquerading as the asshole Ted. I want to be a part of the first shift to follow Maggie.

"Are you sure that's a good idea?" Vinn asks sincerely, echoing my own doubts. We're sharing dry hot pot at a Chinese hole-in-the-wall a five-minute walk from campus. We've each spent enough time in Asia to appreciate its authenticity and it's rapidly become one of our favorite haunts. I don't think either of us considered the irony of our choice of ethnic food while we discuss Maggie. "Both of us have already been marked as trouble by the triad and if they see either of us in the vicinity of Maggie, she, and our whole plan, are toast."

"That's why I won't be in the vicinity, not exactly anyway. First of all, the intent for each member of the crew is to observe without being seen, and I do have some experience in that area. And frankly I'm a little less conspicuous than some of the others. A lot more than all of them, actually. Also, I made clear to Rebecca that I won't be replacing anyone, I'll just be one extra body hanging back away from the action, virtually out of sight. For the first couple of shifts, I want to be nearby, listening in and watching the watchers as much as anything. I need to know that Maggie's in good hands."

Vinn nods as she grabs lotus root with her chopsticks. "I understand. Your student's first sentence creeped me out a little too. Hopefully it's coincidental, not prescient."

"Exactly. According to Rebecca, she's sending out teams of three, not including me. The first one to go out will consist of Chuck, the bodybuilder, Clarise, who I think was wearing a beige sweater at my place, and Nora, one of the hotties." Vinn's eyes flash and she almost chokes on a pepper as she gives me a sharp look, but she says nothing. It may have been the pepper that spared me a scolding. I don't give her a chance to swallow before continuing.

"When it's time, the five of us—I'm including Rebecca—meet up with Maggie so that she can tell us what her plans are, where she'll be going, and who she's meeting. Also, we'll verify that our equipment is working and that we have each other's cell phone numbers just in case one of us gets out of range. I'll verify that everyone knows that this will be the routine every single time she ventures out on our business. No shortcuts."

Vinn looks pensive. "I sure hope we're doing the right thing and that we can trust what you call our 'team.' As I said earlier, I can't shake the feeling that we're throwing Maggie into the middle of a traveling circus. Furthermore…"

My cell phone cuts her off and the "Lola" ringtone tells me it's Rebecca. Tacky, I know, but it guarantees that I'll recognize who's calling. I listen for a minute and the call ends before I can say a word.

"That was the ringmaster. It's showtime."

TWENTY ONE

Vinn and I agreed that Maggie's cover story will be that she's researching a term paper on Chinese immigration, in partic-ular the history of immigrants in Chicago and the parallel history of the city's Chinatown neighborhood. In theory this will be enough to open up access to some of the elders who have knowledge of a broad spectrum of the annals of the neighborhood, including facts about the triad and its workings that they might not otherwise share, as well as to younger Asians who might reveal inside dope about the two youths who constitute our main targets in the murders of the two women. If she's able to find out where they live, or where they hang out on a regular basis, or even anything that allows us to know where they're likely to be at a given time, I'll consider her foray into the world of espionage a success and will quickly pull the plug. Beyond the fake paper, I'm not sure Maggie has thought through even a rudimentary outline of a plan of action. I suggested she begin with Mr. Wei and any friends he may want to bring along in order to give her a comfortable start. A stationary interview at a known location will also allow the first team to get its feet wet without too much stress.

By prior arrangement, Chuck and Nora will be stationed somewhere within view of Maggie's campus apartment to pick up her trail from the beginning while Clarise will be waiting by the el station in Chinatown to join in the surveillance on that end. Since my main goal is to observe and evaluate the watchers, I situate myself between Maggie's place and the blue line to await the first group.

I'm fifteen minutes into an imaginary phone conversation in the doorway of the campus basketball arena when I spot Maggie walking up Racine Avenue toward the entrance to the train station. I wait a few beats trying to find her trailers but see no one. Either they're surprisingly good at staying hidden or they've already lost her, which would be more than a little distressing. I count to ten before pretending to finish my call and head in the direction of the el.

Once I get past the turnstiles, I locate Maggie walking near the bottom of the long ramp to the platform, but no train is due for four more minutes, so I take my time descending. Once at the platform I lean over the edge of the eastbound side looking west for the train, my not so subtle way of keeping an eye on my prey. She's about halfway down. I don't notice any familiar or suspicious faces nearby, not that I expected any, but my relief at not seeing any threats is tempered by my concern that I can't spot any of the team either. Since I know which stop she's exiting there's no reason for me to get any closer. Three minutes later I enter the front car.

Getting to Chinatown requires transferring to the red line at the Jackson station, which entails taking stairs down deep below the already-underground station and walking about two city blocks before ascending again. I scurry to get to the other side first so as to position myself with a view of the tops of both sets of stairs to the red line platform. Still no sign of either one of the crew. My concern is rapidly transitioning into full-blown worry. I move down the platform a few feet to assist an elderly woman carrying a shopping bag who appears to be confused as to which side will have her train when she looks up and gives me a sly wink. Nora. Immediately I think what a pity it is to conceal such an attractive body under rags and wrinkles, but somewhere in the recesses of my mind I hear Vinn screaming at me, so I quickly modify my thoughts to focus on how well disguised she is. I make a mental note to chastise Vinn, probably also only in my mind, for burying herself so deep in my consciousness as to spoil my sexist urges. Still no sign of Chuck.

It's a relatively short ride to the elevated Chinatown stop, where I purposefully lag behind and position myself in front of the train schedule on the platform, eyeing it as if planning my return. After a few minutes I turn to look out over the street below, eventual-

ly picking up Maggie as she walks down 22nd Street. Again, I know
where she's meeting Mr. Wei, so my main focus is on trying to pick up
the team, which should now number three with the addition of Clarise. I'm supposedly well-trained in the art of observation, but I see no
one, not even Nora the old woman. I give up and head down the stairs.

Mr. Wei offered several meeting locations, mostly restaurants
as well as the table tennis club, but none of his options seemed quite
right. In the end we agreed upon the Chinese Community Center,
also known as the Benevolent Association, of which he serves on the
Board, as a more likely place for an interview by a student. Once Maggie enters the building I force myself to cast aside any doubts I have
and assume that at this point she's well covered by the team. I chose to
trust Rebecca and as difficult as it is, I need to stand by my decision.
I kill time by browsing the gift shops and comparing prices on mane-
ki-neko, the waving cats that seem to be everywhere in different sizes
and colors, even though they're not only tacky as hell, they're actually
from Japan. While I'm in one shop a woman with a downstate accent
actually purchases one. Sigh. Tourists.

Now that enough time has passed that Maggie's interview
could be coming to an end, I try to limit my browsing to the area
close to the windows in order to keep the street in view, but so far I
see nothing. I adjust the volume on my earpiece, which up until now
has been silent. We agreed in advance to maintain radio silence unless
communication is absolutely necessary in order to minimize the risk
of being overheard. I'm lost in thought as I pretend to be interested
in an overpriced fake silk kimono and am considering the irony of the
"Made in Philippines" tag when I feel a presence sidle up behind me.

"If you're really interested in buying that, the prices are better
at the shop a block south and across the street. More colorful selection,
too. Otherwise, just thought you'd like to know that Magpie is on the
move back home."

Chuck. I turn, but already the space behind me is empty and

I see no one between myself and the door. I have to concede that he's good. I'm in no rush now but head back in the direction of the el. The team will see that Maggie gets back home safely and afterward will gather in my apartment for a debriefing. I had told Maggie that it would be too suspicious if she was seen in the vicinity of my place, as well as inappropriate behavior for a student and her advisor even under normal circumstances. Unless she uncovers something hot, or feels in danger, periodic updates would be in my office in the guise of discussing the paper with her supervising professor.

An hour later, the four of us are sprawled comfortably in my living room. Clarise—who I try to get a closer look at without staring in order to satisfy my curiosity as to her true gender—sips a glass of water. Nora chose coffee, which instantly moves her down several notches in my book, and Chuck joins me in a cup of Jasmine Pearl tea, to which he added no sugar. He's beginning to grow on me. Before we begin I take a quick peek behind the kitchen island to make sure I don't discover Leo raiding my liquor collection.

I open the discussion with the one critically important question that's been nagging at me since Chinatown. "Magpie?" I ask.

All three of the team members look down sheepishly before Clarise explains. "It was my idea. We knew it was childish, but it made us feel more like spies you read about in novels, you know? Operation Magpie. If you don't like it, we can find something else or drop the pretense."

I smile. "No, it's fine. Any more pressing issues we need to discuss?"

They look at each other with blank expressions. Chuck finally takes the initiative and speaks up. "Everything went fine. Magpie—Maggie—was always within sight of at least two of us. We were in positions to be able to see at least one or two blocks in every direction. She wasn't followed, didn't attract attention that we know about. And we would know."

"Good to hear, thanks. That's to be expected early on since she hasn't put herself on anyone's radar yet. I'm certain that will change as soon as word gets around that she's down there asking questions, term paper notwithstanding. Stay vigilant, and thank you. Unless something unusual occurs, in the future one of you can call me after going out to give me the details."

Clarise gathers the cups and brings them to the sink, teasing me with a little wink on the way, then all three walk toward the door. As the women leave, Chuck once again hangs back for a moment. "Good tea, by the way." He nods his approval. "Have you ever tried Dragon Well?"

My kind of man.

Six days have passed since Maggie's initial foray into Chinatown. While that isn't even a full week yet, all of us are getting a bit impatient at the lack of progress. She's been there twice more, once for an interview with an ancient resident who considers himself the unofficial historian of the community and once at night for karaoke with a couple of her fellow students. These subsequent trips haven't produced much if any useful information but have given each team a chance to trail her once and for me to tag along in the background evaluating them. My initial concerns about their professionalism has been allayed, especially when faced with the challenge of her trip to the karaoke bar. I didn't go inside but understand that one of Rebecca's crossdressing cohorts dazzled in a sequin dress and brought down the house with her version of one of Beyonce's songs. I questioned putting herself in the spotlight like that at first, but she convinced me that it draws more attention not to participate than to get up and sing. I did suggest, though, that next time she consider performing more off-key so as to minimize the attention. My recommendation was not received well.

Each time, Maggie hasn't been shy about bringing triads and

ghost marriages into the conversation, even with people she only met while out at the bar. She and I had a heated discussion on the topic yesterday in my office during our first supposed teacher-student meeting about her paper. I feel that she's unnecessarily bringing herself into the danger zone by raising such specific and sensitive topics among strangers while she argues that it's the fastest and maybe the only way to gather relevant information and to draw out those responsible, directly or peripherally, for the killing of the two women.

"I mean, shit, err, shoot, Professor, this isn't a real thesis, although maybe it should be because really it's kind of fascinating don't you think, people marrying corpses and going through with the ceremony and in a way it's kind of cool, you know? But most of the feedback I'm getting is about stuff I don't care about and that you don't care about but that I need to pretend to be interested in and after a while I just want to ask about the murders themselves but you told me not to but I'm going to at least bring up the weddings and crime because the whole point of my going down there is to draw the attention of the people involved so that you can find them, am I right?"

How to you argue with logic like that, if that's what it is? In the end we admitted to a stalemate, my concern with her safety just as strong as ever and her determination to do what she feels she needs to do "because the best journalists take risks" equally entrenched. When she left my office I'm not sure which of us was the more frustrated. I clearly need another opinion.

"You do see that she's right, don't you?" Vinn is nibbling on a bagel in her usual spot in the campus café. "You don't want to admit it, but that's what we agreed to. Let's be honest, Mal, we're using her as bait. We've danced around it, using phrases like 'drawing them out' or 'getting their attention,' but the only way this is going to work is if Maggie presents herself as enough of a curiosity or potential threat that someone is going to try to forcibly get her alone to answer some questions, maybe with some broken fingers or worse thrown in. And the only way to do that without actually directly saying she's investigating the murders is to bring up the subjects of tongs and ghost weddings with enough people that eventually someone will notice she's linking the two and will pass her information on to the very people we want to find."

Vinn is nothing if not frank when she needs to be. Normally I respect her for that, but today it's a source of annoyance. I realize that I was hoping for her support and it's distressing to hear that her view on the subject doesn't align with my own. Especially since she's making way too much sense.

I sip my tea and feign finding fault with it as a stall tactic, but Vinn's penetrating and way-too-intelligent eyes never leave my face. No convincing retort comes to mind, until finally I have no choice but to face reality.

"I guess seeing the plan play out in real time has accentuated my awareness of the dangers and they're clearly much greater than I wanted to admit when everything was still theoretical. I'm extremely worried about her, Vinn. Scared, actually."

Vinn looks sympathetic and replies in a softer tone. "Me too. And it's my fault, my responsibility, just as much as yours. If it's any consolation, we didn't recruit her. She would have done this on her own if we didn't intervene. She's safer because of the teams we have following her and they wouldn't be doing it if it weren't for us. And Rebecca of course. We're doing all we can." She peers over my shoulder. "Damn. I've got to run to class. Tag along if you want to hear a lecture on analytical technology."

"Tempting, but it might distract from preparing for my freshman creative writing class. I'll see you at lunch."

I have a rule for all of my classes that except under very limited circumstances, cell phones need to be turned off, not simply silenced. It's a difficult concept for most of my students, who aren't accustomed to being cut off from social media as long as they're not asleep or dead, to grasp. There were a few resisters early in the semester, but the dual sanctions of having the phone confiscated for the rest of the school day and having to memorize and recite Elizabethan love sonnets for the class brought them around fairly quickly. I'm not sure which penalty they dreaded more.

The last thing I need, then, is for my phone to announce its presence while I'm teaching. It may not have been quite as great a challenge for me to cut myself off from the outside world for an hour at a time as for my students, but I'm paranoid about forgetting to follow my own rule, so I've acquired the habit of checking that I've turned it off before every class. One consequence of this, of course, is that I'm virtually unreachable while in session.

I'm halfway through a wild debate on point of view intrusion when there's a loud and persistent knock on the classroom door. I excuse myself from the discussion but am pleased to hear the students continue on without me. I'm surprised to see Vinn standing impatiently outside the door.

"Sorry to interrupt your class, Mal, but I thought you should know. Rebecca has been trying to reach you. Maggie's felt like she's being watched here on campus, so Rebecca got a couple members of the team to hurry here to check it out. She was right, someone's following her. We need have a meeting, fast."

It's rare when I have a freshman class that's disappointed when class is cut short, so in the end I let them continue talking while I take my leave. I can still hear raised voices as Vinn and I hustle down the hall.

TWENTY TWO

Vinn's office is larger than my pathetic excuse for a closet, which is only fair considering she's got tenure while I'm still a newbie. She also needs the room to hold her outsized intellect. Besides, it has the advantage of not being under the watchful eye of my boss Stuart, who would be beyond curious about the collection of outsiders holding court in his precious wing of the administration building, especially when one of them has whiskers which don't even match their angora sweater. Vinn had the foresight to direct the team to bring Maggie to her office rather than to my own while she was fetching me. We're the last to arrive.

Maggie doesn't even wait for us to get seated before she starts right in. It's a wonder she didn't explode having to hold it in for this long. "Oh my God I almost didn't notice him at first, you know, but sometimes you get a feeling and then I started looking over my shoulder but I wasn't obvious and it was just like the movies where when I stopped he would stop and even duck into a doorway but I knew he was there and I finally went into a store pretending to shop and that's when I called Rebecca." I almost stopped processing what she was saying as I watched her mouth, intent instead on seeing if she would finish the sentence all in one breath. She did.

Only now while Maggie pauses to reload do I glance around the room to see who else is here. Nora is one of the team members present. The other is a slight, light brown woman with dark cropped hair who doesn't look much older than a college student herself. She has a habit—talent, maybe—of blending into the surroundings and it can take an effort to find her even in a confined space such as this one. The initial meeting in my apartment was almost over before I noticed her at all. She didn't offer her name nor come up afterward to introduce herself. I'm envious of her ability to maintain anonymity and honor it by not asking for it now. Rebecca is not here, as I'm sure Ted can't tear himself away from his job on a moment's notice. She also wouldn't have had a chance to change out of her pricey Givenchy men's suit for her pricier Givenchy evening dress.

"How sure are we that she was actually being followed?" I address my question to Nora.

"As sure as we can be based on such a short observation period." Her voice is confident in her conclusion. "We had Maggie wait to leave the shop until I was in place for five minutes. That whole time there was a guy on a bench looking right at the door of the shop and as soon as Maggie emerged, he got up and walked thirty paces behind her. Didn't seem to be too concerned about being seen, might've even wanted to be. Either that or he's an amateur when it comes to tailing. I lean toward the former."

"Probably some of both," Vinn says. "If he's a thug like we think he is, intimidation would be one of his standard tools for establishing control over a situation. And I doubt that surreptitious surveillance is normally necessary in his world, which involves more strong-arm tactics and bullying than finesse, so he wouldn't have much experience with it. He may want to scare Maggie off, in which case the whole point of his escapade was to be noticed. His approach actually works in our favor. It means next time he won't be careful when he goes back home."

"He wasn't this time." The black woman has one eye on her phone as she speaks. "After we swept Magpie out from his sphere of vision, which wasn't difficult by the way, he looked around for only a few minutes before heading back to Chinatown. Hector took his trail while the rest of us came here."

The lilt in her voice tells me she's from Nigeria, or that she can fake a very authentic accent. I love hearing her speak and my mind races to think of some way to draw out more information from her, such as 'Who in the hell is Hector?' Instead, I ask a question of more immediate concern. "Did you get a picture?"

"Yep. Several. Sending them now." She punches a few keys and instantly I hear several phones acknowledge receipt of a text, including my own. She continues to stare at the screen on her cell and an almost imperceptible smile crosses her lips. "And there's more. I just got a text from Hector. Once back in the neighborhood, he headed straight for a rendezvous with two more young thugs. What do you want to bet they're the goons you're looking for?"

I could kiss her, not entirely because of the good news she just passed on, that we have a connection and a starting point. I find myself wondering if she has freckles hiding beneath her brown complexion. Focus, Winters. I regain my composure and try to sound calm and in control. It's important that no one decides to take matters into their own hands.

"Okay, great. For now, let's keep everything going as it has been until Vinn and I decide what to do with this information. Magp— Maggie, that means you can continue to 'research' the term paper, at least for now, but it's more important than ever that you don't make a move without the team in place. If you change your routine, our target may get suspicious and could go to ground. Once Vinn and I have our next step planned, we'll pass the word on."

I watch Nora and the Nigerian princess file out the door while behind me Vinn speaks quietly with Maggie. I overhear the words "not a movie" and "cautious." I take the opportunity to study the photo of Maggie's shadow before forwarding it on to a number I know well. Two minutes later, I'm heading to my next class.

The cooler weather has me thinking of apple picking and apple butter, and there's no better selection once the farmers' markets move indoors than a tiny Amish grocery and health food store on

Western Avenue a short walk from my apartment. It's not a place to stock the hamper but does carry unusual items that you won't find anywhere else, and that make impulse buying almost a necessity. Raw vegan white chocolate hazelnut spread anyone? Invariably I also end up splurging on some ice cream made from Amish sheep's milk or a fresh baked good, which today includes raspberry nut bars. I put off any sort of decision and move to the shelves with a selection of jams and pickled things, many with a handmade label on a mason jar. The apple butters are there, but I'm distracted by the presence of plum butter, which I've never heard of, and I'm always a sucker for gooseberry fruit spread.

As much as I'd like to just stand here for hours perusing food as a way of momentarily putting the Maggie incident aside, I finally make a decision by not deciding and grab both the plum butter and gooseberry jam along with a jar of apple butter and make my way to the cash register. The friendly woman who rings me up, and who is there often enough that I can no longer ask her name without appearing like an idiot who can't remember her name, which I am, smiles at me.

"No pastry today? We have coconut brownies."

Damn her. "Sure, throw one in, thanks." I avert my eyes in order to avoid having her start a conversation about how fresh the chocolate soft-serve is or the benefits of transdermal magnesium oil and wander over to browse the teas while I wait for her to grab a brownie straight out of the oven. The first one my eyes land on happens to be loose-leaf Dragon Well, which brings on a memory of team member Chuck and, of course, by affiliation the decisions to be made about Maggie's 'friend.' Shit. There's no escape. Time to get back home to do some serious thinking. I pay for my wares, distractedly grab my reusable bag adorned with the Chicago city flag, and head out the door.

My mind may be distracted by more important matters, but when I only buy four items and three of them go on toast, I think I would remember purchasing a lemon ginger dark chocolate bar. Maybe this is the Amish woman's way of flirting with me. I put it in a the drawer I reserve for all of the forbidden temptations that I never meant to buy, make a mental note to pay for it the next time I'm in the shop, and bring a notepad and cup of strong tea—not Dragon Well—to the couch, ready to brainstorm. I have everything I need but the focus, as my thoughts keep wandering back to the stupid chocolate bar. I guess it wouldn't spoil my dinner to break off a small bite if it helps get my mind back where it needs to be.

I unwrap it carefully, but before I move to the foil a small piece of paper tucked inside the wrapper falls to the floor. Curiosity about the paper overcomes curiosity about the taste of the candy. I stoop down, pick it up, and unfold.

A long series of numbers, letters, and symbols greets my eyes. I should have known as soon as I saw the chocolate bar. Carlotta, whom as I guessed isn't as unreachable as she said she would be after all. She knows about my weakness for sweets, especially obscure and fair trade brands, and years ago used to tease me about it. Leaving a code inside a wrapper, though, that's new. In her honor, I take a bite of the bar. Disappointing.

I move back to the couch, picking up my laptop on the way, and navigate to a website only accessible by invitation, a parallel of sorts to the dark web but for intelligence services. Covert operatives use it to send messages and other information among themselves and it's not exactly sanctioned, which may explain why I'm still able to get in. I enter the code number, remembering to skip any odd numbers and vowels, and wait.

Gradually the dark screen dissolves and is replaced by two un-named folders, one white and one red. I click on the white one and am greeted by a short, and not very sweet, message.

"Griff, the first thing I want to say is AVOID THAT MAN AT ALL COSTS." The caps are hers. "His file isn't very thick, but it's full of nasty stuff and he holds some sort of position with the local tongs. Yes, plural. Do not engage or you will be very, very sorry.

"Okay, enough of the disclaimer. Knowing you, it was a waste of my time to type it up in the first place but it'll help me sleep at night after your funeral. His name is Sam Feng but he likes to call himself Sam Bixi, naming himself after some legendary dragon with sharp teeth. This punk's known associates include your two targets so he's a possible means to get to them. His preferred tools of the trade are a samurai sword—I know they're Japanese, take it up with at him, not me—and a sharp awl. Slash and poke. Be wary. Good luck asshole."

I delete the file and move on to the red folder. It contains a few pictures of Sam Feng of better quality than what we have. Most importantly, one of them is him emerging from an apartment building with its address, the number anyway, visible. It'll take a walk around Chinatown, but we should be able to find it without too much difficulty. As to what we do with the location once we get it, I'll need to consult with my brighter side. First, though, I need to shut Maggie down immediately and to change the role of the team from her shadows to her guardians. I reach for my phone, but not before stuffing the rest of the chocolate in my mouth. It's growing on me.

TWENTY THREE

For the price of an eight-ounce bag of loose tea, something so much better than Dragon Well that it would open his eyes to a whole new world and probably spoil his taste for any lesser tea for the rest of his life, Chuck was willing to devote some time to finding Feng's apartment by simply wandering the neighborhood with the picture Carlotta provided in hand. Turns out it couldn't have been too difficult, as it's on Wentworth, the area's main north-south street, just a couple blocks away from the primary business and tourist area. A basic five-story brick box, the developer clearly had no interest in honoring the city's proud architectural history or even adding any elements to reflect its presence in Chinatown. You could pick it up and drop it virtually anywhere in the country and it would fit right in without drawing any significant attention. Kind of like a residential version of Bed Bath & Beyond.

Outside the letdown from an aesthetics perspective, there's good news in that while the outside buzzer directory doesn't have Feng's name listed, Chuck was able to get past the security door to find it on a mailbox labeled with his apartment number of 3C. The bad news is that the building is exposed with little cover for any sort of covert surveillance and that the rest of the names on the mailboxes were all also Asian. We don't have a cadre of Asian team members—I remember one—and a steady stream of Caucasians and blacks hanging around, not to mention crossdressers of any color, would be conspicuous and may even draw unwanted interest from the local constabulary. Ideally, we'd like to observe Feng's comings and goings over a long enough period of time to establish a pattern that would allow us with some degree of certainty to know when we could enter without being disturbed, but that won't be possible here. Like it or not, and we don't like it one bit, Vinn and I will have to wing it.

Our obligations to our students combined with our reluctance to break in after dark force us to wait until the weekend, which also increases the odds that there will be more residents at home and therefore a greater risk of getting caught. We consider going in early, but Feng's young age and lifestyle make it likely that he's a night owl who sleeps in. With a clear feeling of dread, we more or less randomly choose 4:00 p.m. as the go time to break and enter, which will be followed closely by who knows how many other misdemeanors and felonies. The shadows of mid-autumn dusk could provide some cover, and elderly residents staying inside their units to cook an early dinner may also work in our favor. Despite it all, I smile to myself at the absurdity of the entire venture. Mal and Vinn, model citizens or hardened criminals? I can see the episode on '48 Hours' play through my mind. Stuart would probably keep a recording of it repeating on a constant loop.

The fact that neither of us owns wheels, along with the bad guy rule stating that taking an Uber to an upcoming crime scene isn't the best idea, forces us to stow our burglar tools in backpacks and use public transportation to Chinatown. It might be amusing if it also weren't a little pathetic. Our getaway car will be an elevated train.

We take our time wandering past the crowded restaurants and shops, even stopping into Chinatown Bazaar to purchase a silk lantern so that we have some sort of cover, weak as it may be, for why we're in the area. I keep the receipt with the intent of returning it later. Vinn and I put on our best impression of casual wanderers as we move away from the main area, the retail shops and eateries rapidly thinning out with every block. The cluster of businesses disappears completely as we cross 26th Street and a block later pass under the dust and noise of traffic on the busy Dan Ryan Expressway above. It doesn't take long to feel both exposed and conspicuous and we can only hope that the garish shopping bag with the lantern peeking out gives us the appearance of tourists who've lost their way.

Traffic is almost non-existent as we near the apartment building, but we need to worry about pedestrians as well and there are enough of them mingling around that we quickly realize that the front entrance isn't a viable option. City fire codes require more than one way out of a building, so we backtrack to a narrow street that leads west and will give us access to the rear by way of a wide alley. The alley offers no place to hide but at least has less activity. Handwritten signs in Mandarin posted on telephone poles seem to dictate who's allowed to park behind the building.

Vinn pulls out a map and spreads it out over the hood of a car parked close to the rear entrance so that we can pretend to be lost, while at the same time surreptitiously watching the back door. A close observer would conclude that we were in fact very lost, as the map is of Rhode Island. They might also wonder why we don't simply use Google maps on our phones, so we don't want to linger long. No one enters or leaves the back way for five minutes, which under the circumstances has to be long enough for us to move on to the next step.

Past experience has taught us that I possess a better set of lock picks but Vinn the better skills, so I pass her my picks and within fifteen seconds we're inside. An entrance to a stairway stands immediately inside the door to our left and we quickly move into the stairwell, pausing to listen for sounds and to utter sighs of relief at our unimpeded progress so far. One advantage to these newer buildings is the lack of wood anywhere in the common areas, so we're able to climb up two flights of cement stairs to the third floor without worrying about any creaking noises foretelling our progress.

I cautiously open the door, which does squeak, and move my head out barely enough to scan the hallway. No one is in sight and, to my relief, the hallway is carpeted. I nod silently to Vinn and we move to the first door, which to our surprise reads "2G."

"Shit," I hear coming from my right. Vinn grabs the front of my shirt and tugs hard, and together we hustle back to the stairway, not bothering to use stealth upon re-entry. "I guess they use the Asian system of numbering floors," she whispers. We head up one more flight.

This time we don't stop as we move past the first door, which we assume is unit 3G, and walk swiftly halfway down the hall. The sound of a game show filters through one door and the smell of something with an overabundance of garlic and ginger gets stronger as we move further in. Apartment 3C appears on our left.

While discussing our plans earlier, the two of us had a disagreement about how to proceed at this very stage. I argued that knocking would draw curiosity from other residents on the floor, while Vinn felt that announcing ourselves would allow us to know if anyone was inside. If Feng answered the door, she argued, we could always pretend that we were at the wrong apartment. In the end we compromised and agreed upon a soft knocking, which all things considered is probably the worst of both worlds.

No one answers and no curious resident opens a door down the hall, so Vinn works her magic and within seconds we're inside. We stand, silent and unmoving, for two or three minutes with our ears on alert. Either Feng is asleep or away. I move slowly down the shiny wood entryway and veer to my left to where I know the bedroom lies. Not that my instincts are that good; we looked up the floor plan on a rental website last night. I push the door open with one finger and release my breath. A total mess inside, but no Feng.

I give the all-clear to Vinn and we get to work. We've given ourselves thirty minutes, tops, before we leave, absolutely no exceptions. The apartment isn't huge but that still doesn't leave enough time for more than a quick search, especially when we don't know what we're looking for. I move to the bedroom while Vinn takes the living room-kitchen area. I work on the assumption that Feng doesn't have any reason to suspect that someone would be searching his apartment, so looking under the mattress and in other typical hidey-holes isn't necessary. I pull open drawers, do a quick once-over of the closet shelves, and find nothing but clothing and a little weed. The bathroom is also a total wash, so to speak.

I rejoin Vinn, who's apparently given up on the living room and has moved to the kitchen, the final room to search. As I look in her direction she meets my glance and shakes her head. Hard to be too disappointed since we had no expectations to begin with, but it still hurts. We have eight minutes left until our deadline and try to act more quickly as we open drawers and cabinets.

It's Vinn who finds the only possible thing that might prove helpful, an address and appointment book. The calendar pages have nothing written on them, and not for the first time I curse the younger generation and the fact that they keep every important date and piece of information on their phones. I don't have any hope for the address section, but then again why would he have the book to begin with? Sure enough, there are at least a couple dozen names with some addresses and around half of them include phone numbers. My guess is that it's his way of having a hard copy backup in case he loses his phone.

Vinn pulls out her own phone and snaps pictures as I hold the book and turn pages as fast as I can. It doesn't take long and our time is up. She replaces the book, taking care to make sure it's exactly as she found it, and we move quickly toward the door. Being ever chivalrous, I grab the doorknob, pulling the door open for Vinn to pass through first and then swing around to follow. Instead, I run into the rear of an immobile Vinn, who's frozen in shock. Blocking our way out to the hallway, with keys in hand and a look of total surprise on his face, stands Sam Feng.

Twenty Four

For the world's longest moment time stands still, then all hell breaks loose. In an instant, Feng's expression transitions from total surprise to bafflement and finally to recognition of what's going down. During those same few microseconds, my thoughts move from inert stupefaction to disappointment at getting caught to rapid calculation as to the best way to defend ourselves. Vinn and I apparently both reach the conclusion at the same time that the best defense is an aggressive offense, as she and I simultaneously push forward in Feng's direction. He's half a beat ahead of us in making his own decision that quickly putting distance between us is his best option, and before we can reach him is moving in full flight toward the stairs, Vinn and I in close pursuit.

Feng gains a few feet on us as he leaps several steps during his descent, but any advantage is lost in the split second it takes him to pull open the door to the first floor and then to push past the heavy fire door to the outside. He chooses to avoid the alley to our left, which would require him to weave around several parked cars, instead veering to the right through a vacant lot overgrown with weeds. It seems to be a strategic error, as a flimsy chain link fence sitting atop a concrete barrier runs the length of the lot on its east side along Wentworth as well as on the north side along 27th Street, effectively blocking him in on three sides. He'll either need to turn back to face us or climb the fence, which could cost him valuable time and allow us to catch up. Vinn follows him into the lot while I hustle north to prevent him from doubling back or turning west, where he could more easily get lost in the alleyways and yards of the neighborhood.

I'm moving fast now but choosing to protect the alley side forced me to position myself at least two hundred feet from Feng and Vinn. As I round the corner onto 27th to close ground, I have a clear view of Feng leaping the fence in one fluid motion, as if he's done this a hundred times before. Vinn isn't quite so smooth in clearing the barrier but her ground speed is enough to keep our prey within striking distance. Feng glances my way, sees that moving west would bring him directly into my path, and continues north, passing quickly under the Stevenson Expressway. The access ramp to the expressway is on his immediate right and more fencing, higher and sturdier than the one abutting his apartment building, runs without a break on his left, so he's got no choice but to continue up Wentworth into the more populated area. Vinn runs stride for stride with him and is only three steps behind. I'm doing the best I can but can't seem to gain ground. I've always been more an endurance kind of a guy than a speedster.

Feng is quick but Vinn is equally swift, and his periodic glances back over his shoulder to see where she is costs him precious fractions of seconds, allowing Vinn to close the gap ever so slightly each time. It doesn't take long for them to make it back to the edge of the Chinatown business area, where hopefully the more crowded sidewalk will slow Feng down enough to allow Vinn to reach him and bring him to the ground. Just as that thought crosses my mind, Feng darts into traffic. The delivery truck that narrowly misses hitting him blocks Vinn's line of sight and forces her to go around it. I can still see him from half a block away and watch in dismay as he knocks an elderly Chinese man off of his bicycle, deftly taking his place and beginning to furiously pedal away. As fast as Vinn is, I see her gradually falling further behind.

"Keep after him!" I shout. Without a word or so much as a look in my direction, Vinn continues her pursuit, but I know the bike is giving Feng a huge advantage and that it won't be long before he's able to put enough distance between the two of them to lose himself among the crannies of the neighborhood. Fortunately, the long-ago training that allows me to observe details of my surroundings and retain them in a corner of my memory, to be retrieved when needed, brings to my mind at that key moment a vague vision of powder blue only a block away. I double my efforts, sprinting to get there as quickly as I can.

A few years ago a bicycle rental service started business in the city. Seemingly overnight racks of its bikes, recognizable by their light blue color, started appearing in locations all around town. They became an immediate sensation and the service expanded rapidly. A quick swipe of a credit card and a bike is yours to ride to your next destination, where another rack awaits its return. Not having a car, I've used it often, so I don't need to pause to figure out how the system works. Within seconds, my two weary legs are replaced by an equal number of wheels, and I'm back in the game. Feng and Vinn are a full block ahead of me now, riding and running past the shops of Chinatown Square, but I can see the distance between them is getting greater by the second. I'm lucky and get a walk signal at the busy intersection of Wentworth and Cermak and begin to gain on them.

Just past the square, Feng skids on loose gravel as he maneuvers to turn west onto the first street heading that direction on the far side of the mall. I'm even with Vinn now and yell as I go past that I'll take over from here. I know she won't be giving up and, should I catch and capture Feng, she'll be able to help me out at some point. We're pedaling rapidly past neatly kept rowhouses, Feng still a half block ahead. I'm frustrated that I can't seem to gain on him and worried that he'll use his youth and greater endurance to keep going until he reaches an area where he can ditch the bike and lose himself among the cluster of homes.

Feng angles to the right down a narrow street, then takes a slight right again so that he's once more heading due north. My concern grows that he has a particular destination in mind and that either he knows a place where he's sure to lose me or that I'm being lured there. He suddenly turns left, looking directly behind him and right at me as he pedals. Straight ahead is a red brick apartment building as the street turns back south, where a moving truck blocks access, but Feng veers to the right of the building, trading street for sidewalk as he merges onto a wide cement walkway.

Then, finally, I catch a break. Wherever he's headed, it's blocked by a freight train one hundred feet in front of us, with no paved pathway to take in either direction. Feng slides to a halt and jumps off his bike, hesitating momentarily as he looks in both directions, allowing me to almost reach him. He darts to the right onto a narrow patch of gravel running alongside the tracks just as the train's last car moves past, giving him the ability to jump over the tracks and head into the Ping Tom Memorial Park, a narrow patch of green nestled between the residences of north Chinatown and the south branch of the Chicago River.

The gap between us is short enough that I can hear Feng panting, but he shows no sign of slowing as we race one after the other along the path in the park. To our right is an enclosed playground with a scattering of mothers with their young children, to our left a pagoda under which a gathering of elderly Asian men and women are stretching to music. Directly in front of us looms the wide and dirty river. Feng chooses to turn left, but in that direction the park quickly ends under the shadow of an old vertical lift bridge, its enormous counterweights dangling over the banks of the river. Feng has no choice but to turn around. He cuts slightly to his right, across a patch of grass, and gains traction on the path along the water. I'm not losing any ground and am so close that I can nearly touch him.

We're both audibly gasping for breath as we sprint back past the pagoda, now on our right, past a vacant speaker's platform resting in front of a wall painted with images of bright blue foliage, and over footbridges lined with red fencing. The distant skyline of the Loop rises in front of us, and soon too does the northern border of the park, a six-foot fence separating the lush green grass from acres of dirt and dumped construction materials, the apparent future site of an as yet unplanned development.

Feng takes the loop of the path back in the direction we came, but this time I'm ready for him. He manages to make it back into the park almost to the boathouse but no further, as I lunge and tackle him. He turns onto his back, kicks his legs out into my chest to gain separation, using the time his maneuver bought to rise to his feet. No more cat-and-mouse chase now, we move into each other as each of us attempts to gain the advantage by grabbing limbs, necks, or any other available appendage. I pull him close, positioning myself to place him in a head lock, when I feel a searing pain near my rib cage. Through my agony, I hear Feng say "Your little Chinese friend is next." As Feng runs off, I stumble back, slip on the wet grass, and slide down the bank, tumbling helplessly into the murky waters below.

TWENTY FIVE

"It was more of a dead man's float," Vinn tells her audience of two as she concludes her less than flattering recap of our misadventure. "Hard to differentiate him from all of the debris, frankly. I came a little late to the party expecting Mal to have the kid trussed up like a Thanksgiving turkey but instead he decided it was a good day for a swim. The punk apparently decided not to join in."

Rebecca snickers while Leo merely grunts as he skillfully threads a needle he's removed from his now-familiar cigar box. The feeling of déjà vu is unavoidable as we sit in his kitchen while he uses mysterious colored ointments and a primitive sewing kit to patch up the knife wound near my left ribs along with some assorted scratches I picked up on my way down to the river. Unlike the last time we sat in these exact same chairs as he worked his magic, today we have an audience. Vinn appears entranced watching Leo's handiwork while Rebecca seems more interested in staring me down, waiting impatiently for a wince or a whimper that betrays my oath of manhood.

I still have colorful scars from the last slashings Leo mended, but they're healing nicely and no doctor could have done a more professional job. I've never had the nerve to ask him where he obtained his skills due to our unspoken pact that personal information from before we met is off limits as a topic of conversation. The only difference this time is the pinkish gel Leo applied initially that stung like hell but which he swore will prevent infection from the invisible microbes that infest the river water. Leo prefers not to talk as he sews and I like to pretend I'm somewhere else as the needle works its way through my skin, so Vinn's chatter is beginning to get on my nerves. I don't let her know this, though, since without her help I'd still be floating in the frigid canal.

"I would have loved to have been there," Rebecca remarks casually as she continues to study my face for any sign of weakness. "In fact, I should have been. You need to call me before the two of you decide to set off on any more of this cloak and dagger stuff. Safety in numbers, you know."

Vinn's eyes twinkle subtly in the face of Rebecca's scolding and even the corners of Leo's mouth go up a fraction of a millimeter. Vinn and I have confessed our dark pasts to each |other, personal histories involving tales and tasks which would horrify Rebecca if she knew, while Leo's instincts have revealed an uncanny perception of my former life, a life he may have shared, if not in the U.S., somewhere. Of the four of us in the room, Rebecca may be the last person who should be participating in any sort of "cloak and dagger." On the other hand, she remains the biggest enigma of us all and none of us have probed her own past. Her skill as a sniper is the only reason Vinn and I are still around to get ourselves deep in trouble once again.

"Done." Leo says simply as I watch him dip the needle into some sort of liquid before replacing it in his kit. He looks directly at me, his eyes probing and dark. "Question. Why chase him?"

This time I do wince, not from physical pain but from embarrassment. It's just like him to cut straight to the point that exposes our folly. As Vinn and I made our way back to my place after abandoning the pursuit, that's the one question that we kept asking ourselves. We couldn't come up with a plausible justification then, and even now with more time to reflect we don't have a good answer. What would we have done if we had caught him, especially among a crowd of people? What if a well-meaning citizen called the cops? We were the ones who broke into an apartment, chased a local resident across the neighborhood, and were the instigators in the confrontation. I cast a sheepish glance Vinn's way and notice her cheeks are deepening as well. Thankfully, she comes to my rescue and chooses to respond.

"Instinct. Habit. Self-preservation. We had to make him think that we're the ones that are in control, forcing him to be the one always looking over his shoulder to see if we're nearby. If we'd fled, I guarantee that as we sit here he'd be plotting to come after us. Of course, our plan would have worked better if we'd caught him and roughed him up enough that he wouldn't want to risk finding us." She glances at me and I move my eyes to the floor.

Leo doesn't look any more convinced by Vinn's explanation than we ourselves were an hour earlier in trying to figure out a reason for our actions. If we had caught Feng, what then? We had hoped to keep the extent of our involvement in the investigation of the two murders under wraps, but his unexpected appearance as we left his place forced us out in the open. His comment about Maggie shows he clearly made the connection between us. By now we'll be the talk of every tong member and half the citizenry in Chinatown. If we'd had a solid and well-orchestrated game plan in which anonymity was a key component , our careless action in chasing Feng would have blown it. If there's a bright spot in all of this, the only real strategy we did have was to flounder aimlessly hoping to find a lead while keeping Maggie safe. After shutting Maggie down, though, we're left only with floundering, but this time with watchful, unfriendly eyes marking our every move.

I sigh. "Leo, if we had had time to think it through we might have done something differently, but we didn't, so now we've got to live with the consequences of our actions. Even if we hadn't gone after him, the fact is he recognized who we were. We were toast anyway. And it's more than a little disturbing that the triad knows about our role in looking into the killings and has spread the word among its members. But that doesn't mean we need to pull back and give Feng free reign to make our lives difficult or to insert himself as an obstacle between us and solving the killings of the two women. There's no way around the fact that we need to be a presence in Chinatown on and off for a while and as a consequence have to find a way to prevent Feng from dogging us on his home turf."

I clear my throat and look at Vinn for permission to continue. She nods imperceptibly. We debated our proposed action before knocking on Leo's door, with each of us playing devil's advocate and arguing why we shouldn't do it. In a professional debate, declaring that it was crazy and abandoning it would be the winning side. But both of us had already made up our minds and were just going through the motions to pretend like we gave equal consideration to both paths. I make sure I have Leo's and Rebecca's attention. "Most importantly, his threat against Maggie has to be addressed. For what we plan to do, we need your help. And I can't say that it's going to be much fun."

A significant number of my former colleagues from when I worked for the government, or more precisely an unrecognized unit of it, had a drug problem. It may have been the need for escape from the overwhelming stress of the job or simply a result of the easy access that came from associating with criminals on a daily basis. I never gave it much thought and I never judged, as long as their use didn't affect their performance or risk my safety. I avoided getting hooked not because I was an angel, but because I have a phobic fear of being in any situation without having full control of my faculties. That fear has kept me alive.

My inexperience with narcotics makes me woefully ignorant of much of what would be common knowledge among users and junkies. I actually had to hop onto the internet to research what commonly available street drugs can be readily available for purchase on college campuses, which drugs carry the harshest sentences for possession, and what amount of various drugs carry a charge of intent to deliver should you be caught. I'm sure Jenkins has those answers burned into his brain but I have no desire to attract his attention even more than I already have.

Leo didn't hesitate when we asked him to be our go-between in the purchase of illegal drugs, nor did he ask why we needed them.

He understands that given our positions at the university, neither Vinn nor I can risk being recognized by the campus dealer. His response to our request was a simple grunt followed by a slight movement of his head up and down. For Leo, that's about as much of a reaction as you'll get. Rebecca, on the other hand, threw an historic hissy fit at not being asked, her emotional reaction demonstrating one of the very reasons we didn't ask her. She left Leo's apartment in a pout and immediately made sure we could hear her banging her kitchen pans around. I need to figure out if flowers or chocolate or expensive nail polish are the panacea to getting back in her good graces or just to let her mood pass.

It's past 9:00 at night by the time Leo finishes tending to my cuts. Vinn and I are both exhausted, but we don't want to wait for another week to put our plans into place or to give Leo a chance to come to his senses, so we waste no time in fitting him out with a small receiver I retrieve from a secret drawer of my apartment. While Leo himself sews it into the collar of his shirt, using the same kit with which he stitched my wounds, Vinn goes outside and walks down the block to test it, and within the hour we're ready to go. Rather than dragging the old man onto the el, we splurge on an Uber, figuring that no suspicions would be raised if we're later asked the reason for going to our offices at night. Vinn often does it when she gets an idea she wants to check out or simply can't sleep. I seldom hear long-dead authors calling me to campus after dark, but could say that I accompanied Vinn to keep her safe. Leo, I guess, could say that he just came along for the ride.

We stay in the shadows as we get closer to the library, eventually finding an alcove with a view of the adjacent green big enough for the three of us. Not a word is exchanged and no one moves for a long time. Finally, Leo breaks the silence.

"I see him," he whispers. "In the trees. Do you see?"

In truth, no, but I did notice two students nervously looking over their shoulders disappear into the cluster of oaks Leo indicated and then come out a minute later, moving away quickly. I assumed that's where the deals were going down, so Leo's superior powers of observation merely act to confirm it.

"Okay," I respond. "Let's do it. You know what to request, right?"

Leo's answer is a dirty look in my direction as he moves away from the building. As prearranged, Vinn takes a parallel course about twenty feet from him and I stay put. Both Vinn and I will hear everything that happens. It doesn't take long before Leo's gruff voice fills my ears.

"No go. I know what you do. I need something."

"Who the hell are you?" Baxter's loud whisper sounds suspicious, with good reason. Leo is easily three times the age of his typical customer.

"My nephew tell me. I need something" Leo repeats. "Meth? Crack? I buy."

"I don't know what you're talking about. Leave me alone, old man." This isn't going well.

"Look. Cash." We had told Leo not to show the roll of twenties I gave him until he had a deal, but he's improvising. "What can I get?" Damn. He's probably showing the entire wad. I may not be able to eat for a week.

A long silence, or at least one that seems eternal, follows. I'm growing concerned and edge away from the wall, but move back into the dark when I hear what appears to be the sound of a plastic bag being opened.

Leo again. "That all? I need more."

"Fuck you, old man! Forget it, just—umphh!"

I'm already racing in Leo's direction and seconds later arrive in the grove of trees to find Leo standing passively off to the side while Vinn hunches over an inert and unconscious drug dealer. She looks up at me as I approach.

"Sorry, couldn't wait for you. Didn't sound like it was going according to plan."

Leo still has the money in his hands. "Tried to sell me one pill. Not enough."

"No, not enough. Leo, you did well. You too Vinn." I stoop down and quickly go through Baxter's pockets, pulling out a healthy supply of pills and powders in small snack bags, stuffing them in my own pockets. "We'd better go."

Within minutes we're back in front of the campus assembly hall, mixing with a large flow of students leaving either a basketball game or concert. Anyone would assume we were inside with them and I make a mental note to look up the event. We grab a cab and ask to be dropped off outside of a restaurant about three blocks from Vinn's apartment that has late weekend hours. From there she walks home and I summon an Uber, using the restaurant as the pickup location. Once home, Leo enters his apartment without a word. I begin my climb up two flights of stairs, serenaded by the clanging of pots and pans as I pass Rebecca's unit.

Three days later I'm in my office preparing for class when my cell phone rings with the call I've been expecting but not necessarily wanting to get.

"Jenkins, it's been awhile. Are you calling with news on the cases? Did the Chicago cops have a breakthrough?"

"No, nothing like that. Thought you'd like to know about an arrest in Chinatown. Seems like some punk named Feng got nailed for possession with intent to sell. Had a regular candy store stashed under his mattress. Funny thing, though. The officers went there in response to an anonymous call about a woman in distress in his apartment. They didn't find any trace of the woman, but they had no problems finding the drugs. They weren't hidden well at all."

"Huh. And what does this have to do with me?"

"Nothing at all, Winters. Given the amount of time you spend in Chinatown, just thought you might be interested. You take care, now."

Before I can respond, he's gone. I dial Vinn. One problem down, a million to go.

TWENTY SIX

I should be elated at getting Feng out of the picture, but I'm not in the mood to celebrate. Planting drugs was the trap I intended to use for either Shen or Jiang or both. Trying it a second time this soon, assuming we could even get ahold of any, would almost certainly raise the suspicions of the cops, especially if neither of them is known to deal. It's also likely that Jenkins wouldn't be quite so willing to play ignorant and look the other way a second time. Another anonymous drug tip could even give Feng's defense that he was set up reasonable credibility, which would send the one tiny bit of progress we've made right down the tubes. Not that using the same tactic again would be possible anyway. Word of Feng's arrest probably made its way up the triad ladder and a bulletin to be on the watch for two Caucasians bearing illicit gifts issued before he even arrived at the station to be processed. At a minimum, it would certainly make our two targets even more cautious and unreachable than usual. And we still don't even know where they live or hang out anyway.

For now, the only breadcrumbs we're left with are the photographs Vinn took of Feng's address book. The fact that neither of us was in a rush to see if the sole fruit of our break-in ripened into anything useful shows that Vinn doesn't have any more faith that there'll be a payoff in there than I do. Our procrastination is also a clear and disheartening acknowledgment that it's all we've got, so if its contents don't give us at least a hint of a lead, we're back to the starting line. No reason to hurry if nowhere is where we're headed.

We can't put it off forever, but a few more minutes won't hurt. It's Friday night, classes for the week are over, and Vinn casually lounges on my couch while I put the finishing touches on a simple Bolognese sauce. I'd roasted the tomatoes the night before and put the sauce on as soon as I got home, but ideally it should simmer for several more hours. With the mood we're in, we won't taste the difference. Still, as I squeeze a little fresh lemon into it, the magical aroma starts my stomach growling. Vinn must feel the same way, as she joins me in the kitchen to help set the table and to sneak a taste of the sauce when she thinks I'm not looking. I have to keep an eye on that woman or she'll add more salt.

We've been together in enough different situations that I'm usually comfortable with long periods of silence, but today I'm restless and as we sit down to dinner I feel the need to open my mouth for something more than stuffing it full of noodles. I plunge into forbidden waters and breach the subject we've been avoiding. "Have you given any thought to what we might find in Feng's address book?"

Vinn looks pensive as she chews. "Not really. I guess the best we can expect would be addresses for the other two, and I'm not sure where that gets us. Unless inspiration has hit you over the last few days, that's not even the beginning of a plan."

I ignore the jibe; last time I checked this whole investigation was her idea. I attribute her remark to the frustration we both share and stay cordial. "Sorry, no. But it would be better than nothing. A starting point, but for what I'm not sure. I have to say, though, I'm not optimistic."

It might have been better if I'd kept my thoughts to myself after all, as we eat the rest of the meal in a gloomy silence. The only inspiration I'm hoping for right now is a way to further postpone going through the address book. Maintaining a thin sliver of hope, no matter how unrealistic, is better than facing a total dead end with no idea in which direction to go.

Nothing brilliant penetrates my brain, so once the dishes are stacked in the sink and I've brewed an oolong tea, infusing it with some orange and ginger, Vinn sinks back into the spot on the couch she vacated earlier and I nestle next to her. She opens her laptop with a sigh of resignation.

"I've uploaded the pictures to my computer," she tells me, "but haven't looked at them yet. Thought I'd wait to share the excitement." She doesn't sound like she has any excitement to share.

A few clicks later and we're looking at a dark and blurry photograph of the cover of Feng's address book. Vinn's quiet curse doesn't escape my sensitive ears. I wonder sometimes if she was a sailor in a former life. Neither of us says a word, but we both exhale with relief when the next image is sharp and clearly readable. The fact that it's of two blank pages seems secondary.

Within twenty tense seconds we're finally at the beginning of the alphabet. The temptation is to skip ahead to the "J" or "S" page, but Vinn, ever the methodical scientist, resists. We move slowly from page to page, most of them containing anywhere from two to five or six names, primarily but not exclusively Asian. Vinn pauses upon reaching the "G"s.

"Have you noticed? Next to some of the names he's put these little symbols, or a couple of Chinese characters. There's been several with stars, one sun, and a few other things. Any thoughts on what they mean?"

I shake my head before realizing that she's focused on the screen and isn't looking in my direction. "None. Before we go on, though, maybe we could try to translate the listings of characters from Mandarin to English. There's got to be a program for that."

Without acknowledging my brilliance, Vinn opens up her search engine and connects to my internet. A few years ago the sign of getting serious was being given a key to your counterpart's apartment. In today's world, I wonder what stage of a relationship it is when your partner's laptop automatically connects to your wifi network and auto-fills your password. After a minute or two of separating true links from ads, she finds a translator and then moves back to the photographs. Another word muttered under her breath is new to me, but the tone indicates it's a part of Vinn's impressive vocabulary of profanity. I'll need to find an online dictionary of cuss words after she leaves. For educational purposes, of course.

She quickly explains her angst. "I can't cut and paste the characters from the uploaded photo. We're going to have to try to find the ones we want to look up somewhere and copy those to the translator. How many Chinese characters are there? Fifty thousand or something like that? This could take a while."

Which turns out to be an understatement. After half an hour, we've only been able to translate one of the notations, next to an Asian man living in Feng's same building, and if the translator was doing its job the English equivalent is "parrot bird." Our current methodology clearly isn't going to work. I reach for my phone.

"Rebecca, this is Mal. What do you mean, Mal who? Look, I know you're probably busy getting ready to go out and paint the town, but can you do Vinn and I a favor? Do you know if any of that motley crew you put together or your friends from the table tennis club read Mandarin? It would help if they also had some sort of knowledge about tong structure." I observe Vinn as she continues to work while Rebecca considers, and it's not a pretty picture. I think she's ready to toss her laptop across the room. "Ok, great, would you mind giving her a call and asking when we can meet? We need some help with Feng's address book."

I put my cell phone down and reach across Vinn's lap, gently drawing the computer over to my side. Vinn gives me a look that would frighten a lesser man, but her expression soon melts and she nods in my direction. I close the translator and return to the pictures of the book, moving through them a little faster. No sense dwelling if we're going to have to go through them again with someone else.

In my impatience to restart at the top, I move ahead rapidly to locate Shen's name, which is adorned with a long mix of characters next to it, followed by two exclamation points. To our great disappointment, no address or phone number. Our dismay is somewhat mollified when we retrace to the J's, where Jiang's information includes both an address in Chinatown and two phone numbers. Before we can think about whether this find is anywhere near significant, an electronic version of "Lola" sings from my cell phone. Vinn, as is her custom, makes a sour face.

"Yes, Rebecca? What, tonight? Um, yes, of course that's great news, thank you. Wait, what? Are you sure you aren't on your way out for something more exciting? We're more than capable of handling this ourselves. No, no, I don't mean anything by that, of course you're welcome to come, I just didn't want you to have to cancel any plans. Fine. We'll see you soon."

Vinn clearly caught the gist of the conversation, but I fill her in anyway. "Our translator will be here in about twenty minutes, accompanied by Rebecca. I guess I'd better put on more tea."

Twenty-three minutes later, without so much as a knock, the door I must have uncharacteristically (and for the last time) left unlocked swings open and Rebecca flounces through in her usual dramatic fashion, adorned from head to ankles in an orange garment that combines the worst features of a cheap dress and a classic pair of overalls. Someday I'll ask her where she obtained her fashion sensibilities and what she considers to be the proper attire for a meeting among amateur detectives, but for now my eyes shift to a slight young Asian woman hanging back in the doorway, either too timid to enter or reluctant to follow her predecessor's performance. I move around Rebecca to say hello and to put her at ease, feeling the darts in my back as I pass by Ms. Prima Donna with only a murmured "excuse me."

I start to introduce myself before the woman interrupts me. "Yes, I know. I was here for the initial meeting with Magpie, but there were a lot of people crowding the room. I'm not surprised you don't remember me. I don't forget much, so I remember your name. Mine is Karen Wong."

Vinn also bypasses Rebecca to re-introduce herself, gaining a not-so-subtle "Hrummph" from the neglected diva. I make a mental note to myself to make sure that she's included in tonight's discussion for the sake of neighborly harmony.

I fill Karen in on some of the more relevant details as I steer our guests to the couch, where four printouts of the relevant pages of the address book photographs await. I pick one up, move to a chair, and take out my pen. Anticipatory silence hangs in the room for several minutes while Karen and Rebecca turn pages. Rebecca makes notations on her copy, which I assume has no significance outside of a performance for my benefit. If she could read Mandarin, she wouldn't have called in Karen to share the spotlight.

Karen flips back to a page at the beginning and looks up, making sure to swivel her head to include all of us. She's obviously better at group dynamics than yours truly. "I'm not sure I know all of them, but I grew up in Chinatown and still live there, so many of these symbols are familiar to me. Some of my classmates and neighbors, even a few friends, are at least peripherally affiliated with the triad and I'm pretty observant, and like I said I remember things."

She points to a name listed among the 'A's. "This symbol here appears next to several names, more than any other. It designates members of the local tong, but not full-timers. More like hangers on or wannabe thugs who get asked to do errands from time to time. They're the lowest rung on the triad ladder but can at least boast that they're part of the group. If the people with this symbol next to their names were any threat to anyone, they'd be higher up in the organization. You can ignore them."

Karen turns a few pages. "This snake-like thing is the next level up. Foot soldiers, basically. Again, soldiers in name only. Not a threat." She begins moving on, but I stop her.

"Wait, before you leave that page. What about these characters next to this person's name?" I point to a string of four Chinese characters on my copy. Karen grins.

"I'm not entirely sure, but I think that's just Feng making editorial comments on the people listed. The one you're asking about? Its literal translation is 'Pig ready for slaughter.' I know that kid and he's overweight, at least by Chinese standards. If I see anything that seems to have any significance beyond a character judgment, I'll let you know.

"These swirly marks I think are the equivalent of a lieutenant, someone with a little power. They've sworn an allegiance to the triad and can be dangerous if they think they need to prove themselves." She flips to a page further on. "See, Ji Jiang has that symbol next to his name. Don't underestimate him. He doesn't look very intimidating, like a pudgy buddha, but I've seen him stab a kid in a bar just for looking in his direction. He wants to be a big shot but from what I've heard doesn't have the brainpower. That may be why he hangs with Delun Shen."

She moves ahead to the entry we've been most concerned with. "I don't know this symbol, but it looks like a crude drawing of a dragon. If that's what it is, then Shen is an important part of the triad, just a couple notches down from the inner circle, or maybe just highly thought of. Feng's description after Shen's name doesn't make much sense read together, but each symbol separately mean things like good fortune, immortal, genius, that kind of blind praise. I'd have to go through all of the names more carefully to be sure, but I think it's the only positive thing Feng has to say about anyone."

Karen stops and remains quiet, her task here finished. What she's told us has been educational, but not very helpful in giving Vinn and I a thread to grasp onto. I sense a discomfort, though, a feeling that she has more to contribute but is debating whether to say it. Time for a prompt.

"Karen," I speak reassuringly. "Is there something else you want to tell us?"

She looks up to make eye contact, her cheeks coloring, then glances over at Vinn. A slight nod brings me to the edge of my seat.

Karen keeps us waiting for a few tense seconds as she pages back to a page she'd skipped over earlier.

"This name." She points to the sole listing under the letter "G," a name with the swirl next to it indicating this person is into the tong deep. "Xi Guo. It's not that uncommon a name in China, but there's only one guy that I know of in Chinatown with it, and I'd remember if there were more than one. He's about my age, thin, dark eyes, ambitious, and can be violent when provoked. I don't know him really well, but he's kind of an acquaintance. And he was one of the group that met here in your apartment that night."

After a moment of stunned silence, three pairs of eyes moved to face Rebecca, whose own features are a picture of terror. She's having a bad night.

"Don't look at me!" she shouts defensively. "I only put the word out to a few people I know. Chuck invited the rest."

As much as I'm enjoying her discomfort and appreciate utilizing her as a convenient target for my wrath at the moment, she's right. I'll need to have a word with Chuck. "Rebecca, we're not blaming you. There's no way you could have known. If anything, it might be an opportunity. Just promise you'll keep him away from Maggie."

Rebecca nods vigorously, reinforcing her promise with the girl scout pledge, holding up three fingers. The corner of Vinn's mouth twitches but she restrains herself from cracking a smile.

I stand, anxious to consult with Vinn over this new development, but before that can happen I need to cut my apartment's present population in half. "Karen, thank you so much for your invaluable assistance. We may need your help with Guo, nothing dramatic, maybe just passing on a request. Would you do that? Great, we appreciate it. For now, it's late and I'm sure you want to get home."

Rebecca is at the door before I finish my sentence, anxious to leave, tapping her foot impatiently for Karen to join her. Karen shakes our hands, her eyes sad and puzzled, and follows Rebecca down the stairs. I close the door after them, this time verifying that I locked it.

I take the place on the couch vacated by Karen and turn to face Vinn, who doesn't seem the least bit upset that our ranks were infiltrated. "Mal," she begins. "I'm like a kid in a candy store. This isn't a disaster, it's a gift. There are so many ways to work this. Let's get started."

I refill our cups with tea. It's going to be a long night.

By 3:00 a.m. we've considered somewhere between fifteen and two million different ways to turn Guo's gang affiliation to our advantage. We both fiercely advocated for our favorite scenarios, neither of which ended up making the cut. Our final decision won out because it has the unnecessary but deeply pleasing aspect of total humiliation for our target, and if all goes well, could take two players off the board. It does, however, depend upon the unknowing cooperation of the local constabulary, a healthy dose of luck as to timing, and the services of my favorite hacker. Vinn heads off to crash in my bed without even being invited to stay, which again will require some serious thought in evaluating where our relationship stands. On the other hand, maybe she's so sleepy she thinks she's in her own place. Whatever the case, I need to stay up just a little bit longer before joining her.

I power up my laptop and proceed straight to a bookmarked site, where I enter a message board for traveling foodies and pose a question about where to get the best steak in Toronto, crossing my fingers that J.J. still uses the same script for reaching out to him for help. It could be anywhere from five minutes to a week before he answers with the first coded message that will require visiting a trail of websites that eventually result in direct contact, if he responds at all. Normally I would wait for at least an hour or two in case I get lucky, but the sounds of soft snoring from my bedroom induce a severe case of envy of the sleeping source of the sonorous breathing. I close my laptop, tap it twice for good luck—habit—and shuffle slowly down the hall to join my friend in slumber.

TWENTY SEVEN

J.J.'s response wasn't waiting for me when I awoke way too early on Saturday morning, which cast a bit of a pall over snuggle time with Vinn. We took a walk along the lakefront, trying to enjoy the spectacular view of the skyline before the winds of winter make it impossible, but even then I spoiled what was meant to be a few hours of respite by checking email on my phone every five minutes. Nothing. All my obsession did was ruin what could have been a pleasant fall day. Vinn quickly grew tired of my inattention to her, even though she seemed as anxious as I was for word from J.J., and eventually sent me packing. Sunday was no better, so to distract myself I actually reviewed my syllabi for the week and mentally prepared for class, which proves that there's a first time for everything. Stuart would have been proud. Or not.

I'm presently sitting at my desk on Monday during my open office hours listening impatiently to Gail, a student in my first year composition class, whine about the B she received on the most recent assignment, and how unfair it was and how she's never received less than an A- in her life, except maybe in gym class in second grade. She's currently circled back for the third time to the irrelevance of the class in relation to her future as a surgeon and how her life will be ruined if this grade keeps her out of medical school, mirroring the repetitiveness of the paper which formed the basis of the grade I gave her. She's been talking mostly to hear herself speak for the past ten minutes, rarely even making eye contact, and I might as well not even be in the room. I use the opportunity to surreptitiously reload a page on my computer and am startled to find an email waiting for me. Time to bring Project Complain Long and Loud Enough and He'll Change My Grade to an end.

"Gail," I begin, but she's too engrossed in her own speech to hear me. "Gail!" I say more loudly. "I understand your angst, but the grade for that paper is only worth about five percent of your final grade. You show signs of being a talented writer"—okay, fibbing is a part of my job—"but you're still a little raw. Read the comments I made. And I tell you what. If you want to revise the paper and resubmit it, I'll take another look."

Gail's face brightens with relief and a smidge of triumph, which shows me that she never bothered to read the syllabus for the class because I let all of my students rewrite and resubmit a paper. She quickly picks up her backpack and hurries toward the door, perhaps afraid that if she lingers much longer I may change her mind. She would be right.

I waste no time in opening J.J.'s email. After following the usual links and providing answers to security questions that only I would know (and which make me wonder how he does), I land on a page containing a short "I'm on it" message along with the cost of his services, which elicits a bit of a gasp on my part. He's the best and charges like it, so I shouldn't complain. Maybe if I tell him his fee will keep me out of medical school and ruin my future plans as a brain surgeon, he'll cut me a break.

I bite my lip, take out the credit card I use for all illicit purchases, and pay the fee. Immediately the site automatically redirects me to a coded message that takes me twenty minutes to decipher, and all I get is an acknowledgment of receipt and that he'll let me know when he finds anything. For the moment I guess that's as much as I can expect. I text an update to Vinn then head off to my last class of the day.

J.J.'s nothing if not savvy. He must have mined enough information about my private life, presumably including my relationship with Vinn, that when he sends a message telling me that he'll be emailing what I've requested at 8:00 tonight, I know that he already has it, but that his timing allows both Vinn and I to be together for the grand unveiling with a few extra hours beforehand for a nice dinner. I make an executive decision to quit mentally castigating him for the depletion of my bank account but replace that with an equal amount of pique for his having invaded my personal space.

Vinn and I do go out for dinner, a hearty Polish meal of beet-root soup with dumplings and assorted pierogi, made more pleasant by our agreement, more of an edict from my better half, to turn off our cell phones for the duration of our time at the restaurant. I assume that choice was driven by my behavior at the lakefront, so I have to hide my smirk and choke back a pithy comment when Vinn reaches for her phone before we've even had time to exit out the door.

We're back at my place by 7:30, but I know it would be a waste of effort to check for J.J.'s email early. If he says 8:00, that's what he means. I keep busy by brewing a decaf sencha tea, which Vinn accepts without complaint. She still prefers coffee, but I'm working on her.

The anticipation is such that as the anointed hour approaches, Vinn begins staring at the second hand of the clock on her phone. To avoid being accused of cruelty—because of course I'm not at all impatient—I navigate to the proper website at least thirty seconds early, finding exactly what I expected. Nothing. It doesn't take long, though, before a little ping announces a new email, eliciting a "he's two seconds late" from my couch companion. I decide a response isn't called for. I'm getting better at preserving the peace.

We open up the email, once again follow the usual path through several various sites displaying J.J.'s playful side, including a message board which requires proof that you own at least ten cats before you can post, and finally get to the main event. We quickly scan it as I scroll down, then I send the information to my printer before going back up to the top to look at it more closely.

It's a good thing the Chicago police department and the cops it employs don't use sophisticated security barriers and impossible encryption the equivalent of CIA systems, or it might have taken J.J. an hour longer to break into them. From the three results he sent on, it's clear that he went through not only official websites, but also internal communications, union message boards, and private cops-only sites allowing the men and women in blue to post opinions and information that would cause scandals if they were ever outed. Somewhere among all of the noise, J.J. was able to find a few standout possibilities for what we're seeking.

Vinn and I remain silent as we read. After a few minutes I rise and take the five steps to my printer, returning with hard copies of the same information hovering on the screen of my laptop. I'm a tactile person and prefer to have something in hand that I can grasp and write on if I choose. Vinn sets the copy I tender to her aside and continues to stare at my laptop, pulling it closer to her. To each her own.

After about ten minutes, she looks up and I nod, ready to discuss. I go first.

"The first option, the award ceremony for the two beat cops who saved that kid from drowning, is probably a little too public. The number of officers there might provide a decent level of protection for us, but that many cops in one place could also either spook Jiang off or cause him to panic and start a massacre. I vote no. There's a better one in there."

"Agreed," Vinn replies. "The next one is a little better. Fraternal Order of Police union committee meeting, something on the agenda about drafting a response to an article criticizing absenteeism of patrol officers. Smaller group and limited to the cops themselves, so less chance of the public getting hurt if something goes south. But that's the issue for us, too. We're not cops. No access.

"Which bring us to number three, the bachelor party. This is clearly the winner, don't you think? What do you want to bet that J.J. found this one right away and then padded his email with the other two imperfect options so that we'd have no choice but to select this one?"

"That, and to justify his fee," I smile. "Yes, the setting seems perfect, with both a public and private element, and it has the additional advantage of happening next weekend. That doesn't leave us a whole lot of time but should be enough if we hustle."

Vinn concurs, and within seconds we're giggling like schoolgirls as we imagine various scenarios of what could happen. Only when we start considering the possible ways our idea could go wrong do we come down to earth. By 10:00, with the tea long gone, we have our plans in place. I send a quick note off to J.J. noting our selection along with a request for a room number for the party and use of his skills at breaking into the hotel's reservation system to secure a room next door or across the hall, the system showing the room is prepaid of course. Next, I call Rebecca to ask her to set up a meeting with Gao for the following day, stressing how she's the only one that has the connections and skill to put it together that quickly. Vinn rolls her eyes as she listens to me lay on the insincere flattery, but after we hang up we hear Rebecca singing in the apartment below.

Satisfied with ourselves and with a sense of optimism for the first time in months, Vinn and I head downstairs to Leo's for a nightcap and a healthy dose of advice.

TWENTY EIGHT

If Guo actually did infiltrate our team in order to provide inside information on our activities to Shen, our guess is that he would jump at the chance to meet with us and that we could pretty much name the day and time. Working on this assumption, Rebecca first reached out to Karen to find out when she could be available. Once Karen committed to coming by on Saturday at 1:30, Rebecca called Guo, who as expected readily agreed to meet us at 2:00. It's now 1:50. Vinn has briefed Karen on the fact that she's here mainly as window dressing and that her only job will be to deny knowing Shen when we reach that point in the conversation. Her role is minimal and no-risk, but her constant hand wringing betrays her frayed nerves at what lies ahead. Finding out someone you know is a gangster can do that to you and the prospect of sharing a couch with him doesn't help. Rebecca sits on the comfy chair in the corner, whether present for moral support or as supposed eye candy, I didn't ask.

I'm just looking at the time on my phone for the fifth time in the last three minutes when we hear a loud and long knock at the door. Each of us unconsciously takes a deep breath as I move to let our guest in. I glance in Karen's direction and give her what I hope is a reassuring smile.

"Xiu, thank you for coming on such short notice. Please, come in and make yourself comfortable. I think you've met everyone here." Guo glances around, flashes of recognition in his eyes, then grabs a seat next to Karen. Hopefully he doesn't notice her involuntary flinch. I waste no time in addressing both of them.

"As you know, our initial strategy to rope Jiang in was to have Maggie pretend to be researching a story on triad activity in Chinatown, then to have her go down there with some amount of frequency in the guise of doing research in order to get on the gang's radar. We hoped her continual presence there would make certain tong members a little nervous, or at least curious enough, to draw them out, with the hope that Jiang would be among them. We had our own people standing by to follow him back to his place, yourselves included, so that once we knew where he lives we would have the advantage we're looking for.

"It didn't work out and now circumstances are forcing us to abandon that tactic. Neither of you were on the team the night Maggie was followed close to her apartment on campus, but I'm sure you've heard about it. We didn't anticipate a level of interest high enough that it would bring the threat out of the Chinatown neighborhood, and we don't have the resources to watch Maggie around the clock. As a result, we shut the operation down. Since then, we haven't been certain what to do."

I take care to keep moving my head back and forth between Guo and Karen, as if she doesn't know what I'm going to say any more than Guo does. Karen continues to look nervous, but fortunately Guo isn't paying her any attention, his focus solely on me. "Vinn, Rebecca, and I have been brainstorming and finally came up with a new strategy that we're optimistic will be successful. Clearly, the cover story of Maggie's research drew the attention of the tong, so we're going to keep that part of the plan intact. We know that Jiang is affiliated with the triad in some capacity, so he's probably looking for a way to impress them with his initiative." I pause for a moment. I could just as easily be describing Guo, or at least I hope so. Everything depends on it. "Anyway, we're going to try a more direct approach. We'd like to use the same ruse of the research paper, but in a way that will bring Jiang to us."

As prearranged, Vinn takes over from here and two sets of eyes move in her direction. "We're going to keep using Maggie as bait, safely of course because either Mal or I will be with her, but this time it'll be in a different setting. Instead of her going to Chinatown, she's going to ask Chinatown to come to her. The premise is that her advisor—Mal—told her that the paper needs some first-hand accounts of gang life, which means interviewing tong members. If this were a real paper, she would post a notice somewhere or ask a local to make some connections for her.

"That's where the two of you come in. We don't think Jiang, or any triad member for that matter, would respond to a solicitation by someone who's not Chinese and we don't want Maggie to face any more exposure. You're the only two Asians on our team and have the advantage of living in Chinatown. Do either of you know Jiang, even casually, so that you could ask him to be interviewed without raising his suspicions?"

I find myself tensing. This is the pivotal moment. For a long moment, no one speaks.

"I think I've seen him around, but I don't know him," Karen tells us. "But I realize that this is important so I could probably ask around or see if someone I know knows someone that might know someone that knows him." I'm impressed. That was improvised, and it has the intended effect of making Guo speak out so as not to be outdone by a girl.

"I've met him a few times," he begins. "I doubt he'll remember me, but I could probably approach him and ask if he could help." I scan his face for some sort of tell, but he's good. I know that on the inside Guo is salivating at the prospect of bringing the heads of Maggie and either Vinn or myself to Jiang on a silver platter.

"Whew," Karen sounds genuinely relieved. "Thank you. I really didn't want to have to do it. Those people scare me." Bless her, she's tying the knot.

"No problem," Guo replies without looking her way. "So what do I need to do?"

I take the baton from Vinn. "We can't hold the interview at any of our places, because frankly none of us want Jiang to know where we live, and it's possible he won't come alone. Besides, it'll look more realistic for Maggie to conduct them in a neutral location but not somewhere where the public could be endangered. We'll book a hotel room for next Saturday afternoon and let you know the time and location after that. Once you talk to Jiang, confirm with me whether he can make it. Maybe you could follow him on Saturday or even offer to accompany him and then text us when you reach the hotel. Find an excuse not to go to the room, though. Once he's inside and settled in front of Maggie, his guard will be down and that's when Vinn or I will pounce. If you're there and don't help him, he'll wonder why. You don't want the local triad to think you were a part of bringing Jiang down."

"Sounds like a plan," Guo says as he rises and puts on his coat. "Karen, you want a ride?"

Karen momentarily turns pale, but recovers to politely decline, saying that she needs to use the bathroom. We all hold our breath as we listen to Guo descend the stairs. Once we hear the creak of the gate, an explosion of exhaling fills the room.

Three days have passed since the meeting and still no word from J.J. I confess to having checked the email of my ghost account over a hundred times before Vinn taught me how to set up an alert for when I receive mail. Nevertheless, I'm back online now to make sure technology hasn't let me down, because of course there can be no other explanation for his silence. Still no news. I take small comfort in knowing that considering the exorbitant amount I paid him, it's almost certainly not a delay on J.J.'s part. He has a reputation to protect. I'm sure he's eavesdropping on every verbal and written conversation of our unwitting accomplices and is checking the message board he hacked into previously, so as soon as a time and an agenda are set, he'll pass the information on to me before fading away into the ether.

I'm not the only impatient participant. Guo has called once

and sent four texts asking whether he can set up a meeting yet. He claims that he'll need time to find Jiang and to somehow convince him to do the interview, which would make sense if I didn't already know that he's in Jiang's pocket and that Jiang has his own plans for how this rendezvous will go down. He'll need no convincing to meet at the hotel and will make it his top priority. Any pressure Guo is feeling is probably from Jiang himself and he's simply passing it on to me.

I'm forty minutes into a lively discussion in an honors seminar as to whether a straight author can accurately depict a gay character when my left pants pocket comes alive with a persistent vibration. It catches me by surprise since I always turn my phone off in class, and it takes me few moments to realize what my pocket is trying to tell me. My facial expression is probably betraying my confusion for all of my students to see, but since the kids in this class are generally smarter than me, a look or befuddlement is pretty much standard and they'll have no reason to wonder if something is wrong with me. I stare at the clock and watch the second hand barely move. My position on phone usage in the classroom is well-known, so pulling my own out to check email would be awkward at best. Nine and a half minutes to go. Nine minutes twenty seconds. Nine minutes eight seconds…

Just when memories of a third-grade me clock-watching on the last day of school before Christmas vacation nibble at the edges of my mind, the volume of the class discussion rises and the tone of two of the loudest and most opinionated students becomes antagonistic, even angry, forcing me to pull myself back into the present.

"Vickie, Stan, please remember that there's no correct answer here. The point is to exchange views for the purpose of enriching our understanding of the obstacles a writer faces and decisions he or she has to make. It's essential that we remain civil during class discussions." My god. Did those words come out of my immature mouth? Time to move away from establishing myself as the intolerant parental figure and to solve my impatience with a single bold move. "It's almost the end of class and tempers are starting to rise a little too much. Let's call it a day today, cool down, and we'll reconvene next class. For next time, draft a position paragraph on today's topic. Exactly one hundred twenty words. No more, no less."

The groans that greet my pronouncement give me a perverse pleasure and also discourage any hangers on. The last student is still crossing the threshold when I push the door closed behind her and pull my phone out of my pocket in one swift motion. Normally I would wait and open up the email with Vinn at my side, but I'm not sure I will survive any further delays. She would do the same.

As I read, my smile grows broader. J.J. outdid himself and is not only passing on details of where and when our men in blue will be, but also a schedule of events down to the minute. The run-down motel on Ohio Street west of the Loop appears to be perfect for their purposes: a cheap, relatively off the grid, no questions asked kind of a place. It also dovetails in with our cover story perfectly, as the cost per night matches what a poor student such as Maggie might be willing to spend for a series of interviews. My smile broadens even wider when I read that the festivities peak in the afternoon hours, avoiding having to come up with a reason why she chose to schedule interviews at midnight. That would have raised suspicions too difficult to explain away.

The good news for my pocketbook and our anonymity is that our room, perfectly situated immediately next door and sharing a wall, has been paid in full under the names of John and Laura Winthrop through the miracle of hacking the reservations system. My mind is already spinning with possibilities for the perfect set-up. I need to bring my thoughts under control and to run them by someone with more common sense than myself. I send a text to Mrs. Winthrop.

TWENTY NINE

"She insisted on coming," I explain in response to Vinn's look of surprise as she sees two faces at her front door instead of one, the extra body dressed in a knee-length wool skirt with a white blouse and dark jacket as well as the ever-present heels.

"I feel responsible," Rebecca jumps in before Vinn can respond and possibly turn her away. "At least a little. I helped assemble those people and it never occurred to me that one of them would be on the naughty list. I want to be there when this goes down, whatever this is because Malcom won't tell me, in case I can help in any way or at the very least so that I know that Guo gets his due."

Vinn's only reaction is to look at me with a blank expression, shrug her shoulders, and to grab her coat. If all goes well, we could bring along a whole room full of people and it wouldn't matter. My only worry is if our little charade is sniffed out, in which case we'll have brought Rebecca into the line of fire. She's shown herself to be resourceful, though, so my level of concern is minimal.

Vinn and I are lost in thought and don't exchange a single word on the el ride down, and Rebecca's constant chatter eventually ceases as she reads her audience. In the course of any assignment with my previous employer, my mind would automatically go through the process of closing out all extraneous distractions as I approached the zero hour, and it gives me some sort of satisfaction to find myself entering that familiar zone again. I assume Vinn was and is the same way. Rebecca, clearly not, but at least she finally picked up on the mood and is giving us some space.

As we cover the few blocks from the station to the hotel on foot, I suggest to Rebecca that she remain out of sight while we check in so as not to raise any complications with the desk clerk, who's expecting a married couple. It's also best under the circumstances not to be the slightest bit memorable. No sooner does she reluctantly agree than our destination comes into view. A two-story throwback to the 1950s with a small boxy office set apart from the rooms by a cramped parking lot, it gives no indication that it's been updated since it was built ages ago. For some lodgings that might translate into a sort of nostalgic charm, but at first glance and based on its reputation and reviews, that's not the case here. The closer we get the dingier it looks. Rebecca's repulsion is obvious. She walks past the office entrance as if she doesn't know us.

The desk clerk, a worn-down man in his 50s we have to rouse from reading a magazine with a racy cover that makes Vinn cringe, is straight out of central casting as the seen-it-all, sees everything but says nothing character running a sleazy motel. I make a note to myself to look for peepholes in our bathroom. True to the stereotype, once he brings us up on his computer and verifies that we've prepaid, he simply tosses us the key, tells us that the hotel would lose half its business if they asked for identification, and that there's no reason to keep a credit card on file because there's no minibar or other amenity which would necessitate ringing up a charge. Vinn is out the door before I even have a chance to pocket the key.

Rebecca's waiting for us behind the office and falls in line be-hind Vinn as we troop up the single set of stairs to Room 204. Before entering our room, I walk past to verify that Room 203 is in fact next door, see what I need to see, then return in four short steps. I hesitate before putting the key in the lock—no fancy electronics here—and pull out a handkerchief to use for turning the doorknob. Might be overly cautious, but out of the corner of my eye I see Rebecca subtly nodding in agreement.

Sometimes an otherwise plain hotel surprises and opening the door to the room reveals an unexpected gem inside. Not the case here. A double bed fills most of the room and is positioned to face an ancient, wobbly dresser sporting a television that became outmoded over a decade ago sitting on top, with no remote in sight. Dingy yellow, or perhaps yellowed, curtains that needed to be washed five years ago block all outside light, and a bedside lamp with a low-watt light bulb provides the only illumination to fend off the gloom. A chair with a long tear in its back and food stains on its seat sits in the corner, the only option for parking our posteriors other than the bed. Rebecca alternates staring at the end of the bed and the chair as her mind clearly debates the lessor of the two evils until Vinn returns from the bathroom with two threadbare towels, spreading them out over the bedspread. "I assume we'd know if these hadn't been washed," she says to the room without conviction.

I place the small suitcase I brought on the bed behind where Rebecca is now tenuously perched and begin unpacking as Vinn brings her ear to the wall separating us from Room 203, working her way down and over as she knocks gently. Once she's traversed the length of the room, she returns to a spot behind the television, knocks again, then finds me with her eyes. "Here."

I bring a dinner plate-sized piece of brushed aluminum over to where Vinn has marked an x on the wall in pencil, peel back four pieces of heavy-duty double-sided tape, and affix my toy to the wall. Remarkably inexpensive considering its usefulness, it's served me well. I run a cable from the plate to a box I've set up on the dresser and turn a switch on to test its batteries before handing Vinn one set of head-phones while I hold on to the other.

I turn to face Rebecca, whose narrowed and questioning eyes send a thousand questions my way, but they'll have to remain unan-swered. I know she suspects or even assumes certain aspects of my personal history, but she's never probed and I wouldn't tell her anyway. "Sorry, I don't have a third pair," I tell her. "But these walls are so thin you'll probably hear just as well as we do."

I check my phone for the time. We have about an hour before our neighbors arrive and another 90 minutes or so after that before

Maggie's fictional interview with Jiang. My aversion to vermin has me veto lying on the bed for a nap, so I take out the book I packed, spread two washcloths out over the chair, and begin to read, although my mind is jumping ahead and making it difficult to concentrate. I glance at Vinn, sitting next to Rebecca on the edge of the bed, and note that she's grading papers. Ignoring the fact that she invited herself last-minute on this little adventure, Rebecca appears annoyed that we didn't prepare her for the current lack of action, so she's decided to sulk.

And so we wait.

I've glanced at the time on my phone at least a dozen times in the last hour, a nervous habit I've just acquired in the course of this investigation, my impatience garnering looks of annoyance from Vinn. Rebecca is equally unhappy with me, as her periodic questions of what time something is going to "go down," and what exactly that something is, have been met mostly by vague responses on my part. Within the last twenty minutes or so, though, she's been quiet as she senses an increased tension on the part of both myself and Vinn, correctly assuming that the bewitching hour must be drawing near.

At 2:04:33—not that I'm counting—we hear the door to the room next door open and a cacophony of drunken male voices immediately follows. They're loud enough to hear the slurred speech punctuated by profanity through the walls without the need for amplification, but Vinn still moves to the gadget by the television, puts one set of headphones on, and adjusts the settings. Once I get the thumbs up from her, I move to her side and push the button to start recording. If their scheduled entertainment is on time we still have another fifty-five minutes, but she may be early and we don't want to miss getting every single second on tape.

I pull out my cell phone to make a call but have second thoughts given the clatter from next door. "I'll be right back," I tell Vinn, who understands and nods. Rebecca tilts her head with a question on her lips but I shake her off and step outside, moving away from the raucous shouting of our men in blue. The background noise of city traffic is more appropriate to my purpose. I dial.

"Xiu, this is Mal. We're almost to the hotel. It'll take Maggie and I a little time to set up once we check in, so about 3:15 would be perfect. She's pretty jumpy and I'm mildly concerned that she'll change her mind if she has to wait too long, so it's important that you be on time. He's with you now? Great, thanks. No extra bodies? Good, that'll help with Maggie's nerves. You got my text confirming the room number? That's it, yes. Don't forget, just in case things don't go according to plan you're not going to want to be here, so find an excuse to have him enter the room alone. Okay, we'll see you in about an hour."

As I reenter our room, Vinn looks up. "They're pretty well lubricated, which could be good or bad. I count about nine different voices, and hopefully a couple of the men attached to those voices are still functional. How did it go?"

"They're on the way and promise to be on time." I look at Rebecca to throw her a crumb. "That's 3:15." Back to Vinn. "I reminded Guo not to enter the room with Jiang. I'd say the odds of him sitting this one out are close to zero, but they'll still be outnumbered. Let's hope that the element of surprise works against them and cancels out the fact that they'll be the only sober ones in the room."

We go silent again, only half-listening to the raucous bachelor party going on next door, and I resume my clock-watching, this time joined by Rebecca now that she's been cursed with knowing the schedule. Vinn turns her back on us and pretends to read. I know her better than that.

As 2:55, as if we planned our movements, we both rise. Vinn drags the chair over near the television and dons one pair of headphones while I stretch the cord for the second pair over to my place on the edge of the bed. Rebecca puts on her pouty face, gets no reaction from us, so instead moves to sit next to me in order to be a part of the action. I put my finger to my lips and she nods, turning an invisible key in front of her mouth.

At exactly one minute past 3:00, there's a loud knocking at the door of the cops' room followed by about ten seconds of a hushed murmur, then as their guest enters the room the noise level redoubles, with whoops and cheers and a few belches thrown in for good measure. Rebecca remains good to her word and says nothing, but her expression throws a question my way. I remove the headphone from one ear.

"Stripper," I whisper, and she rolls her eyes. I wonder whether Ted shares her view or if he's jealous of the goings-on next door.

The next ten minutes or so are painful to listen to, both in the volume of the party guests emanating through the headphones and in the misogynistic catcalling and sexual commentary that embarrasses all of us voyeurs. Each of my glances in Vinn's direction show her cheeks getting more and more flushed with anger, until she catches my gaze and sends a bone-chilling silent glare of reproach my way that somehow silently blames me for the behavior of my gender. I decide to keep my eyes focused on the wall between the rooms and to avoid any further eye contact for now.

The initial shouting diminishes to more casual but still sexist commentary as the stripper proceeds with her show, probably at this point focusing her attention on the bachelor guest of honor. Not that I have experience at these sort of events, of course. I no sooner feel a sense of relief that the happenings inside the room have become quieter and less obvious when a second knock fills the room and causes momentary confusion among the cops within.

"Another one?" someone finally shouts. "Let her in!"

One set of footsteps moves toward the door, and chaos immediately follows. The sensitive equipment we have set up allows us to hear the door knob turn, and a split second later the door slamming open as it bangs against the wall, someone moving quickly into the room, and then shouts and a woman's screams mixed with what is most likely furniture being moved, chairs being overturned, and the rush of nine inebriated bodies going into action when years of instinct overcome alcoholic haze.

"Gun! Get them! On the floor, now!" Overlapping voices make it hard to distinguish everything that's being said, although it's obvious that a lot of it starts with the letter "F." Vinn and I both involuntarily cringe away from the wall as a loud crash fills our ears when a heavy object, most likely Jiang, is thrown against it. In all, the action takes less than fifteen seconds before a comparative calm permeates the room and the voices become easier to understand. Puzzlement gives way to professionalism and the clear click of handcuffs accompanies questions from at least four different directions with a lot of them ending with the word "Mother" or something similar. I finally get the nerve to look once more in Vinn's direction, and notice a small smile forming at the corner of her mouth.

We listen intently for about five more minutes, long enough to hear what appears to be the sounds of one or more people taking a beating, then remove our headphones as at least some of the cops, presumably accompanied by the intruders, move out of the room. We can listen to the rest later.

In all the excitement we momentarily forgot about Rebecca and only now do Vinn and I turn our attention to her. She sits slack-jawed on the end of the bed, her wide eyes fixed firmly on the space in front of her as if her vision could penetrate the drywall to observe the scene within. Vinn and I cast amused glances at each other, waiting for the inevitable question. It comes a moment later.

"Was that—" Rebecca starts.

"Yes," I respond. "You didn't expect us to invite Jiang into our room, did you? You have to know that Guo would have told him about our plans to use Maggie as bait to lure him to the room, where our intent was to send him a message through physical violence. We proceeded on the assumption that he would see an opportunity to turn the tables and to assault or even kill both Maggie and either myself or Vinn, whichever of us was acting as the bodyguard when he arrived. Couldn't let that happen, so we redirected them. Might have inadvertently given them the wrong room number."

A smile gradually spreads across Rebecca's face during my explanation. "Thank you for letting me come," she says softly. "I feel better now. And let me know when you plan to play that recording. I want to be there."

We stay another hour or so to avoid running into any police who might get curious about our presence in the room next door, or someone canvassing the area for witnesses, then when all is quiet sneak out the door and briskly walk through the chilly hair toward the el and our ride home.

"You must pray to the right gods," Jenkins says as he lowers himself into one of my student chairs and tosses a thin manila file across my desk. "First the drug arrest for that guy who showed too much interest in your little operation with that student. Now this."

I put on my best impression of a bewildered innocent—I knew this moment would come and have been practicing in front of a mirror—as I open the file and begin reading the arrest report inside. I decide to remain quiet as I read except for a low whistle of apparent surprise. Jenkins chooses to fill the silence.

"Seems like these two young gang bangers from Chinatown threw open the door of a motel room full of cops enjoying a little entertainment for a bachelor party, automatic guns at the ready, and were in such a rush to enter that they were all the way into the room before they realized what they interrupted and who was there with them. They were on the floor in a flash, although they must have put up a fight considering the physical condition they were in when they got to the station. Bond hearing is next week. I don't expect the judge will be inclined to let them out. Facing some serious time."

"Hmm. That is something. One of these punks' names had come up in our investigation before we quit. And to think we'd given up figuring out a way to find justice for those two women. Karma I guess."

"Uh uh," Jenkins grunts as he rises and turns to leave. "Just lucky for you, you mean. Involved or not, nothing wrong with getting a few of their type off the streets."

I watch as he ambles out my door then move to my computer, punch a few buttons, and anonymously send an audio file to his personal email address. It provided much amusement for Vinn, Rebecca, and I over a few drinks, and I would expect that Jenkins will appreciate it as well.

THIRTY

"Okay, Mr. Magic, do you have anything else in your bag of tricks?" Vinn asks as we sit in our usual spots in the café before Monday classes. Our euphoria over how well our plan to get Jiang off the streets worked, with the bonus of having the traitorous Guo swept up along with him, has faded somewhat with the reality that Delun Shen still roams free. Along with his status as our primary target, he remains the most dangerous threat to continue the string of ghost murders, has more intelligence and street savvy than Jiang and Guo put together, and is by now on high alert that there are motivated forces out there aiming to bring him down. Getting Jiang and Guo is all fine and good but means very little unless we're able to cut off the head of the beast. We've been procrastinating by going after the underlings first because of the difficulty we face with Shen, but now there's no one else left.

"None," I admit. "He's not likely to fall into a trap as easily as the others, and any direct confrontation to take him out would put us in harm's way not only from he and his minions, but law enforcement as well. They're not fond of vigilantes, no matter how justified or well-intentioned. And we still have Maggie to worry about—we used her name to lure Jiang in and I'm sure that didn't go unnoticed. Maybe for now we need to focus on a strategy that protects her from any further attention from Shen and his crew while we figure out what to do."

"Hmm," Vinn mutters, whether in response to what I just said or the fact that she caught me eyeing her blackberry muffin, I'm not sure. She reaches for the sweet-smelling baked good but rather than push it toward me or break it in half, she drags it out of my reach. "Maybe it's time for this story to come out into the open. For evil people accustomed to working in the shadows, the spotlight is their worst enemy. What if we spread the word about the motive behind the killings of the two women, how their murders are connected, and its link to the Chinatown underworld? It might force Shen to lie low for a while and that'll give us the chance to come up with a plan."

I look at Vinn thoughtfully while I consider her idea. She notices me looking at her and takes the opportunity to stuff the entire remainder of the muffin into her mouth. I hope she chokes. "It might work," I reply, warming to the proposal. "At the very least, it couldn't do any harm. And I also think that the whole ghost bride aspect would be a great lure to a journalist anxious to get their name in the byline. It doesn't solve our problem as to the method to achieve our primary objective, but like you say it may buy us some time." I pause, considering the next step. "Do you have any contacts in the news business?"

Vinn looks at me like I'm an idiot. I would be offended, but I'm still working on the hurt of her not sharing the muffin and I'm used to it with her anyway. From the viewpoint of someone with Vinn's brainpower, most of the planet's population are idiots. "Yes, I do," she finally says. "And so do you. Meet me back here during your lunch break."

It doesn't surprise me to see Maggie sitting next to Vinn when I bring my bag lunch into the cafeteria. I may be slow, but Vinn's opinion notwithstanding, I'm not a total moron and made the connection long before lunchtime even though I'm sure Vinn knew I was hoping for a seasoned and more influential reporter or columnist as opposed to a novice freshman, especially one with a target on her back. I slowly unpack the leftover eggplant dish I brought from home and uncap my thermos of tea, which elicits a glare and unspoken threat from Manuel. Vinn gives him her usual disarming smile, his expression softens, and he turns his attention to other patrons who offend him. Without my association with Vinn, I would have been banished long ago.

The verbal onslaught instead comes from a different direction. "Oh my gosh, this is just like, well you know, so exciting, I mean it's a real assignment this time, right, not a fake one like last time? I've already got so many ideas in my head and I just know this will be so good but I'm not sure what you want and do I have to run it by you first I mean that might be okay but I need to be my own person, if you know what I mean. Right?"

If she hadn't needed to take a breath, I'm not sure when Maggie would have stopped jabbering. I jump in before she has a chance to reload. "Yes, this is a real article, Maggie. And we're not looking to cramp your journalistic style. But there are a few essential points that we need you to include in order for the piece to be effective. So yes, we will need you to run it by either myself or Vinn before submitting it for publication."

I hold up my hand to stop the objections I see coming so that I can finish. Surprisingly, it works. "Run with the ghost bride details in whatever way you think will be the greatest draw for a reader. Emphasize the oddity and be as lurid as you desire. In fact, when it comes to the killings of the two women, stress the horror of the murder of innocents and push it as far as you can. Most importantly, link them to Chinatown. I don't want you to set yourself up for a lawsuit, but emphasize the rumors that the killings were by someone associated with the triad, and do whatever you can get away with legally to shine a spotlight on them."

Maggie's eyes dim for a moment when I mention the triad, but she recovers quickly. The prospect of fame will do that. "You can count on me Professor. Professors. I already have so many ideas and the article will write itself well not really I mean it still takes skill to put it together so it won't literally write itself but it'll be something I can do and I'll start right away. When do you need it by? I have a history exam this afternoon. Is tomorrow too late?"

She's exhausting and it takes me a moment to realize she asked a question. Two questions. Vinn takes advantage of my hesitation and steps in. "You can take a little longer than that to get it just right, Maggie. Now, once it's ready to print, do you have any ideas how we can get it into a paper that will circulate in Chinatown?"

"Ooh, ooh, I know this one! I mean, I know someone. The guy who puts out the Chinatown News, he's my neighbor's mother's cousin. I think. Maybe my mother's neighbor's cousin. The paper's all in Mandarin and has a lot of ads kind of like those shopper's guides, you know, but people still read it and it's free but there's also the Gazette that covers the south side but it's in English but I'm sure I can get it in one of them."

I may be gaping. "That's great, Maggie. I tell you what, let's think about it but for now why don't you get started and then email Vinn and I when you have a draft together. If we can get something finalized by the end of the week that would be ideal. It doesn't have to be perfect, but reporters have to learn to work on deadlines, right?"

Maggie is already on her feet. "Right Professor. I gotta go. You can count on me!"

Vinn and I watch in a refreshing silence as Maggie exits the café. "One of the editors of the Sun Times uses me as a source sometimes," Vinn says finally. "I can probably get her to help."

Maggie must have worked on the article well into the night because a draft that had been emailed at 4:21 a.m. was waiting for me when I awoke this morning. I don't want to bemoan the future of journalism, as she's new to it, but even with a quick once over I could tell it would need more than a minor edit. Vinn apparently has the same opinion, as I found a Post It note on my office door in her handwriting with the command "My place 7:00." She's wildly sexy when she takes charge.

"She tracked me down in the café before classes this morning anxious to get our feedback," Vinn says as I shed my coat. "I didn't have the heart to confess that I only glanced at it on the el, and that what I saw wasn't encouraging, so I told her that you were enthusiastic beyond belief but that we might have to tweak it a bit." Vinn compressed her lips before continuing. "I'm no expert, and I welcome your input, Mr. Creative Writing Professor, but I fear that she's about to get an unpleasant lesson in the editing process."

"Agreed. And thanks for preemptively shifting all the blame onto me." I flop on the couch and pull out a red pencil. Might as well play the part of ruthless editor. "Shall we?"

By the time we finish nearly two brutal hours later, not counting the break for pizza, the finished product bears little resemblance to the article Maggie submitted other than the fact that we kept her byline. Vinn's already spoken with her connection at the Sun Times, who was less than enthusiastic but eventually succumbed to Vinn's powers of persuasion, aided by a little extortion in connection to the next time she needs Vinn's assistance understanding basic science. We scored a spot for 750 words in the city scene section of the weekday edition. Considering Maggie's draft was over 2,400, we were forced to be merciless, but the hook of the oddity of ghost weddings and the connection to the triad in Chinatown made the cut. For the sake of Maggie's feelings, we hope that just getting something into print will assuage any hurt our editing may cause.

While Vinn emails the article off to the Sun Times, I call Mr. Wei to give him a head's up. He of course knows the editor of the local news tabloid and will make sure some version of the article gets translated and inserted into the edition due out on Friday. Along with the Sun Times agreeing to use their journalistic might to duplicate what they print in the Gazette, we should have some pretty good exposure in and around Chinatown.

I close my phone at precisely the same time Vinn shuts her laptop. We look at each other and telepathically admit that we need to discuss what happens after the publication date and to map out a plan, but we also read each other's eyes to see that our mutual interests lie elsewhere. Without exchanging a single word, we rise together, interlock our hands, and head to the room of the condo where work is never discussed.

THIRTY ONE

*A*s a stopgap measure, mostly to feel like we're doing something other than just wringing our hands in angst, we enlist Rebecca's help in bringing the crew back into action by having teams of two make themselves conspicuous around Chinatown on a daily basis. With Maggie absent, their job now is simply to be seen and to create a buzz, the exact opposite of what we originally told them to do. Simultaneously, we ask Mr. Wei to anonymously start rumors that these are vigilantes hired by concerned citizens to keep an eye on extreme gang activity in the neighborhood. Despite reservations as to the wisdom of this tactic, Mr. Wei relents and admits that he knows a few gossips who, with a poorly-veiled hint or two, would have the fabricated story spread far and wide within less than a day, and that soon thereafter it would be thought of as fact by half the local population.

Rebecca vigorously advocates having the crew members wear an armband or other identifying mark to raise their profiles, but it doesn't take a genius to see that her main purpose is to give her an excuse to add a fashion accessory. Vinn and I quickly veto the idea. We explain that we want the locals to start seeing every outsider as a possible vigilante so that eventually it will seem like the neighborhood is crawling with spies ready to report any criminal activity. What we don't say is that many of the team won't have any problem standing out from the crowd. Hopefully the extra attention, both real and imagined, will temporarily make the triad cautious about attacking any more women while we formulate a more permanent solution. We expect a pout and get it, but she brightens up when we suggest that she create special ID cards for the crew if it would make her feel better.

The program's been in place for about a week now. Despite some mild concern that we may present targets too tempting for the tong's members to resist, Vinn and I insisted on doing our share and today is our turn in the rotation. Earlier today we separately took quick trips to Chinatown during gaps between courses and just wandered a bit to look visible, but only she had the foresight to bring back scallion pancakes for lunch. Class schedules have prevented us from going down there together, so we had to wait until my senior seminar ended at 3:50 before teaming up for one final visit.

I give my best impression of a secret knock on her office door, two taps followed by one tap and then three more, which only elicits a disappointing "come in Mal" from Vinn. "What, you don't know the coded response," I chastise her as I enter. "Some spy you are."

"If it makes you feel better, I can show you my credentials," she responds with a smile, producing a wallet-sized pink card with black profiles of sunglasses and a passport and the letters "S.CREW" in script. "Did you ever ask her what 'screw' stands for?"

"I'm afraid to, because once I know I may be even more resistant to carrying it than I already am. Let's just assume it's 'surveillance crew.' Anyway, are you ready to go?"

We pull our jackets close to guard against the chill as we walk to the el. Less than half an hour later we exit at the Cermak stop and begin the task of looking furtive and conspicuous at the same time. Mainly that involves just wandering around, stopping in shops now and then pretending to be interested in the merchandise, and standing on street corners for extended periods of time staring at nothing in particular. It gets old fast, but has the benefit of helping us get to know the area well in case that ever becomes important.

"Mal, if I have to see one more paper lantern or waving cat I'm going to go insane," Vinn finally says, interrupting my efforts to perfect the best inscrutable expression. "What do you say to some dinner?"

"Sounds good. Sichuan, Cantonese, or something else?"

"Right now, anything served where it's warm inside."

Despite her impatience to move indoors and to sate her appetite, Vinn rejects the first couple of possibilities, finally settling on a tiny noodle shop that appears to be popular with the locals. We grab a table for two against the wall, gladly accept an offer of hot tea, and peruse the menu.

Our order of sour and spicy rice noodles and pork buns has barely been placed before us when a shadow falls across our table. "May I join you?" Mr. Wei has appeared out of nowhere, as has a chair that allows him to lower himself to our level. He looks at our food and nods his approval. "Next time may I suggest the curry noodle. Good here."

We're not sure why he's here, or how he knew where to find us. I assume that the gossip mill he referenced is as efficient as he described. Vinn and I remain silent for several moments until she breaks the impasse by offering him a bun, which he politely declines. Our past dealings with Mr. Wei suggest that he doesn't hurry conversation, he'll start when he's ready, so we wait for him to take the initiative as our food grows cold. He notices us stealing glances at our plates and motions us to eat.

"The articles have generated much excitement in Chinatown. The presence of so many watchers has also been noticed. Much talk among the neighborhood. I hear triad is curious. They start to watch the watchers."

I pause my chopsticks in mid-air before the noodles reach my mouth. "Do you mean that the tong has people spying on our people?"

Mr. Wei nods again. "Soon a man will enter to pick up order to go. He will be your shadow tonight. I do not wish to be here, so I must leave. Before I go, please inform me. What is your idea? How will you make sure there will be no more killings?"

My mouth is full, leaving Vinn to try her best to explain that we have a long-range plan that needs time to implement, but we don't wish to burden him with too much information. Hopefully coming from her, the lie seems more plausible, but Mr. Wei's eyes reveal the disappointment he feels.

"I must go," he says, rising. Just as he does, his cell phone buzzes and he takes the call. His posture tenses, his lips tighten, and he looks frightened. He stares at us for several moments, his face ashen.

"That was a friend. Ji Jiang has been released from jail."

The entire room immediately grows eerily silent. Rather than wait for our reaction, Mr. Wei, growing paler by the second, turns and stumbles uncertainly out the door. A low murmur brings a semblance of sound to our surroundings, but Vinn and I can only stare at our plates of half-eaten food. How could that have happened? And what does it mean for how we proceed from here?

Our reverie is broken by the distant sound of a cell phone ringing. It takes me a long moment to realize that the ringing is coming from my pocket. I manage to answer before the caller hangs up, uttering a weak greeting. "Jenkins," I mouth to Vinn.

"I assume you've heard," he starts in without bothering with an introductory hello. "Happened about an hour ago. His lawyers managed to convince a judge that he's no risk to the community and had bail set at a million. Was paid within thirty minutes. Just thought you'd like to know he's back on the streets."

Jenkins hangs up without waiting for a response, which is just as well because I remain dumbstruck. Vinn pushes her food around on her plate before looking up at me. "Well, that's a game changer," she finally says. "But I'm not sure how it alters the rules."

"Me either," I admit. "But if it's all the same to you, I'd rather not stick around here any longer."

I throw a twenty on the table as we hurry to leave and head for the train. Stalling is no longer a viable option, but neither one of us is any closer to knowing what to do next.

Over Vinn's feeble protestations, I walk her home from the el before heading back to Ukrainian Village. The sun is low in the sky as I mount the stairs to my unit, but even the late afternoon gloom doesn't hide the figure standing on the landing outside my door. He sees me at the same time I spy him and puts his hands in the air with palms out, a wise precaution given my mood and the fact that I've seen Jiang in every shadow since leaving Vinn's place. It would have given me great pleasure to shoot someone right about now, which is one of the reasons I avoid carrying a firearm unless absolutely necessary. Only as I get closer do I notice a small package sitting as his feet. My hand goes to the hilt of my knife as he stoops to pick it up.

"Many blessings, Mr. Winters," he says in a heavily-accented Chinese dialect whose precise origin I'm unable to place. "I bring a gift from a friend. Please accept it with his best intentions." As he speaks he extends the box out to me. I ignore it.

"Who is this friend?" I might be more snarly than the occasion calls for, but I'm on edge.

"Many blessings, Mr. Winters," he repeats, stammering this time as he struggles to get back on track. I realize that he probably doesn't speak English and has phonetically memorized just the three sentences he's already conveyed. "I bring—"

"Yeah, I know, a gift from a friend," I interrupt. "Thank you. You can go now." He looks at me, puzzled, so I put him out of his misery and take the proffered box, waving my arm down the stairs. With a clear expression of relief, he hurries down without so much as a look back or a goodbye.

I put the gift back down at my feet as I take out my keys, wondering if I should take the chance of bringing it into my home. Before I have time to make a decision or to even get through my door, a concerned Rebecca followed by an impassive Leo climb up the stairs to meet me. Leo rarely makes the trip up without a good reason, maybe because most of our interactions involve over-imbibing and navigating down two flights might be a challenge, but his special effort this time adds to my worry about what might be transpiring. Mainly to keep it from getting trampled, I bring the box in with me and am immediately followed by my two tenants.

"Ninety-four minutes," Leo growls as I remove my coat. "I check him eight times. Never moved. Held onto box whole time."

I set the box at issue on my kitchen island as we gather around to stare at it, as if a label marked "Explosive" will magically appear. I know everyone's thinking the same thing, but no one's saying it. Until Rebecca chimes in.

"Oooh, should we go behind the couch when you open it, or do you think it might be a viper or something? You know, Malcom, you do get yourself into some nasty messes, don't you think?"

"Open the fuckin' thing," Leo commands, pulling out a large pocket knife that has almost certainly been involved in multiple felonies. Without another word, he slices the cord, pulls off the butcher paper, and uses the hilt of the knife to push a small container about the size of a milk carton in my direction. I take a breath before moving my hands toward its top. Rebecca's viper comment was ridiculous, but naturally is playing with my mind at the moment.

Once it's apparent that none of my companions will be seeking shelter, I extend my arms to their full length and use a pen to flip the top onto the counter. Nothing happens, and after a brief pause all three heads simultaneously lean in together to peer inside. A bundle resembling a dealer's undersized stash of pot sits inside with a plain white envelope leaning against it, my name printed neatly on the outside. Fear of snakes allayed, I reach inside and pull out the bundle. A label with Chinese characters is the only indication of what lies within.

"Well?" The question comes in stereo from two directions.

I'm momentarily speechless, wondering if I might be misinterpreting the words set forth in front of me. "If I'm right, and if whoever sent this isn't pulling my leg, this is Da Hong Pao, a type of tea."

"What, tea?" Leo takes offense at the tension a few tea leaves has caused and reaches out to grab them.

"Aaakk, no, wait." I quickly slide the tea out of his reach, protective of my gift. "This isn't any ordinary tea. It's extremely rare and impossible to find, even in China. It's harvested from ancient trees that are almost extinct. The last harvest was fifteen years ago. Gram for gram, this tea is far more valuable than gold. This small amount here is probably worth in the significant six figures."

"Who would want to send that to you, and why?" Rebecca asks. Seeking an answer, she pulls out the envelope and slits it open with a false nail. Her invasion of my privacy is a conversation for another time. Instead of a note of explanation, two small rectangular pieces of cardstock fall onto the counter.

"Tickets? To what?" she asks to no one in particular. "What the hell?" Sometimes a bit of Ted reveals himself from under the layers of foundation and rouge.

I pick up the tickets and read them. "For this Saturday. The architecture cruise on the river. For two." I assume that the second ticket is meant for Vinn. I'm loath to mimic Rebecca, but the same two questions, plus a third, occupy my own thoughts. Who sent them and to what end? Are we being lured into danger, or even death?

Leo looks at me with the wizened expression he gets sometimes when he's made a decision that may tempt fate or put me in danger for my life. "You must go," he says simply. "But we will be watching."

He exchanges a knowing glance with Rebecca but offers no further explanation, a signal that it's better for all of us if I don't know. When those two start conspiring together making plans to protect me, at least a dozen laws are probably going to be broken or at least challenged, and it really is better if I'm kept in the dark.

"Enough of this. Enough talk of tea. Time to get real drink." Leo mutters as he heads toward the door, Rebecca in tow. I hold back long enough to store my precious tea properly and to text Vinn before following, wondering what headache-inducing moonshine is on tap tonight and whether I'll be taking part in my own anticipatory wake.

⑨HIRTY ⑨WO

The options for a commercial cruise on the Chicago River or the lakefront are many and varied, including dinner cruises, cocktail cruises, and speed boats, but the only one I've been on that I've truly enjoyed is the one hosted by the Chicago Architecture Foundation Center. Docents share their vast knowledge of the histories and significance of the multitude of towers as we float gently up and then back down the river under their shadows. A highly popular diversion for tourists and locals alike, it's normally a pleasant and fascinating way to pass seventy-five minutes on a warm summer day in the city.

The calendar for this particular Saturday, though, shows that we're well past summer and the gloom and chill outside my door confirms that this will be no pleasure cruise. Not that nicer weather would have made me look forward to it to any greater degree. This is not only the first time I'll need to wear a warm jacket on the river, it's the first time I need to consider what weaponry to pack. I text Vinn, who's struggling with the very same issue. We finally decide that I'll bring a mini arsenal of small-caliber pistols while she'll select a few of the sharper blades from her enviable collection of knives and daggers. I search my memory bank trying to recall if the boats have any sort of metal detectors or other types of screening but come up empty. If they do, we'll be giving the guards something to talk about with the family over dinner tonight.

Leo and Rebecca have been tight-lipped about what precautions they've arranged, maintaining their opinion that the less I know the better in case something goes awry. I have my doubts about the logic of that sentiment, unless they don't want their names brought into play if Vinn and I end up in either the morgue or the slammer. All I've been permitted to know is that there'll be a presence both on the water and on shore all along the route. What kind or who is apparently beyond my need to know. It takes an effort on my part, but I bite my lip and don't complain. They don't have to do this and I appreciate the effort in whatever form it takes.

By arrangement, I arrive early at Vinn's apartment so that we can each evaluate the other's aptitude in hiding our armaments.

"I have to tell you, Mal, I'm not at all comfortable with this," she tells me as she pats me down methodically, deliberately squeezing much too hard near one of my more intimate hiding places. "Any way you look at it, we're idiots to go through with this. Totally vulnerable. I'm sure this whole set-up has a voice from your training days screaming at you to stay away. Mine does."

I flinch as Vinn again presses a bit too diligently, then it's my turn. I may be the idiot she accuses me of being, but I'm no fool. I'm much more gentle with her. She not only has her feminine wiles, she's carrying knives. "Agreed. If there was any other option, I'd still be under my covers this morning enjoying the warmth of my comforter. But I'm totally out of ideas and with Jiang on the loose, we're out of time. This may be our last or only chance to break something open. On the other hand, we may be walking into something we're not walking out of."

Vinn sighs in resignation as I complete my search. "Right. Whatever happens, know that you didn't force me to go along. I'm doing this for the same reason you are. I can't get the images of those two women out of my mind. For their sake, and that of any other woman falling within the crosshairs of these monsters, we need to take the chance. You ready?"

We summon an Uber, eschewing the el for once. Might as well splurge on what may be our last day of existence. We're both fidgeting as we ride, ignoring the chatter of our young driver, who assumes we're visitors to the city based on our destination. Neither one of us engages him, and he eventually falls into a sullen silence.

All too soon we arrive at the corner of Upper Wacker and Michigan, pausing only for a moment before descending the stairs to river level. I search my pockets for the tickets as well as to reassure my compulsive side that all of my sidearms are in place, while Vinn checks the board to locate the number of the pier where the boat is docked. The Riverwalk has a few joggers and other wanderers, but some of the boats have already called it a season and the smarter tourists have found warm museums more inviting than the river breezes, so it's not at all crowded. We still have fifteen minutes but decide to get to the boat early to get seats in the rear where no one will be behind us. Safety first.

We arrive at our dock in less than ninety seconds and weave the gangplank easily, as we appear to be the only customers boarding. The ticket taker checks us in without comment or searching for contraband, hands us each a flyer, and we board the boat, heading upstairs to the upper deck. As we reach the top of the stairs, Vinn in front, she stops abruptly, forcing me to do the same. I immediately discover the cause of her actions. Far from being the only people on board, the seats are virtually full. Curiously, or perhaps not, every other visitor on this tour is Asian. The only two available seats are about halfway back in a row of four, where two large men in suits sit in the inside and outside positions, leaving us no choice but to sit between them. Vinn glances back at me, clearly sharing my concerns, and I shrug. We're committed. I casually feel for my closest weapon and notice Vinn doing the same.

We take our time strolling back to our seats, surveying our fellow passengers as we go. The only thing of note is that no one shows even the slightest interest in us, to the point of studiously avoiding eye contact. If there was any doubt that we weren't in the middle of a Chinese tour group, that small detail seals my assumption. As the only white faces here, we should be the subject of at least some curiosity or a cursory glance or two. The two men seated in our row are clearly the muscle, the rest of the passengers merely props who will deny seeing anything unusual should they be questioned by the cops later. Someone with clout is obviously behind today's meet, if that's what it is. I haven't ruled out the possibility of Vinn and I taking an unwanted swim halfway into the tour.

"Good morning, a bit chilly today, but at least it's not raining, right?" I bluster as I move to take my seat. The thug sitting on the aisle doesn't make any effort to make squeezing past him easier nor to acknowledge my greeting. Likewise the guy along the rail. Between them, they must weigh close to six hundred pounds, all of it muscle. I can't see any evidence of a weapon on either of them but given their size they may not need one.

Vinn and I snuggle close, partly to ward off the cold fall winds and partly by necessity. We discover with some degree of relief that the bulkiness of our companions acts as an effective wind break. We may be in fatal danger, but at least we're comfortable. On the other hand, being pressed so close together makes retrieving a weapon virtually impossible, which I presume is by design. We engage in nonsensical small talk and pretend to read our brochures. It seems like forever before the guide appears at the front of the group, microphone in hand.

"Good morning, and welcome to today's tour. We'll be casting off in just a moment. Can you hear me in the back?" No response, which doesn't seem to faze the docent. "Great. We get travelers from all over the world on our boats. Where are all of you from?" Again, complete silence. This time the guide is clearly uncomfortable, obviously unprepared for the lack of reaction to her cheerful effort to draw everyone into her spiel. The possibility that no one on board speaks or understands English may be dawning on her. She recovers and continues speaking—not in Mandarin—as the boat starts to move out into the river. "We begin in 1838, when the railroads first came to Chicago and from here began to expand to the west…"

Normally I'd listen in rapt attention, but my thoughts at the moment aren't on the composition of bridges or neo-classic architecture. I'm mostly concerned with staying alive, and secondarily piqued with curiosity about what we're doing here. As we cruise upriver beneath some of the world's greatest architectural feats, I scan the build-ings above not in admiration of their design, but to see if I notice anyone up high that shouldn't be there such as snipers, friendly or otherwise.

After about fifteen minutes, I'm growing restless and Vinn is fidgeting. Our guide hasn't been asked a single question or had any sort of visible reactions from her audience, although by now they've begun to show some interest in the towers above. With two massive exceptions, who continue to stare straight ahead nearly motionless. I resist the temptation to check a pulse. I decide instead to tune into the poor guide to at least show her someone is listening.

"...convex curve due to...a public park because subterranean railroad tracks prevented putting a building on top...adaptive reuse..."

It's no use, I simply can't focus. Just as I'm ready to get up to stretch, mostly to see if that elicits a reaction, a small middle-aged man in the front row rises and heads in our direction. To no one's surprise, he stops even with our row. The muscle doesn't so much as cast a glance in his direction.

"Mr. Malcom, Ms. Vinn." Despite the circumstances, I have to suppress a grin. However well-connected our mystery host is, even he or she hasn't discovered Vinn's true name. "Please," he continues softly, "come with me."

Without waiting for an answer, he turns and begins walking back up the aisle, compelling Vinn and I to hustle in order to catch up. He moves past the puzzled docent, who to her credit doesn't miss a beat as she discusses the six months it took to defrost an old cold storage building before it could be remodeled. We descend the stairs to the enclosed first level, where our escort beckons us to enter before closing the door behind us, with him still on the outside. The first thing I notice is that the windows have been covered in a temporary film to keep prying eyes from peering within. Even after my eyes have adjusted to the dim light, I have difficulty seeing anyone else in the room. A frail voice from the rear brings my focus in that direction.

"Please, sit. Have some tea." As we draw nearer, first the outline then the features of an ancient Asian man sitting in the last row of benches appears, a makeshift tea setting by his side. A few wisps of gray hair protrude wildly from each side of his head, his face a topographical map of wrinkles. His hands shake from the effort of lifting a small cast iron tea pot as he pours a heavenly-smelling brew into three china cups. Behind him stand two gigantic, imposing, and stationary men who make our topside escorts look like kindergartners.

Vinn and I take seats on the other side of the tea setting and I pass her a cup before taking a sip myself. I close my eyes momentarily, savoring both the warmth and the flavor. I look directly into the old man's eyes and ask the first question that anyone in a similar situation would pose. "Lingering Clouds?" I ask.

The corners of the old man's mouth turn up ever so slightly. "No, my own blend. But there is similarity, yes. You have a good palate. You will find pleasure in my gift." Our shared interest in tea and his reference to my future enjoyment of the Hong Da Pao gives me hope that we may make it out of here alive after all.

A slight shifting of one of the massive hulks brings his focus back to the present and the old man's expression turns serious. He lowers his cup, pats his lips with a linen napkin, and his eyes take on an almost frightful intensity when he looks again in our direction.

"I am Hop Leung. We have not met, but our interests have overlapped. For a while you were like a flea, annoying but no threat. Even now I could swat you without worry." He demonstrates with a wave of his hand. So much for the camaraderie of tea buddies. I may be turning slightly pale but try to compose myself and to focus on an exit strategy. "But you have had success in interfering with my business, drawing attention where it is not wanted. That must stop."

He pauses to raise his cup and take a sip of tea, reminding me that I have a cup in my own hands. I sip as well, hoping to reestablish our commonality. If he notices, he doesn't react and instead continues speaking. "You seek justice for two women. You want no more killing, no more ghost weddings. I understand." He pauses and frowns in distaste. "That was not my doing. It was rogue. Is that right word? Rogue?" He looks up at one of the giants, whose almost imperceptible nod meets Leung's approval. "I can give you what you desire.

"We are a people of tradition. Some older customs are difficult to part with. But this one, these marriages, they can be done another way. A way that does not involve killing. These two times, these women, they were done for people in the old country. I have sent word. Do what they wish but keep it there. I have influence even back home. No one here will kill again for that reason. You have my word.

"Sometimes ambition or money leads to bad judgment. Both were the case here with Ji Jiang." He pauses to turn his head and spit. "Reckless boy, a cousin of my wife. For that reason, I could not allow him to stay in American prison."

I start to object but he anticipates me and holds up his hand. "Yes, I arrange his release. But do not worry, he will still pay a price for his actions. He is no longer in this country, no longer a threat. His fate back in China will not be a pleasant one. He will stay alive for the sake of my wife, but he will sometimes wish he was not. For that, you must trust me. My word is good.

"Xiu Guo, another flea. No escape for him. Wild, causes much trouble for my people. You do me favor by sending him away. He will serve his time."

Leung falls into silence for a long time. I hear the distant voice of the guide above mention thirty-five drawbridges. Vinn speaks for the first time since we sat down and true to her nature comes straight to the point. "And Delun Shen?"

The old man's voice is strong and bitter in response. "Delun Shen no flea. Ambitious, impulsive, uncontrollable even by my people. Even before you, brought too much attention. Bad for business, bad for Chinatown. He will not be problem anymore. He has been handled."

That apparently is all the explanation we'll be getting, as Leung rises and one of his goons quickly and efficiently packs up the tea set. Leung moves out into the aisle then turns and faces us once more. "You are always welcome in Chinatown. Eat, shop. But cease all else. All your issues settled. Do not cross me. My reach is far."

Leung continues his walk toward the front of the boat. I wonder if he's headed upstairs, as by my estimation we still have a good thirty minutes left on the tour. Vinn and I follow his progress and watch as he and his bodyguards move out the door and out to the riverside rail. I race to the window where there's a gap in the film and watch in astonishment as a small tourist boat pulls alongside, a crew member lowers a ladder, and the three men vanish from view. It takes less than thirty seconds. The small craft pulls away and within seconds is gone.

I turn back, expecting Vinn to be at my shoulder, but she hasn't moved from her seat on the bench. Her eyes are focused not on me, or at the point on the rail where Leung disappeared, but on the area where the tea set had been. In its place is a plain brown box about twelve inches square wrapped heavily in tape.

"I haven't moved but still didn't see anyone put it here," she tells me. "I was looking at Leung as he left, just as you were. I don't think it's more tea."

"No," I reply. "It's obviously meant for us to open. But not here, not now."

We choose not to go back upstairs, instead sitting quietly holding hands with the box at our side while the faint drone of the docent plays above us.

THIRTY THREE

For the second time this week, a small gathering in my apartment stares at a mystery box sitting on the island in my kitchen, the only difference being that Vinn has joined our little group. I'm not happy about bringing her into the fray, as I'm convinced that in opening too many packages from underworld figures, eventually the odds will catch up with me and one of them will explode. I figured the pyrotechnics coming from Vinn would be worse than that of any bomb if I tried to keep her away, though, thus explaining her presence at my side.

At this point, my feeling of dread at discovering the contents of the box outweigh my curiosity, which gives Rebecca the opportunity to describe, in painful detail, her heroics in following the progress of the tour boat this morning. For the most part, I've been tuning out.

"...about every seventy-five to a hundred yards, on both sides of the river, because you know we wanted to make sure we had a clean shot if it came to that, and we didn't know where you would be. It was kind of like leapfrog. As soon as you passed out of range of one of us, that person would hustle to a position further down the route. We had it meticulously planned so that you'd always be protected. Except, of course, when you went downstairs behind the darkened windows. That we didn't plan for."

Rebecca looks at me with a frown as if I were to blame for throwing a kink in her master plan, as if I had a choice in how things played out. Leo sits passively on the couch watching us. Whatever role he had in this morning's activities I'll never know. Leo's not one to volunteer information, especially as to anything that may border on the criminal. This is supposedly because he doesn't want to risk his alleged status of being under witness protection but more likely because he simply chooses to stay in the shadows. It's enough for me to know, from his presence here now, that he was involved.

I realize that while I've been lost in thought, Rebecca has been staring at me waiting for a response. To what, I'm not sure. Vinn comes to my rescue.

"We deeply appreciate all that you and the crew have done, thank you, Rebecca. When all of this is over, I'm sure Mal will join me in showing our appreciation with some sort of a celebration." Vinn smirks at the dirty look I throw her way. By "join me," I know she means 'throw a party at his expense at his place which I may or may not attend.' I consider giving her the honor of opening up the box while I watch from another room.

Rebecca seems mollified for now and retreats to the bathroom to freshen up her lipstick while I retrieve a sharp knife to cut the cords. As soon as she returns and Leo joins us in the kitchen, all four of us signal that we're ready and I begin the process of opening it up. As I slice and remove the thick layers of butcher paper that have been taped so heavily they must have set a four-year-old loose on the wrapping, the slightest trace of an odor reaches me. I glance at my companions. Clearly Vinn and Leo detect it as well and recognize it for what it is. Leo gives an almost imperceptible shake of his head as he tilts it in Rebecca's direction. He wouldn't think of putting Vinn in the same protective category as Rebecca. He considers her one of the boys.

I stop what I'm doing and make sure I'm including everyone in the little speech I'm preparing in my head. What I'm about to say is solely for Rebecca's benefit but I don't want her to think I'm singling her out. "You know, I'm having second thoughts about this. I think I'd better have this opened up by the experts. It's probably nothing and maybe I'm overreacting, but I don't want to be responsible for your deaths just in case." As I speak, I begin to fold the paper back into its original position, pressing down the tape.

"I don't believe you, Malcom," Rebecca sneers. "After all we've done for you, for you to chicken out like this speaks volumes. I'll never forgive you!" Upon saying her piece in the most dramatic voice she could muster, Rebecca turns and stalks out the door, her hips swaying exaggeratingly in ultimate diva fashion.

We all look in the direction of the door for several seconds to make sure she isn't planning a curtain call after that performance before turning our attention back to the box.

"Well played," Vinn says in approval. Leo nods and grunts.

"Just open the fuckin' thing," he adds, bringing on a sense of déjà vu.

A little quicker this time, I unwrap the package and use the knife to cut the last pieces of tape holding the flaps shut. As the smell begins to fill the air around us, I maneuver the tip of the blade to fold the flaps open. A heavy plastic bag sits inside, its contents obscured by dark smears. Leo moves closer and without ceremony lifts the bag straight up.

One of us, perhaps me, gives a bit of a gasp, although in truth the "gift" from Leung is exactly what I had anticipated it would be. As our three sets of eyes peer inside the bag, the eyes of the severed head of Delun Shen stare vacantly back at us.

Darkness has long ago descended by the time I'm allowed to leave the 19th District station at Belmont and Western. Our efforts to signal the triad of our interest in Shen and his comrades apparently didn't escape the notice of a beat cop in Chinatown, who ratted us out to her superiors upon hearing of his death. No one is waiting outside to greet me. Belatedly, I remember having to turn off my cell phone when I was deposited into the dingy, unpleasantly fragrant interview room earlier this afternoon. Upon powering it up, I have a text from Vinn telling me that she's waiting at a nearby coffee shop. The text is from three hours ago.

"Still there?" I text back, my creative writing skills showing off how I can efficiently state my inquiry in a succinct two words. UIC is so lucky to have me.

The response is thirty seconds in coming. "No. Closed. Meet me at 90 Miles on Clybourn."

A quick check on my phone reveals it's only a five-minute walk and I head off in that direction. Easy to spot, the brightly-colored shack with colorful murals of native Cubans populating the outside walls has the look of a structure that barely survived years of Caribbean hurricanes. The similarity to the Kuban Kabana is unsettling, although the aromas that greet me upon entering are much more pleasant. It's not hard to find Vinn, as the only seating consists of bar stools tucked under counters lining the walls, which are covered in old newspapers. Considering where I've just been, I'm more than a little disconcerted to see the familiar figure of a black man in uniform sitting next to her.

"Vinn. Jenkins." Plastic baskets of half-eaten sandwiches sit before them along with plates of black beans and green plantains. The spot next to Vinn hosts an enticing platter of something that smells absolutely amazing, although given that I haven't eaten since yesterday my epicurean bar is low. Vinn notices me eyeing the dish.

"We ordered for you. Masas de Puerco. Pork with pickled red onion and mojo de ajo, a kind of garlic gravy. Rice and beans and fried sweet plantains too. Before you dig in, though, come give me a hug."

I move toward her, only to have her put her hands on my chest and gently push me away. "Whew," she says gently, "you smell. Best we save any physical encounters until you get a shower. To emphasize her point, she uses her left hand to slide my meal down one more seat away from her.

"Ten years in the big house, and that's how you greet me?" I growl, but with a smile. I grab my designated place, isolated that it may be, and begin cramming the steaming pork into my waiting mouth. My goodness, I didn't realize Cuban cuisine could taste this good. My sole recent experiences have only been with Leo's cooking. Between mouthfuls, I manage to pause long enough to ask Vinn a question. "How come you got out so long before me?"

"I sold you out," she says with a straight face. "Seriously, I was only in there about twenty minutes. There's only so many ways you can say 'I don't know anything about a severed head.' I guess they believed me. You must have a guilty face."

I only grunt in response. I essentially said the same thing to the cops, that I was totally ignorant about how a box with its grisly contents ended up on the front stoop of the local precinct captain's home, but I was kept for over six hours and questioned by four different officers of three different ranks.

"They even had me in to ask what I knew about it," Jenkins chimes in with a bit of disgust in his voice. "That's how I met up with Vinn. Your name did come up, but I told them the truth. I don't know anything about anything. Now that I've given my statement, is there something you want to tell me?" My glare must have served as enough of an answer, and he began to rise from his stool. "All right, well, I'll leave you two alone. Stay out of trouble." With a sly grin, Jenkins moves to the door in two strides and is gone.

"Do you think they know?" Vinn asked once Jenkins was out of earshot.

"Absolutely. They know that we're involved somehow and have probably guessed that the head passed through our hands, but any details elude them. And I don't think they're likely to push it more than they already have. I'm sure the cops are happy to get a troublesome thug off their hands."

"Yeah, that's what I think too," Vinn responds. "So this ends it. Killers brought to justice and a promise that no more ghost wedding-related murders will occur under Leung's watch. We can't take all the credit for the outcome, but I guess we did set the necessary wheels in motion. We need to celebrate." Vinn reaches out to put her hand on my arm, then immediately withdraws it and crinkles her nose. "First things first. You can take a long, soapy shower at my place, we'll have our own one-on-one celebration, and then we'll open a bottle of champagne and watch an old movie. Sound good?"

"Sounds wonderful," I respond as I toss my trash, having cleaned my plate. And it does sound absolutely perfect. But leave it to Vinn to continue on and to ruin the mood.

"And then we have a party to plan."

THIRTY FOUR

An early November snow has done little to deter any of the gang that shadowed Maggie months ago from turning up at my apartment for the "wrap party," as Rebecca insists on calling it. If anything, despite the notable absence of Xiu Guo, there's no question that there are more people here tonight than at the first meeting. Apparently when Rebecca spread the word, rumor has it through social media, she conveniently forgot to express my preference to limit attendance to the "spies" themselves and not to any friends or extended family. The Italian beef was gone within the first hour and the cookie tray soon followed, but that hasn't seemed to dampen anyone's spirits, as long as the alcohol supply lasts.

Which inspires my idea to bring the gathering to a swift end. As midnight approaches, and the temptation to grab an automatic weapon to clear the room increases, I begin to quietly stash a bottle or two of booze in a drawer or under my bed when no one's looking, or open a bottle of beer as if to drink it then pour it down the drain. Despite my best efforts Leo catches my eye as I act, but his trademarked nearly imperceptible nod of approval encourages me to redouble my efforts and soon he joins me. After thirty minutes or so, guests are noticing that the supply of spirits that seemed so endless does in fact have a limit, which triggers a mass exodus for the door. Shouts from the stairway as to which bar to continue the celebration at gradually fade, leaving my home suddenly very quiet. Leo settles his weary bones in a corner chair while Vinn and Rebecca flop on the couch.

I make my way to the kitchen and soon reappear with a bottle of champagne from my secret stash along with four flutes, then one trip later place a quick charcuterie platter of two cheeses, assorted sausages, crackers, and Greek olives on the table. As I pour and drop into a chair myself, Rebecca pipes up.

"Mal, I saw you ogling Sandra." She's nonplussed by my puzzled reaction. The entire evening has been a blur and I'm certain I wasn't ogling anyone. "You know, the broad in the red cocktail dress with the big boobs. I can set something up for you if you want, but you should know she's trash. You might also want to know that she has spare parts down below, if you know what I mean."

Her comments bring all activity to a halt. Vinn freezes, a piece of cheese halfway to her mouth, Leo pauses mid-sip, and I simply gawk. The silence is broken as Vinn begins to giggle drunkenly, followed by Leo's loud guffaw, and then I lose it myself. All of the tension of the last few months evaporates as we break into a long and loose round of laughter, eventually joined by Rebecca as well.

Wiping my eyes, I'm suddenly filled with an intense feeling of respect and love for the other people in the room, whom I realize are the only three friends I have in the world. Vinn, intelligent beyond comprehension; Rebecca, who only truly comes alive in a dress; and Leo, the only person capable of grounding me, frequently at the same time that he stitches me up. We've been through a lot together over a fairly short period of time, to the extent that I've lost track of who's saved whose life how many times, and what favors I may owe or be owed. I decide to put my feelings to the test and raise my glass to propose a toast.

"I just want to say..."

"No!" Leo interrupts. When Leo wants to speak, which isn't often, I don't stand in his way. "Me. You are good man, Malcom. But trouble finds you, always will. We will be here." He raises his glass as he moves forward in his seat to get within range of the rest of us. "To survival, in past and next time."

We clink our glasses, down the bubbly, and sit back in silence, each of us knowing that yes, there will be a next time, and whatever that may bring we'll be there for each other. With the echo of Leo's speech hovering over the room, we settle back into our seats, lost in the alcoholic haze of our own thoughts.

PREVIEW OF THE NEXT IN SERIES
THE COSMIC KILLINGS

Reluctant sleuths Mal and Vinn are once more coerced into investigating a death, this time of an Amish teenager found murdered at a zoo in Chicago. Navigating the unfamiliar world of the Amish and the tradition of Rumspringa proves difficult, especially for two outsiders. On the verge of giving up, a police officer informs them of the murder of a young suburban man with no apparent connection to the teenager other than a singularly bizarre and grisly detail that links the two killings. Trying to tie a girl's life of horse-drawn buggies and no electricity to that of a man barely out of high school living in his parents' basement brings together the old gang and a collection of college students as they traverse a dark path that draws them into the realm of a cultist whose belief that celestial beings will visit Earth offers both a possible solution and the risk of death to everyone involved.

Lightning Source UK Ltd.
Milton Keynes UK
UKHW010012270721
387818UK00007B/503/J